WHO KILLED ANNE-MARIE?

CM THOMPSON

*For Marie and Fran
who have mysteriously left the country for some strange reason.*

*And for the K Thompsons
Who would if they could.*

CHAPTER ONE

The overcooked eggs are not so much sunny-side up as misery-side down.

Misery is what emanates as his knife slices through the cold yolk. It is the main ingredient in that tough bacon sandwich but Daniel still savours every single bite of the over-salted burnt mess.

He burps mightily, releasing another stench of misery into the air. The only other sound comes from the loud rhythmic chop of a knife hitting a plate a little too hard. He had made this for her: he had waited patiently for her to come downstairs, had eaten his own breakfast calmly, promised himself repeatedly that he wouldn't be the first one to crack, only to find himself snatching and shovelling her share, now too angry to notice that he is already beyond full.

This is all too good for her, she doesn't deserve such a feast. He does so fucking much for her and she just spits it right back in his face. If she did come downstairs now, she would only sit on the edge of the chair, nibbling morosely at a dry piece of toast, if she ate at all. No, these greasy remains are his alone to savour, he won't let her wreck another one of life's joys. He has so few left now. Good food is reserved for the person who does the washing up – not just the breakfast items that he dirtied but also those slimy plates and that mouldy bowl she promised to wash days ago. He is going to clean everything today, that's why he deserves both portions. In fact, he deserves more than breakfast, especially if he also cleans and sanitises the sticky kitchen. Hell, if he dusts the house then he deserves a frickin' medal.

So many jobs she has been promising to do "later" when she is "feeling better" that he will have to do now. It's not like he hasn't been working all week, it's not like his job is hard or demanding, oh no. He just wanted to spend the day relaxing in front of the telly, just a nice day off. But no, he has to do all of her jobs, he is the one who has to find the source of that smell while she just... while she just lies around, doing... what? What has her attention 24/7? What does she do all day? Maybe he should be asking who has she been doing all day? He has heard the rumour regarding his wife and Paul next door but he dismissed it with a chuckle. But maybe, maybe there was someone else, someone aroused by her unwashed smell and... Daniel's eyes stray over to the overflowing recycling bin. No. He knows what she does all day. An affair would be almost preferable to this. Cheaper too.

The two portions of breakfast sit uneasily in his stomach and he slurps his coffee, hoping that the cooling, bitter liquid will help wash his own bitterness away.

It is not worth this. He can't stand the thought of another fight. He just wants one peaceful day; it shouldn't be this hard. It won't take him that long to tidy up and it would make everything so much easier. He could give the kitchen a quick going over and find out what's causing that smell in the bathroom, then get the washing machine going, do the shopping and spend the rest of the afternoon relaxing in front of the telly. Maybe, she might join him, they could watch the match together like they used to, cuddle up with a few beers; maybe just for once she will even stop at a few beers, and maybe they could order a take-away and maybe, now he is really fantasising here, maybe they could talk to each other without shouting. Just like they used to.

Upstairs, he hears a door softly open and then a pause. Daniel holds his breath as she pitter-patters down the stairs, what kind of mood is she in? Please let today be a good day. She slinks into the room, her head bowed low, making eye contact impossible. There is a sharp scent as she scurries past. She hasn't bothered washing or even brushing her hair. She is wearing the same pyjamas as she was three days ago, and they had stunk then. The smell assures him that today is not going to be a good mood day.

The smell smothers him with memories, and the old feelings of anger flood back, memories of the last argument. The insults she had screamed. Now she is pretending he doesn't exist, just like his mother used to. He hates that and she knows it. She has spent years finding out his pet hates, just to use them against him. He was willing to put the argument behind them and move on, but she isn't. She is going to continue with her childish antics. Why? What did he do this time? Is it because he accidentally woke her up, clattering the breakfast pans? Well, he has to eat sometime and it's not like its six o'clock in the morning. Or is it because he hadn't saved her any breakfast? She might be even more annoyed when she sees that there is no more food left. Well she should have gone shopping, shouldn't she? Like she promised. It's not his fault.

But it's up to him to break the silence. He can do this, he

urges, he can be the better partner. "Good morning," he mutters, trying to force a smile on to his face.

Wordlessly she opens the fridge and he is answered instead by the waft of something rotten, then the unmistakable sound of something pouring. He knows there is no milk in the fridge, no juice. She is starting early again. Despite what they agreed.

Daniel will say nothing about it, this time. He knows what she will say: "I have a headache" or "I am just having one". Or she will cuss him out, knowing he hates hearing her swear. Let her be the one who talks about it, wait for her to be ready, that's what they tell him.

Unprovoked she slams the fridge door shut; oh she knows she is doing something wrong but she doesn't give a shit, he thinks. Still ignoring him she scuttles back upstairs, taking not just her glass but the bottle as well, along with his already diminished hopes for a peaceful day.

Daniel sighs, the anger draining back into his usual resignation. Is this really still all his fault? Is she really still his problem? He knows he should leave but she would kick up such a fuss. Daniel really does not like fuss. Maybe he should start looking, just for somewhere to escape to. Somewhere to go on the really bad days, but then he can't leave her alone on those days. He could ask friends for help, but that would mean admitting... and besides, they don't have any friends left, even the neighbours have lost their friendly smiles.

She would never agree to a divorce either, but then he has never asked. He has screamed it a few times and so has she but they have never taken the idea seriously. He could ask quietly, for once, in a tone that is not fucking around. Maybe then she would cry and promise to change. Maybe he could use it as a way of encouraging her to seek help, professional help this time. Maybe she will agree to a divorce, since she "fucking hates him", and has told him repeatedly that she doesn't need him. After four and a half years of marriage, Daniel can see that. She has never needed him, only his wallet. No, that is not true, that is unfair. But still. Still. Maybe. No. Just keep telling yourself that you love her, he thinks, that's the easiest option.

He switches on the radio to drown out the accusing silence. He is tired of trying to figure out how to solve a problem like Anne-Marie. He is tired of cleaning up after her. He is tired of doing everything for her and getting nothing but abuse in return. The problem is he has married a woman who acts too much like his mother, and he won't act like his father did, no matter what. Even if the bitch does deserve it. Best not to think about the similarities or about his parents, dead and forgotten is best – dead, rotten and forgotten. Whilst his wife is alive, rotten and... no, no more, concentrate on the washing up.

It is disgusting. Why have they let it get this bad? He should have stepped in earlier, but she said she would do it. He shouldn't have to do everything around here. It only takes a few minutes to wash the dishes, it wouldn't have taken her much effort or time, she could even attempt it whilst drunk, it wasn't that hard, but no, she would rather host a pity party in her bedroom. Her bedroom! His and her bedrooms! Whose stupid idea was that? Her mother, dear old Sherri. It had been her sneered suggestion when Anne-Marie had claimed that she needed so many nightcaps because of Daniel's "snoring".

He doesn't snore! He knows he doesn't. Any excuse to separate them. Sherri always closed her eyes to her daughter's drinking; it was always Daniel's fault, not her precious Anne-Marie's.

He needs to man up: he should tell Anne-Marie to leave, kick her out to live with Sherri. He shouldn't have to be the one who leaves – he pays for this house; he maintains it while she does fuck all. His hand scrubs angrily against dry crud firmly embedded onto the bowls. She should be the one who leaves, goes back to her mother. Let's see how well they cope with each other again after all these years. Then they'd acknowledge that he is a saint, and they'd stop with their snide comments, their guilt trips. Their affair accusations. It was just one fucking kiss. It meant nothing.

Yes, he is going to tell her to leave right... tomorrow. No, he isn't even going to tell her, he is just going to pack her bags and put her in a taxi. Change the locks, disconnect the doorbell, take the phone off the hook, hammer the windows shut. Hell, why take such petty precautions? He should put the house up for sale, change his name, grow a beard, emigrate to a warmer country. Maybe her father had the right idea. He rants as he scrubs. He decides that the heavily chipped mouldy plates are not worth keeping and throws them in the bin instead. She won't notice as long as she has a wine glass and it doesn't even need to be clean anymore. It takes over an hour of scrubbing, running more water and draining away gallons of greasy, filthy water before he finishes. An hour of fantasising about getting rid of his wife, one way or another and shacking up with a cute blonde.

Nothing changes upstairs despite his clattering and clanging. She is still up there with that bottle, like an evil presence in the house. A fermenting storm. He turns the vacuum cleaner on with a little glee, something to make her "headache" worse, maybe even make her feel guilty that he is the one doing the cleaning – again, despite what she promised. Maybe the constant noise will be enough to drive her out of her room and hopefully even out of the house. Daniel turns back to his fantasies about throwing her out, triumphantly slamming the door, yelling, "Don't come back!" to the applause of the neighbours. Of her quietly exiting, in a taxi, tears running down her face, vowing never to touch a drop of alcohol again. They joyfully reconcile a month later, never to part again. Then they will have two kids and a dog, and he will never have to see a spirit bottle or his mother-in-law again. He can dream. In reality, she will be scratching, biting and cursing from the moment he tries to pick her up, and there would probably be kicking too. There is no way to get her out the house without a fuss. Even if he took the coward's option of changing the locks the next time she left the house, she would just smash in the windows, or scream on the pavement until he gave in and opened the door. No neighbours would applaud that. They would probably take her side too; everyone always takes her side. It isn't fair.

He can't do it anyway; he doesn't have the guts. She took away his spine and his already diminished balls the minute he said "I do" at the altar. He can dream all he likes about leaving her, but he can't do it. End of. Still, on the bright side, the amount she costs to maintain is still cheaper than a divorce.

He is stuck with Anne-Marie, but it's not like she gets in his way that much. Yes, the arguments are bad sometimes, but they are fairly infrequent. Yes, it would be nice to come home to something more welcoming, but it could be worse. Maybe they should get a dog, a replacement for the baby they are probably not going to have, but could he trust her alone with a dog? It isn't worth finding out, and he would have to walk the darn thing every day. It would be another thing he would have to clean up after, and Anne-Marie would probably train it to attack him. But it would be a friendly face. Maybe when they start talking again, he could hint about a dog, see how she reacts. It might even help her, be a motivation for her to leave the house.

He finishes vacuuming in thoughtful silence and then he

mops with little fanfare. No longer will he tread in something disgusting when he comes in, late at night, on a snack run. The kitchen could do with a better clean, one involving a stronger disinfectant, but it will do. She will only mess it up again anyway.

Upstairs, to the bathroom, he can do this. Taking a deep breath, he darts in, trying not to inhale as he forces open the grubby window. Oh God, what has she been doing in here?

Normally he avoids this bathroom, using the en suite in "his" bedroom, but the smell penetrating the hallway has become too strong to ignore.

Is this traces of sick? When was she sick? Why hadn't she told him? Why couldn't she clean up after herself for once? No wonder it smelt like something died in here. He didn't think it had got this bad again. Well he did, but there is no point in admitting it – it's another unapproachable, like the baby, their marriage, his parents. So many things they don't talk about by mutual agreement. One of those subjects that if he even breathes a mention of, she will start screaming at him, saying he doesn't understand. She is right, he doesn't understand, he barely even cares. He just can't reach her anymore, can't even have a normal conversation. It is pointless to even try.

Is it so bad he needs to invite Sherri over? He can't stand the thought of that chain-smoking witch polluting his house, cackling about his shortcomings, and encouraging Anne-Marie to drink that little bit more, but it would mean that Anne-Marie might willingly come out of her room and socialise for once. She never misses the opportunity to complain about him to Sherri, and Sherri will coo and scold, maybe even suggest that Anne-Marie stays with her for a few days. Sherri could scold her about being too thin and make food that she will actually eat, without sounding "insensitive". Sherri would be able to get her to shower without argument.

Not today, he won't call Sherri today he really needs a day off. Maybe next weekend if Anne-Marie hasn't improved, maybe. He could pretend that he has to go on a business trip and ask Sherri to stay with her for a few days. Then he could have a few days alone in a hotel room with room service. But then, what will he say when they start asking questions? Laying out the guilt trips, they might even start again with the affair accusations. Sherri is a suspicious woman: if she saw so much as a hotel receipt she would explode, but then, maybe he could use that to his advantage, maybe he could go away stay in a hotel then "accidentally" leave the receipt on show. The shit wouldn't just hit the fan, it would bury it. Sherri would insist Anne-Marie leaves for good this time and there would be no pleas from her brother Peter, to take her back because she "needs" him and she has changed. But then there will be confrontation, yelling, everyone thinking the worst of him and they would tear him apart in the divorce courts, take every penny he has, expose him as a cowardly worm. No, the fake affair is a bad idea. He needs to face the facts, there is no way of getting rid of his wife that easily. And it's not worth involving Sherri.

The bathroom smells lemony fresh again, the house is vaguely presentable. He is going to go; maybe if she hears him leaving, then maybe she will come out of her room, maybe even shower now the bathroom is clean. Maybe she will be in a better mood, maybe she will stop at one glass, and maybe pigs will fly.

At the supermarket he picks up enough easy-to-cook meals to last him the week and a couple more in case she feels hungry — easy things for her to heat no matter what state she is in. Anything to stop her attempting to cook again. He finds a couple of snacks to go with telly watching. He deserves them after all the cleaning he's done this morning and because he knows he is in for another lonely night, he adds a pack of beer. And it's cheaper to buy two packs so he might as well get two. Then he pauses. This is the decision he doesn't want to make. They are out of wine and spirits; she won't be happy with just beer. If he wants a quiet night, he needs to buy a few bottles. But then, that's not being supportive or is it being supportive? If he buys them, she will scream at him for buying a temptation, but if he doesn't buy them, she will scream at him for ignoring her needs, for making her headaches worse. Maybe he will buy them and let her have one bottle at a time, an offering when the volcano erupts. The last time he didn't buy anything she tore apart the house, looking for hidden caches – they still haven't replaced the lamp or the drawer. And then she will go without showering or changing out of her pyjamas, back to the corner shop. He was beyond mortified when she was caught stealing, he can't let that happen again. Maybe a couple of bottles, he could hide some in the car, after all he will probably need them for himself too. She is easier to love when she is drunk. Even easier if they are both drunk.

They had met in a bar, no surprises there. Anne-Marie had made the first move, came over to talk and he brought her a drink and another and another. Daniel fell straight away for her smile. He wasn't used to anyone smiling at him. She had fallen straight away for his wallet. But there was so much he had admired then about Anne-Marie, she was not afraid of anything. He, having spent most of his life hiding in fear, loved her reckless fearlessness. It was like being able to kiss a tornado in those first few months, wild, exhilarating, never knowing which way she would turn, so passionate, so exciting, so fun. Things he had only ever thought about before, he finally felt because of her.

And alcohol.

Which is why he needs the beer.

They were drunk when they had fallen in love and they can't sober up now.

Whilst he waits in line to pay, he practises what he will say if the cashier asks if he is having a party, eyeing up the excessive amount of snacks and alcohol. He did go a little overboard, but he can't be bothered to put anything back. He plans to say something jolly like: "Yes, I am having a little family get together, ha ha, of course you can come, ha ha!" Something like that. Luckily, today the cashier is disinterested, only looks at him briefly to check he is over the legal drinking age and goes back to scanning his goods. The thing Daniel misses most is human interaction; no one has spoken to him today, no one has smiled at him, it has been months since his last hug.

On the bright side... He is tired of looking on the fucking bright side, of pretending everything is just fine. Of having to tiptoe around in his own house, of trying to figure out what to do or what to say. He doesn't want to go home to more silence. In desperation, he takes a detour to pick up two fish and chip meals. He tells himself that it's just in case she is hungry when he gets back, that he is too tired to cook today, that it's not so he can hear a friendly voice. The woman behind the fish shop counter can always be counted on for a genuine smile and a "How are you, sweetheart?"

He will never get a "How are you, sweetheart?" from the stony face that watches him unload the car. The face belonging to their neighbour, Mrs Ludmilla Bryski. Anne-Marie has a different name for her, Lady Bitchski. So many times Daniel has arrived home to Anne-Marie rambling on about the Bitchski next door, at a volume they both know Ludmilla can hear. Or the muttered allegations against her "creepy" husband Paul. Daniel had tried to say that Paul is just old-fashioned but apparently that meant he was on Paul's side and they were all disgusting creeps. Daniel is reduced now to just giving Paul an embarrassed, apologetic smile and avoiding any other form of contact.

Anne-Marie hates all their neighbours, but Ludmilla next door and Penelope "Lying Penny" at number ten are the worst. The feelings are mutual. Daniel originally liked Ludmilla, she had welcomed them to the neighbourhood with home-made cookies and they had been on friendly terms for a short while. Daniel saw her as the grandma he never had. But then too many sleepless nights, too many empty bottles carelessly flung into Ludmilla's pristine garden, too many shouted insults, then adding in the not-quite-true but juicy rumours spread by Lying Penny, had considerably soured their friendly neighbour. Daniel didn't think it was his problem that Ludmilla was a light sleeper, who woke up at the slightest bit of noise. In the last row, he had tiredly snapped that maybe Ludmilla should consider moving her bed away from their connecting wall, or maybe she could try ear plugs, or maybe she could try shutting her face. Ludmilla then made it very clear that Daniel and Anne-Marie Mills would never again be welcomed into her home, and Anne-Marie made it very clear that Ludmilla Bryski was welcome to go to hell. Daniel now pretends he can't see the Bitchski watching him, judging him and hurries back inside.

The house is quiet and he unpacks the shopping quickly, not wanting the fish and chips to go cold. Maybe he should go upstairs, ask her if she wants anything, but what if she has gone back to sleep? She would be angry if he woke her. Daniel is sure other husbands don't have this problem, they don't spend their days in a constant dread of their wives. He doesn't want to disturb her, doesn't want to share, his conscience guiltily whispers.

Wearily he settles in front of the telly, both plates and a

tepid beer balanced on the side table, the rest of the pack and some post-match snacks cooling nicely in the now-full fridge. He tries to relax and stop thinking. Tries to stop listening for the door upstairs to open, waiting for the next confrontation with dread.

Daniel is a simple man who just wants a simple life, a quiet life.

____

CHAPTER TWO

Anne-Marie breathes in, inhaling the overpowering stench of stale bacon. She woke up feeling tired and sick and this is making it worse. It means that Daniel is awake and he is in the kitchen. She can't face him right now, can't face anything right now, not right now. Later, she promises to herself as she lies back down and closes her eyes, willing both the smell and Daniel to go away. But even that slightest movement makes her head scream in pain. A throbbing urgency emanates from her bladder, forcing her to struggle out from the unforgiving bed.

Pain, so much pain, from her head to her lower back, even to her toes.

Downstairs Daniel eats on, not caring the slightest bit. The smell of his breakfast clings to her as she falls into the bathroom, struggling to close the door behind her, she sits. Her hands supporting her too heavy head. She can hear Daniel clattering downstairs. You would think that her loud flight to the bathroom would bring on some support, that he would bring her something for her head, some painkillers, a glass of water or even something simple like some tea and toast. Something that would take very little effort, but no; even if she asks, she would only get a long whine about how there is no food in the house because *she* didn't go shopping when *she* promised. He would go on and on, moaning about nothing. It is not her fault; she hasn't been well. He just doesn't understand, doesn't know how easy it is to lose track of everything.

She tries over and over to lift herself from the toilet, her body bursting with pain. Finally she manages, clutching the wall in an attempt to stay up. She lurches out of the bathroom into the hall, keeping her eyes firmly averted from the mirror. She wants to go back to bed, she should go back to bed, she deserves to go back to bed. If only she had a caring husband who would look after her on these bad days, someone who would bring her breakfast in bed and maybe even a comforting word or two. That has always been too much to hope for from Daniel; he doesn't even know what a comforting word should sound like. Where does she go? Downstairs where Admiral Undermining is no doubt waiting, his sarcasm cannons ready to fire, or should she go back to bed, where there is no food or water? She really needs something to eat, something to drink. She needs pain pills too, strong ones, because she doesn't know what the fuck has happened to her legs but she is walking on painful stilts, so bruised, so swollen. Did she fall? Did someone take a hammer to them whilst she slept? She doesn't remember falling but she doesn't remember going to bed either. What happened? What did she do? Did Daniel hear her do it? She crawls back into her bedroom. Moving is bad, very bad. She needs to rest for a little while longer. She needs a jug of water. She needs a fucking worthwhile husband, not that useless lump.

Where the fuck are her painkillers? She wants to cry with frustration as her hand gropes around on the dirty floor, stirring up dust. She finds only empty packets and the mere effort has her dry heaving again. She peers around desperately in the gloom, focusing on the bin, overflowing with mistakes. Another smashed mistake lying close by, she recognises it as the bottle she was drinking from last night. How can it be empty? She didn't drink that much! She doesn't remember smashing it either. Someone else must have done that. They all hate her around here, she is surrounded by enemies, coming in, drinking her alcohol, hiding her painkillers, making her look bad; they must be laughing at her right now. No one believes her about them, Daniel never believes her, he always takes their side. They are all just looking for an excuse to get her. She tries tipping up the bottles, eager for some relief for her dry mouth. They can't all be empty. She didn't drink all of these. She can't let Daniel see. Got to hide everything, got to get something else to drink, got to find something to eat, got to get water. But that means having to go downstairs: he is waiting downstairs, Mr Judgemental, locked and loaded, Mr Disparaging all ready to start his lecture, but she needs to go downstairs, get it over with. She can't bear this pain any longer. Maybe she will be lucky, maybe he will take pity on her today, maybe he will love her today and take care of her, and maybe that fucking burnt bacon will turn back into a winged pig!

She will have to go downstairs, get another box of painkillers, some water – and nothing stronger than water, she tells herself – something to eat, something that hasn't been fried in a ton of lard. Maybe she will even apologise to Daniel for the state of the kitchen, although it wasn't as bad as he made out. Maybe she will even apologise for what she said the other night; she didn't mean to call him a fat bastard, it just slipped out, along with the other things she didn't mean to say. Besides he deserved it, he said some hurtful things too.

Her legs don't seem to work right and she is too tired to remember how to walk. She half steps, half falls down the stairs and then slowly slops through the living room into the kitchen. He doesn't even look at her as she limps past, no smiles, no good morning, no acknowledgement that she even exists. He just keeps chewing, stern-jawed, at his grease.

Fine, be like that. She is not going to apologise if he is going to act like this. She staggers forward to the fridge. Her feet sticking accusingly to the floor. He is probably still mad about the state of the kitchen, she will clean it when she feels better. Just get off her case already!

"Good morning," he finally mutters, sounding like a sulky child.

Where is her breakfast? Has the greedy pig eaten everything? No wonder he is looking, staring. Is he looking pointedly at the washing up? Why can't he leave her alone? She just can't cope with this argument right now.

She just can't cope with Captain Bring Down at all, all poised, ready to jump down her throat for not doing the washing up. She said she would do it, she will, when she feels better. God, what's the rush? She just feels like shit right now, for fuck's sake leave her alone. Doesn't he know how badly her head hurts?

She opens the fridge to look for food, her hands out of habit reach for a half-empty bottle. She doesn't remember opening this one. Maybe Daniel had opened it? Why isn't he saying anything? She waits for the sarcastic comment. He always has one ready. He just doesn't understand how bad she feels.

Nothing. Is he ignoring her? Where is the "Starting a little early, aren't we?" or the "Do you really need that?" She waits for the verbal assault, but it seems he has other plans. The silent treatment. This is why she doesn't want to leave her room when he is around, he just has to be so pathetic. Why can't he ever be nice to her?

Maybe if he said something like "Good morning, Darling,

would you like a little breakfast?" then she would sit down with him, talk to him. But no, he just has to be hurtful and hateful, that is what he specialises in. Tears threaten her eyes, she grabs the bottle and leaves, as fast as her poor head will allow.

Back inside her room, she flings herself into the dirty sheets and gulps angrily at the bottle, waiting for the cold bitter liquid to soothe her. She loves him so much, why does he always have to be so nasty? Downstairs she can hear him running hot water, muttering, probably complaining to himself about the washing up. She said she would do it, damn it! Why does he always have to interfere? Why does he have to be so belittling? Why has their marriage become a silent squabble over the washing up? Why doesn't he love her anymore? She takes another strong swig and waits for the pain inside to dissipate. Tomorrow she will win him back, tomorrow she will stop drinking. She will shower and clean the house. She will look at the job openings, work on her CV. Tomorrow she will see a doctor about her headaches. Oh God, what if Daniel is going to leave her today? Tomorrow would be no good.

She needs to make him love her again and never stop. It's his fault too, if only he could provide support for once. Their marriage can still be fixed, they can still go back to the happy times if he would just stop with his stupid little comments.

She hears the vacuum start up, the noise is piercing; she can't think anymore. She takes another robotic gulp. What time is it? Maybe she should eat something but he is vacuuming close by and is sure to give her evil looks. She is so hungry though. So tired, everything just hurts. Why does he have to be so mean? It won't kill him to do the housework, just this once, will it? No, she can block him out, she is safe in the dark room, he wouldn't dare come in. Maybe she should go back to sleep for a while, sleep will make her feel better. The liquid is making her sleepy.

If only he would shut up with the vacuuming. Yes, she got the fucking hint, okay? Shut up! Shut up!

She grips the bottle firmly in her hand. She should yell out his name, and when he comes to see what's wrong, she should throw the bottle at his stupid head. Hard. Then he will finally understand what it is like to have such a headache. She should get up, tell him to shut up, and fuck off. He needs to be quiet! She is trying to figure out how to fix their marriage. She could sleep right now if it wasn't for him. He is making her ill on purpose now, just to get revenge.

Ahh, finally the unwelcome noise stops. Finally! She lies back, embracing the dark, cold silence. Sweet peace at last! She starts to close her eyes, her heart calming down beat by beat, suddenly jolting dramatically as the front door slams. Where is he going? Why didn't he tell her he is going out? Why would he just leave her like this? He can't be going to the shops; he didn't ask her if she wanted anything. He must be going to see her again, going to spend his afternoon huffing and puffing his sweaty mass over another woman. How could he do this to her? She takes another gulp and then another, downing the last of the bottle.

The throbbing pain in her head begins to numb. Her eyes feel heavy. He can do whatever he fucking wants now. She can sleep this headache away, and it will be all right tomorrow. Daniel isn't seeing anyone he will come back; he always comes back. He has probably just gone to get something else greasy to eat. She hugs herself drunkenly. It's okay, she can save their marriage. It's okay, she is just going to sleep this off, everything will be fine...

She wakes with a gasp. It is dark. She doesn't want to be awake. Is it morning again or evening? Oh God, she fumbles out of the room and into the bathroom, just in time to heave the morning's drink out into the toilet. Heave and heave, gasp, heave. Her stomach is in agony, her head screams as she spits out the last of the nausea. Fervently, she takes a gulp of cold sink water, then another. It trickles comfortingly down her burning throat. She longs to return to bed, back to the heavy sleep, but her stomach screams for food. Food, and a painkiller or three. What wouldn't she do for a painkiller right now? Stumbling out of the bathroom, she sways in the hallway, downstairs she can hear the television. Daniel must be down there, waiting. Why did he have to come home? What if he has brought someone home with him?

Muffling back a sob, she starts the shaky descent downstairs. No, don't let him see tears. Why is she such a prisoner in her own home? She should call Peter. Get Peter to teach him a lesson. But Peter told her not to call him anymore. Peter said he is tired of these "stunts". They are not stunts! It was just a stupid joke, and Peter takes everything too seriously. She was going to give it back. What a fucking useless brother he is. She should call her mother. That will piss the piggy off. Get them both in trouble. Her mother is the only one who cares.

She feels sick again. There must be something wrong with her head, there must be an angry mass of tumours growing in there, it's not normal for it to hurt this much. She should go see a doctor. Then the piggy will be sorry, sorry he didn't believe her, serves him right.

The stench of chips hits her as she passes the television room. She peers into the flickering darkness to see him, slumped, snoring like a pig. She creeps forward, there is a carton of half-eaten cold chips, bobbing up and down on his sizeable belly. A half-finished beer at his side. She stuffs a handful of chips in her mouth, then takes a swig of warm beer. Another handful of chips, another, desperately feeding her hangover. Now they are all gone but she needs more! She creeps into the kitchen in search of more. Oh fuck.

He has brought another bottle. How many times has she told him?

No, she is not going to take it. He must have brought it because he felt guilty about seeing that woman. No, she won't take his dirty booze. He is trying to placate her or keep her out of the way. No! She won't take it. She is going to call her mother about this! Hush drink, that's what this is, hush drink and she won't hush!

She is not going to take the bottle this time...

But it would make her headache go away. Just a couple of gulps, then she would feel better, just a few mouthfuls. She could even go and sit with him in thanks, be the good wife for a while. A few more mouthfuls, a little more food, some water, then she will be okay. She might even be able to cope with him if he doesn't start being Mr Sanctimonious. Maybe they could even share a beer, like old times. She hears another snore. So sexy! So romantic! She turns her attention back to the fridge, what else did he buy? More disgusting junk food. Well, the pig must feast. He won't notice if she took a few items back to her room. And the bottle.

Daniel doesn't stir as she creeps past with laden arms.

He wakes up later in time for the nine o' clock news. A report on a morbid story, about a man who killed his wife in a fit of anger and tried to disguise it as a burglary gone wrong. Daniel has been following the story with interest, as have most people, he's even sympathising a little with the accused. After wondering where his chips went, he goes into the kitchen to grab some popcorn and another beer. He notices the bottle has gone. He is in for another lonely Saturday night, a night of wondering what it would be like to be surrounded by a loving family. Watching all those happy families on the television, watching and wishing and hoping that there is still time.

He waits a few hours, listening but not hearing as much as a drunken laugh from her, so he decides it is safe to go to bed.

She stays quiet all night, which worries him. He spends Sunday pretending to watch TV but all the while waiting, holding his breath, waiting. He checks where he hid the other bottles, but they are gone. Stolen by a thief in the night, a drunken thief of happiness. He doesn't dare confront her; they will never speak of this again. He goes to bed on Sunday night thinking that he has avoided the worst of it. He is just so tired of the arguments. This is what he needs, a quiet weekend with no drama.

Anne-Marie is drunk. She can't remember what she has been drinking or even why. All she knows now is that she wants another drink and the bottles are empty.

She feels like a helium-filled balloon, rising above everything, like she is falling in love for the first time, limb-shaking, heart-racing, word-slurring, stuttering love. She floats out of the room, gliding down the stairs, hands gripping the smooth walls to steady herself. Then she is down, barely remembering the journey, not remembering what she wanted. Where was she going? Why is everything so dark? Where is Daniel? Danny? Danny? DANIEL?

"SHUT UP and go back to sleep!" comes the irate yell from upstairs. He is not going to get up at 4am to deal with her shit AGAIN. He has to go to work in four hours and ten minutes.

Danny, it's so cold. Danny, it's so dark. Why has she come

down? What did she want? The alcohol has made her lips tingle, thirsty for more. Why is it so dark? Her hands rise up, groping the wall. Why is she on the floor? Why can't she get up? Her hand hurts, something is trickling. Why can't she get up? A plaster, she needs a plaster...

"DANIEL!"

CHAPTER THREE

"I want a plaster," she wails as Daniel rushes down the stairs. "I want a plaster."

He panics at the sight of the smeared blood.

"PLASTER!" she screams after the ambulance arrives, pointedly showing the paramedics the glass-embedded wound.

"I just want a fucking plaster," she continues to screech as they load her into the ambulance, Daniel glumly following behind. "Plaster, piggy, PLASTER."

The neighbours peek out from behind curtains, pretending not to see. No doubt they are rejoicing that Anne-Marie is being taken away and hoping that they don't bring her back.

Then the questions start.

"What happened, Mrs Mills?"

"No, really how did this happen?"

"How much did you drink, Mrs Mills?"

"Do you often drink that much, Mrs Mills?"

"How are you feeling, Mrs Mills?"

"Where is Anne-Marie?" Peter asks impatiently, his eyes wrinkling in disgust at the sight of Daniel. He would not have agreed to dinner if he had known Anne-Marie was not coming. He reluctantly agreed to see his sister at his mother's insistence. He has not forgiven her for her last "joke" when she "borrowed" money from his wallet and he is not expecting an apology. He grits his teeth and waits for the weary "She is unwell", or "She has another headache" or "She will join us later if she is feeling better."

Instead his brother-in-law mutters, "She is in the hospital. I would have called you but I didn't get the chance." Peter wouldn't have thanked him for a 4am phone call. "I thought it would be better to tell you in person. It's not serious, she is only being held for observation." Daniel tries to reassure.

Peter loudly grits his teeth.

"I thought we could eat then go and see her. Visiting hours aren't for another two hours."

Typical Daniel, always thinking of food, Peter thinks. "What happened?" he asks finally.

"I don't know. I really don't know what happened. She doesn't remember." All Daniel really knows is that she just wanted a plaster.

Everyone keeps asking what happened? What happened? Daniel feels guilty every time he has to admit he was asleep. But it was four in the morning when she fell. "She fell down the stairs."

At least Daniel hopes she fell. He doesn't know what happened before she fell, all he heard was "Danny, Dannnnnnnnnyyyyyyyyyy, DANIEL," using that voice that told him this was more than drink-induced sadness. That's what finally made him get out of bed. He knew that tone of voice too well. It always meant trouble. He knew he had to get up before the neighbours called the police, again. He dragged himself out of bed, finally flippantly flipped the light switch, expecting to see her doing something stupid, not expecting to see all that blood, not that he would tell Peter this. Peter is not a sympathetic ear. To Peter, Daniel's behaviour is always inexcusable. Anne-Marie's behaviour is inexcusable too, but she is family.

Daniel thought it would be easier to lie to Peter here. Yes, they could have met at the hospital but the food is better here. Anywhere just not at the house, Peter can't see the house! Nor the state of Anne-Marie's room. No twisting of the truth would be believed if Peter saw the full carnage. Daniel had gone home briefly, to shower and change, and had been overwhelmed. He was grateful the paramedics didn't have any reason to go upstairs otherwise he would have had even more difficult questions to answer. It didn't take a genius to realise what had happened though. She broke a bottle, probably to get out the last drops or because she was enraged that there was no more, and she had cut her hand on the glass, quite deeply. Then, like a naughty child with a crayon, she had smeared the blood across the wall as she struggled to get up, continuing to the hallway then stopping abruptly halfway down the stairs. A puddle of stagnated blood marked where she had lain, screaming for him and how long it took him to answer. It had scared the breath out of him when he turned on the light, a nightmare trying to stay strong enough to pick up the phone, to stammer to an indifferent operator that he needed an ambulance.

"It's not as bad as it looks," the paramedic had said, as his wife tried to smear blood onto the man's face. But they still needed to take her to hospital. Six stitches and a minor sprain, mercifully held for observation. His wife refused to say another word to him or co-operate with anyone. She just wanted a plaster. Daniel needs to clean up the blood before she gets released, he can't let Peter see it. He can't let anyone see his shame.

Peter is pretending to study the menu, but he is really adding the evidence in his mind. A fall late at night, the guilty expression on his brother-in-law's face, excuses he has heard before.

Peter gives his order to the waiting waitress as pleasantly as he can, but as soon as she moves away, he starts. "How drunk was she?" His voice is stern.

Daniel's face answers for him, he can't look his brother-in-law in the eye.

"How did she get it this time?" Peter's voice drops. "You bought it for her? After everything we agreed?"

"I bought it for back-up."

Peter watches the worm snivel. "Back-up? What the fuck do you mean, back-up?"

"You are not there when she can't get a drink, you don't know what she is like, what she might do."

"I told you to call me."

Actually you told me not to call you, Daniel wants to say, you said you were done with this shit. Daniel knows it is not worth protesting. Peter is like his mother, they are never wrong, they always know best, they are never anything but "reasonable". There is no point pointing out their inconsistencies, it is not worth a fight.

"I haven't told your mother yet."

How typical of you, you fucking coward, bet you are waiting for me to volunteer to tell her, Peter thinks, clenching his teeth, sealing in his retort.

There are a few minutes of silence broken by the food clattering down in front of them, the now nervous waitress quickly tip-toes away without a comment.

Daniel isn't one to let food go cold, so he bows his head, avoiding Peter's accusing glare and starts shovelling.

Peter picks at his food, composing his next attack and wondering what he should he tell his mother. Sherri is prone to seizing the wrong end of the stick. Telling her Anne-Marie had an "accident" will not go down well. It is not something he can keep hidden from her either. Go to the hospital first he decides, see how bad it is. No need to set his mother on a rampage unnecessarily. It is for the best that Daniel doesn't tell her, she can barely tolerate him and his excuses on a good day. Peter can feel the headache building, an angry bubble of pain behind his eyes. Anne-Marie's drinking isn't the only thing that is becoming a big problem.

"I know things are difficult right now... but..." No, that isn't the right approach.

Daniel immediately tenses, readying himself for stronger defences on hearing the "but".

"Do you know Anne-Marie is thinking of leaving you? She thinks you are not being sympathetic enough, that you are making her worse. She is only thinking about it at the moment," Peter lies softly, hinting that maybe Daniel could still change things. His mother is not the only one who can manipulate, she is just better at it. A lot better.

This is news to Daniel. At first it hurts, she can't leave him, not after all they have been through. Then he reminds himself of how much he has been thinking of leaving her. He is tired of always being taken advantage of.

"Well maybe she should." Daniel stabs angrily at the remains of his food.

Peter had not been expecting this kind of response. Normally his brother-in-law is more docile, more apologetic. Anne-Marie must have really gone too far this time.

"She is just depressed."

"She is always depressed. She has been depressed for over a year now."

"Well, whose fault is that?"

Daniel's fork hits the plate with an extremely angry ding. "I said I was sorry." This reply escapes through gritted teeth, while the knife scrapes across the plate.

"Well why don't you act like you are sorry, instead of..." Peter doesn't venture any further. This is not a good time to be pushing his brother-in-law further by listing his many faults. As fun as it would be.

"There is only so much I can do."

"But you don't do anything. You can see she is hurt, that she is depressed and what do you do to compensate? You ignore her, you mutter stupid comments and hurt her even more. How is that helping?"

"FUCK OFF." Daniel is done with this family. She has been spreading lies again, hasn't she? "I do nothing to help her? Without me, she wouldn't even eat, she would sit drinking in squalor, day in, day out. Why don't you help her for once?" Daniel is not the one who hasn't spoken to Anne-Marie since she was caught stealing money from a wallet, Peter's wallet.

He slams back his chair and pulls on his coat.

"Where are you going?"

Daniel doesn't answer, he just keeps walking. Let Peter go to the hospital and deal with Anne-Marie and her moods for once. Let him do the comforting, the soothing, let him do all he can to cheer her up, only to be let down again by her lies and then afterwards, when he remembers what a lying bitch Anne-Marie can be, he can be the one snivelling with an apology, broken, begging for help.

Daniel marches towards his car, lowers himself in and slams the door. Not that Peter could hear him but it felt good. He is not a man to be messed with tonight. The Fowlers need to learn that he is not a man to be messed with at all. He starts the car, over-revving the engine, and squeals out of the car parking space.

Fuck playing nice, fuck Peter, fuck it all. It's all Peter's problem now. He should just kick Anne-Marie out of the house, send her to live with Peter. Peter would soon change his tune, when he has to deal with Anne-Marie on a daily basis. Sure Anne-Marie was easy to love when you only saw her once every two or three weeks but on a daily basis? Peter would soon learn the importance of having a back-up drink supply then. The fool wouldn't even last a week with her, he would be begging Daniel to take her back. Daniel speeds down the road, smiling for the first time that day, fantasising over and over in his mind how Peter would grovel. He should do it, while she is still in the hospital. He could just gather up the remains of her stuff and dump it, along with the mountain of empty bottles all on Peter's doorstep; better yet, dump it on Sherri's doorstep. Then he should just coolly bellow, "She is your problem now." Just imagine the look on Sherri's face. It has been years since anyone stood up to the old bitch. She would be stunned into silence. Then he would leave quickly, before she regained her senses.

But then if he did that, the neighbours would think he is a monster, so would the nurses. "I see why she drinks," they would chorus. Anne-Marie and Sherri playing the roles of the innocent victims, villainising the cruel, cruel husband, who purposely got his wife drunk, let her fall down the stairs and then abandoned her. "Disgusting don't you think so, Nurse?" Milking it for drop of pity, the whole town would be on their side. Wherever Daniel went, everyone would whisper about him. Worse still, what if Sherri got in one of her moods, she knows where Daniel lives, she would just go storming into his house screaming out his faults, the neighbours listening intently. He would have to watch his step every time he left the house, fearful that she might be hiding in the shadows, readying for a fight. Imagine how the police would treat him? "Waah waah baby can't cope with his mother-in-law?" Even if they did believe him, if they went round to caution Sherri, she would ply them with cookies or pie, something mumsy. Sherri has had a lot of practice over the years at manipulating police officers, if you believe his wife. Then over coffee, Sherri would launch into a well-practised sob story: "He just kicked my daughter out, Officers, no warning." All this whilst urging Anne-Marie to show the nice young men her current bruises. The next thing Daniel knows is that he is in jail for assault, and Anne-Marie is getting a divorce and his house. It just wasn't worth it.

Fuuuuuck.

What did he do to deserve this?

Daniel slams his front door shut and then immediately regrets it. What if the neighbours heard him? He can't face any more questions about last night. He needs to clean up before anyone sees the shameful mess. He waits for a few minutes, but no, no one rings his doorbell. Everyone is pretending that they heard nothing, that he is not home. The neighbours are past the polite all-is-forgiven smiles, past the *you-are-off-the-Christmas-card-list* stage and onto the *next-time-she-does-this-I-am-calling-the-police-this-time-I-swear* stage.

Daniel stares at the bottom of the stairs. The blood has dried into a blackish puddle. The sight of it reignites Daniel's anger. He hits the back of the front door with his fist, hard enough to leave a bruise on his hand. He curses silently at the world, Anne-Marie, alcohol, his parents and every single action that brought him here.

But that doesn't change anything. His curses don't magically clean his house, no fairy godmother arrives, mop bucket in hand, to help. He moves into the kitchen and turns the radio on for distraction. There is so much to clean – the floor, the walls – then he will have to go into her room, sort out the broken glass and other stains. Take out the recycling. The radio blares out a gushy dedication to a husband loved with all her heart. Bollocks, despite their twerpings and twutterings, they didn't really love each other. It is all a fucking lie. Happy couples are a lie; they just call up radio stations with their lies to annoy everyone else, to gloat. They weren't really happy.

They sold him into this lie with an "I do". No one said in the "for better or worse" part that it meant he would be stuck washing his wife's blood and vomit off the floor in the name of love. He plunges the mop deep into the bucket of warm soapy water and returns to the stagnant mess. In the background he can hear the radio drone with a gloomy song about a man, left at the altar, that just goes on and on. Daniel doesn't know why the singer is so miserable, he got off lucky.

Anne-Marie's blood is determined not to leave, refuses to budge without a fight. Every time Daniel thinks he is finished, he sees another droplet, mocking him. The whole time he is scrubbing away at his anger, but is creating a bigger mess. Maybe he shouldn't have left Peter like that. He needs all the friends he can get – but Peter is not his friend, a dark thought interjects, no one from the Fowler family is his friend. He should go to the hospital, first give them time to conspire, then show up with a bunch of flowers, prove them all wrong. Yes, he will finish the stairs then go. The fingerprint smears on the walls can wait until he gets back. Why is he clearing up after her again? He spent all weekend cleaning the house, so she should be the one scrubbing. Why is he thinking of going to the hospital, he should take this opportunity to leave? Why is he even thinking of apologising? He has nothing to apologise for, they should be apologising to him. He shouldn't go to the hospital; he should let her stew. If he goes, she will only sit there, complaining about him to Peter, screeching the old *he-never-takes-cares-of-me-anymore*. Daniel slams the bloodstained mop back into the dirty water, then thinks about kicking the bucket. He thinks about creating a huge bloody mural to their marriage and then leaving everything, including her, out to dry.

He didn't force her to drink the whole bloody bottle or the other bottles. He didn't break the glass. He didn't push her down the stairs. So why should he feel so guilty? Why is it his problem? Why does he have to spend all his time and money on her without getting anything in return? Fuck Anne-Marie, fuck Peter, fuck them all. If Peter cares so fucking much about his sister then why didn't he help her? No, that is Daniel's job while her family sit on the sidelines, criticising him just like his mother always did. Fuck them all. He is quitting. Yes, he is going to clean the house, put it on the market and sell it before Anne-Marie is released. Get out of the range of Sherri's fists and go where no one bleeds, criticises or drinks. An isolated farm, in the middle of nowhere, just him and a dog.

Daniel closes his tired eyes and sighs. If only he had the balls. He tries to go back to the old fantasy, the one that has kept him going for a few years, the fantasy of a chubby little angelic girl, with Anne-Marie's hair and his eyes, asking politely for a bedtime story; for a little boy to declare that he is the greatest daddy in the whole wide world. A happy wife and a loving family to come home to, that's all he wanted. He tries to believe that he can still have that, if he can get them through this. They could still have a happy future together. That's all he wants, why can't they have that? Why can't they try again?

He goes back into the kitchen, carefully empties the red water into the sink, then washes out the bucket and refills it. He arms himself with bleach, a disinfectant spray and as many old rags as he can find. He can't let the hand smears stay on the walls. He needs to wash away the shame before anyone else sees.

The paramedics last night, they saw too much, they were probably talking about him right now, the pathetic loser and his blood-smearing drunk of a wife. Shame burns at his cheeks as he scrubs. Memories come flooding back of all the times he wet the bed as a child, and then tried to scrub away the evidence before the slaps came. As he scrubs at the blood, he is tensing, waiting another stinging slap, of feeling that his skin is about to burn with more than a sense of shame.

There is something forbidden about washing away blood. He feels like a murderer, trying desperately to hide his own guilt; he didn't do anything wrong... except buy her the bottles. That had been a mistake, but he didn't force her to drink it all. Shame and guilt propels him to keep scrubbing at the hand smears until even the cheap green paint starts flaking off. They can't keep going on like this. The image of Anne-Marie, lying bleeding at the bottom of the stairs, looking up at him with those pleading eyes, flashes into his mind. Maybe he will get lucky this time, maybe they will keep her at the hospital for a few days. Maybe he will get very lucky and they will keep her there for a long time. Maybe they will fix whatever is wrong with her. Maybe the old Anne-Marie will be the one who comes home this time. Just keep telling yourself that you love her and you can still be happy together, he thinks. She really does need me, he lies to himself, I can't leave her.

Until death do they part.

CHAPTER FOUR

A nne-Marie is asleep when Daniel arrives at the hospital, or at least she is pretending to be. Peter is there too but not Sherri, thankfully. Peter must still be keeping her in the dark. Peter avoids looking at him, pretending he didn't hear Daniel plod in. Daniel wonders how long he has been here and what kind of lies Anne-Marie has already told him.

Perhaps he is holding his breath, waiting for either a confrontation or an apology, this is not really the place for another argument. Not that anyone would hear them over the drunken singing, the crying and the medical staff shouting. The hospital was just like being at home, right down to the stench of bleach.

"I am sorry I snapped at you," Daniel murmurs, not really meaning it. "I'm just really tired. Anne-Marie woke me up at four this morning." He rubs his eyes in an exaggerated movement. He wants to say more, wants Peter to realise how hard it is to live with Anne-Marie, how much he just wanted a relaxing day off. How much he hates feeling like a wuss just saying the word "sorry" and how Peter should be grateful he is making an effort. But Daniel is a coward and leaves it at that.

Peter murmurs something vaguely comforting, Daniel takes this as encouragement to take the seat opposite and they sit in silence, listening to the hum of the hospital, the bleeps, the drunks' encore and Anne-Marie's steady breathing. It is a fragile, begrudging peace in the midst of chaos.

Why did he come here? Was it still the misguided thought that he could save their marriage? Was he still playing the long-suffering but heroic husband? Was it her blood? The belief that he could still fix all of this? His hands still reek of bleach, thankfully masked from Peter by the other hospital smells. It wasn't easy getting the smeared blood off the walls. He would make a good murderer, he thinks darkly, if he could learn how to cope with the guilt. He has done a good job of cleaning up everything, no one will be able to tell. He needed to repaint the hallway anyway, it's long overdue, something he will eventually do when Anne-Marie is not around to complain about the fumes.

Peter is quiet, too quiet. Probably thinking about what he is going to tell Sherri. There isn't much left for them to talk about anyway. They can't talk any more about the accident without getting angry. They can't talk recovery options in case Anne-Marie wakes up. Silence is for the best. Daniel can't talk about his clean-up operation since Peter probably shouldn't know about that. He can't talk about what he found in Anne-Marie's room either: bottles, lots and lots of bottles, all empty. Daniel is going to have to make a lot of trips to the glass recycling when he gets back. So many empties and he knows he didn't buy them all. He idly wondered why in films the alcoholics always have scores of full bottles to empty into the sink? With Anne-Marie, the bottles are always empty. That was the problem, she couldn't keep anything in stock.

Thankfully they are not discharging Anne-Marie tonight; he has time to finish cleaning up the blood and glass in her room, maybe he will even wipe away the thick layers of dust. Anne-Marie won't appreciate that, no, she will probably accuse him of snooping but Sherri will insist on visiting and she can't see the room in that state. Maybe he should have left it all as evidence, or taken pictures to show the nurses so they knew exactly what they were dealing with.

Daniel sighs and studies his wife. Is she really asleep or does she just not want to talk to them? To him, she probably still doesn't want to talk to him. He hopes she is really sleeping; she doesn't look good under the hospital lights. Too thin, too brittle, too washed out. Is her skin slightly yellow or is it just the light? Daniel looks up to see Peter studying him closely. Ah shit. He hopes his face hadn't given off any hint of disgust. Another arrow for Peter to use. If only Anne-Marie would wake up, that would defuse the pit of awkwardness. Who is he kidding, she is the queen of awkwardness. It is going to be a long hour if she doesn't wake up. A long, tension-building hour.

They sit in silence, occasionally one of them thinks about speaking but then decides against it. Eventually, Daniel fumbles around with his wallet quietly and then hesitatingly passes Peter a few notes. "Sorry I left you with the bill, this should cover it." More than cover it, maybe even cover some of the notes she took from Peter's wallet before she was caught. Peter knows he didn't miscount, despite Sherri's reasonings.

Peter accepts with a nod. It's best to forget about it. Peter hadn't been that upset anyway, it meant that he could eat in peace and actually enjoy his food. Peter doesn't mind the silence either, he is tired of trying to maintain the illusion that he is friends with Daniel. Eventually the two men rise from their chairs as if they are squaring for a fight. Loser wins Anne-Marie perhaps – that would be Daniel, he never wins anything. Daniel breaks eye contact first, turns away, narrowly missing a nurse. Without looking, Daniel knows Peter will have that cruel

Fowler smile on his lips. He briskly mutters goodnight and doesn't look back.

Anne-Marie could happily sleep for ever but they won't let her. As soon as she wakes up, just as she is picking away at a breakfast tray, the nurses tell her that they are coming.

"Just a few questions for you, dear." She didn't expect them to act this quickly. She has seen them before and doesn't want to see them again. They had so many questions before, so many silent threats. It will just be the same dance again. Why can't they leave her alone? She just wants to go back to sleep.

When they arrive, they are more obnoxious than she expects and she knows immediately that she doesn't want to talk to them. She knows she has to but she is not confiding in them. She doesn't need their help. Where is Daniel? Why isn't he here?

They encourage her to go with them into a private room. It is all forced smiles, polite conversation. Do they really think she is fooled by any of their fake attempts to "get to know her better?" That they are on her side? That she would think of them as friends?

It would be easier to cope if she had a drink. Not that they will give her one. The nurses have given her some kind of medication that makes her feel airy, making it hard to think. She hopes it will wear off soon, she needs to focus her thoughts. It is not going to be easy to fool them again.

One of them smiles kindly and points to the seat furthest from the door. "Why don't you sit down there, sweetheart?"

She smiles back but inwardly fumes. "Sweetheart?" She hates all endearments, but sweetheart is particularly sickening. She doesn't trust them; she has seen more genuine smiles from politicians. She has to keep smiling, smiling like hooks are pulling up the corners of her cheeks. She has to get out, she can't spend her days locked in one-to-ones with these people.

When she was younger, she learned how to cry on command, mainly to get Peter into trouble. It is a skill she has had much use for over the years and it's always perfect for situations like these. It is always good to add a tear or two when you are pretending to bare your soul and confess that you have let your drinking get out of control, that she didn't mean to but she has realised now how, sob, bad it had got and she won't, sob, let it get that bad again.

She can't overdo it though, she has to keep it believable. These ones look like they won't be swayed easily. Even though they appear friendly, well they have to, no one would to talk to them if they didn't. They always appear to be non-threatening, until after the first chair is thrown. It's all a game, the bullshit game.

She readjusts her face, trying to look like she has been paying attention. They have been babbling on about how all her answers are confidential, no one is in trouble here, trying to be all reassuring and nice. She nods thoughtfully. She discovered last time that they don't expect her to lie, and she will use this to her full advantage. They think she is at rock bottom and desperate, always a truth-telling situation. But she is fine, thank you, and she just wants to go home.

"I would like to ask you some questions about your drinking habits within the last year." She hasn't been drinking that much or that long. "I would like you to be as honest as possible."

Got to keep that face neutral. She is fighting the urge to roll her eyes and snort. Like they are really that concerned, this is just a job to them, they don't care about her at all.

"By alcohol consumption, we do mean all wine, beer, cider and spirit-based drinks."

Well, duh. Like she would actually admit to drinking cider; nasty, weak stuff.

"Do you have any questions before we start?"

What's the point to all this? Can I go home? Is that a comb-over? Why are you reading out the questions to me? Why can't I just read them? Are you aware of how nasal your voice sounds? Do you not think that this is a waste of Daniel's taxes? Anne-Marie gives what she hopes is the weak smile of a brave survivor and shakes her head.

"How often do you have a drink containing alcohol?"

"Oh, only a couple of times a month," she lies and everyone in the room knows it. Every single goddamn day is the real answer and more often if she could.

"How many units of alcohol do you drink on a typical day when you are drinking?"

"Only a couple of glasses." Then a couple more. Like anyone really pays attention to alcohol units.

"How often have you had six or more units on a single occasion in the last year?"

She has to pretend to think about that one. "I try not to do that; it is very bad for you. Though sometimes you just get carried away," she says with what she hopes sounds like a light-hearted laugh. "Maybe about eight times in the past year."

Maybe every single day, unless Daniel stopped her. Did he put them up to this? What had Daniel told them? Sergeant Sardonic probably relished telling them all about her, he just loves to debase her to an audience, loves to get all their attention and sympathy. He had probably given them notes and video footage. Anything to make himself look like the good guy; he wouldn't miss a chance like this to bring her down.

"How often during the last year have you found that you were not able to stop drinking once you had started?"

"I have control over that, I can stop when I need to," she

tries to say assertively. Well, everyone needs to stop when the bottle is empty.

"How often during the last year have you failed to do what was normally expected from you because of drinking?"

"Never," she says proudly. This is true, no one expected anything from her anymore.

"How often during the last year have you needed an alcoholic drink in the morning to get yourself going after a heavy drinking session?"

"Oh, I don't drink in the morning." Daniel better have kept his big mouth shut. She is going to make him pay for this and if they dare try and hold her here, well... she is just going to have to call her mother!

"How often during the last year have you had a feeling of guilt or remorse after drinking?"

"Only after this happened." She holds up her bandaged hand. She can't ignore this particular elephant in the room. She thought it would be best if she brought it up first, showed willingness to talk about it. "I got a little too carried away." She has ruined their flow now, they were going to bring this up later, as proof she was lying. Do they now question her further on last night or continue with their questionnaire? Which opportunity should they miss? These people are robots. They have to keep to a certain order but they surprise her slightly by biting the bait and asking:

"In your own words, can you tell us what happened?" Big mistake, she has practised for this one.

"I drank a little too much and accidentally broke a bottle." Anne-Marie starts faking the tears of remorse. "It was such a stupid thing to do, I cut myself trying to pick up the shards and went downstairs to get a plaster." It was that fucking plaster that got her into this mess. "And I tripped on the last step. It was such a silly thing to do. It won't happen again," she assures through the tears. That's what they want to hear the most, isn't it? That's what Daniel and Peter will want to hear: "It won't happen again", and what is that other phrase she needs to use? Oh yes: "I promise."

She scores twelve points on her Alcohol Use Disorders Identification Test. Had she been answering a little more truthfully than it would be closer to thirty-three points. Had she been more honest then counselling and other help would have followed along with concerned monitoring.

But instead they can only tell her that she is in a danger zone and caution her on the dangers of drinking. They can't do anything else other than send her home with a sternly worded pamphlet – a pamphlet that Daniel sees her stuff into the bin as she leaves.

She is looking better though. The nurses had convinced her to wash and de-knot her hair and she is finally wearing clean clothes. She is looking better than she has in weeks, despite the bruises and large bandage. She gives Daniel a smile as she climbs in the car, and he finds himself smiling fondly back.

Maybe this time...

CHAPTER FIVE

Anne-Marie has been wearing the same faded grey pyjamas since Tuesday; not last Tuesday or the Tuesday before, but over a month ago last Tuesday. She is barely wearing them anyway: she has lost so much weight, they hang loosely off her scraggly frame. She is vaguely aware that she smells. She knows her hair is in dire need of a wash and she has split ends on her split ends but she just can't bring herself to give a flying fuck. Nothing matters, none of this has ever mattered to her. What is important is that she has a drink in her hands. Danny has left her! How could he leave her now? After all they have been through? She didn't even do anything! She is going to tell her mother! Daniel was so angry with her and she didn't do anything and certainly didn't deserve it. He always seems to be angry with her these days, for no good reason, so what does it matter? She is dimly aware that her hands hurt, so do her feet, but can't think what she did this time. She knows Daniel hurt her but that's not it.

But what does it matter? Did anything really matter? Maybe things will matter again tomorrow but today, right here and now, the only thing that matters is having another drink. Daniel didn't matter, he is always snapping at her, yelling at her, such a wanker. He hurt her hands. Wait 'til she tells her mother.

Was that the door? Anne-Marie tries to stop crying, breathes in deep, trembling breaths. Danny? No one else would dare come in, it must be Danny. Danny must have come back to yell at her some more. Maybe she should apologise before he starts. She knows she did something stupid but can't remember what. It wasn't her fault. She probably should apologise anyway. Daniel is one for holding stupid, petty grudges. She will apologise but she is not sorry. She doesn't know if she can get the words out either but he will understand, he has to understand. She will apologise, even though he hurt her! She takes another gulp and firmly sets the bottle down, then unsteadily gets to her feet. She can hear the thud of feet slowly climbing the stairs. She freezes slightly, Danny's footsteps sound too quiet, too calm, he was so angry before. What is he going to do? She doesn't want Danny to leave, like her father did. She is not going to let him go that easily, not without a fight. Danny is hers. Hers alone.

"Danny?" she calls, staggering out into the hallway.

"What happened?" a voice answers.

"None of your business..."

Wrong answer, bitch.

CHAPTER SIX

DCI Sam Colvin stands outside the Mills' home. The sounds of a child crying echoes down the empty street. She can see a few curtains are twitching, she ignores this and looks instead at the Mills' front garden. It is covered in paving stones, the only plants are weeds growing out from the cracks. From a police perspective, this is annoying, no evidence to indicate an intruder had been here, no footprints trodden in the mud beneath their windows, no flora traces since there is no flora. Only thing to check is the windows, for signs of forced entry. Moving closer, Colvin can see only a thin layer of grime covering the windows on the outside – they haven't been cleaned in a long time. They haven't recently been touched by any human hands either, no fingerprints and no forced entry. A voile curtain stops her and any curious bystanders from seeing inside the house from here.

Colvin knocks on the front door gently and is met by an impatient police officer on the other side and a waft of something strong.

"Forensics have finished." Finished and cleared out. What kept you? his tone of voice implies.

Colvin nods and carefully treads onto the stepping plates. She knows the forensics team would have already spent hours going through the house, taking digital photos, which are already waiting at Colvin's desk, lifting footprints, fingerprints and bagging anything of interest, but there is another reason she doesn't want to step on the floor.

Colvin tries not to inhale, as the officer moves to guard outside, sealing Colvin inside with the overpowering smell of blood, alcohol and something else. She can't blame the officer for being eager to leave. Doesn't really matter, Colvin prefers silence to nervous or nosey chirping anyway.

Directly in front of Colvin, just in front of the stairs, is the main focal point of the hallway: a large, mostly dried, bloodstain, littered with paramedics' debris. The stain is accompanied by matching splatters and smears. There is no doubting that the victim had lain here, unmoving, for some time. This is the point of impact and there will be nothing momentous and long lasting there to mark her last moments, no cracked floor tile or indentation, nothing more than a pool of blood and a ruined stairway carpet.

Colvin takes out her notepad and camera. It has never hurt to take her own photos. She trusts the forensics team completely, they take more professional photos than her own point and shoots, but they focus more on the crime, the blood, the evidence. She likes to have a few more reminders of the victim and the accused, if possible, anything that hinted of their own personalities. A home tends to be a good representation of people's marriages and their mental states, not just from what was in their living space but also what is absent. The forensics teams didn't need to know who the victims were, but she does. Photographing, making notes, doing these things makes her pay closer attention and it helps her to mentally keep her cases separate.

Colvin takes a few upwards pictures of the dirty cream stairway carpet, speckled with red, and moves downwards to photograph the blood, the forensics' markers, the paramedics' debris. The paramedics' wrappers suggest that maybe she had still been alive when they arrived or at least still warm. That someone had tried to save her. Annoyingly it would also mean that numerous people had moved the victim before the forensic team had started their photographs.

The hallway is bare, apart from the red speckles, the walls a grimy green colour. No family pictures, no works of "art". No hints in this hallway of the two people who had lived in this house. Just a dying plant placed forlornly next to the front door.

The living room is also bland. No outstanding features, nothing but white walls and cheap wooden flooring. The room's main features are a green sofa, sun-faded, stained and dotted with cigarette burns, plus an expensive looking television. Already she can guess at the main priorities in this house. There is a noticeable change in odour in this room; the smell of the staircase still lingers but there is a stronger smell of grease and spilt beer. She looks down at the imprint in the sofa cushions, someone has spent of lot of time sitting there. Next to the sofa is a badly repaired side table. There is nothing to make this room look pretty or stylish or even homely.

She moves into the kitchen. The walls are a garish yellow. A dirty frying pan and several cracked plates sit in the sink, adding power to the greasy smell. Some saucepans sit on a worktop, gathering dust. A fruit bowl in the centre of a worktop contains three yellowing apples that were no doubt bought with good intentions. She takes a photo of the fridge and notes the empty freezer had been turned off, quite some time ago. There are a few bottles of beer in the fridge and some take-away containers. So far all she can deduct is that the people in this house didn't take care of themselves or their possessions.

A small pile of opened post lies on the kitchen table. Colvin flicks through – there are the usual bills, but nothing issuing a final demand, a few advertisements and take-away menus. No letters from jilted lovers or angry spouses, nothing to make this easy. She looks out of the kitchen window onto an equally neglected garden. The cobwebs around the kitchen door are undisturbed, there is no point going out there.

Time to go upstairs.

She takes a wide step carefully around the blood pool, then steps over the bloodstained step and slowly and carefully climbs up the staircase. When the forensic team were here, they had the job of photographing any stain that looked even slightly suspicious. She does not envy them. They didn't just have to photograph each stain, they also had to take diligent notes of each stain's shape and size, what the stain was (if known) and what item had been stained. Each stain has to be given its own marker and number. Colvin is betting the numbers ran quite high in this house. She notes the random holes in the carpet, where samples had been cut away. These photographs and notes are helpful in deciding how the wound was inflicted, the possible weapon used and whether the injured was moving when hit, or if they moved after being hit. The carpet makes it hard to tell, as the blood soaking into the fabric has distorted its shape. Colvin could only describe the blood splatters here as a light rain of blood. Someone had moved around quite a bit, whilst bleeding heavily. She is trying not to form a judgement just yet, but the sight of so much blood makes her feel angry and sick.

On the upstairs hallway, she stares, mouth wide open in disbelief, at the blood stains criss-crossing the carpet, the splatters and dents in the hallway walls. Numerous fist-shaped dents. A dark feeling shudders through her body as she remembers similar cases where she has seen similar holes. She takes a deep breath and steps into the master bedroom. Colvin starts with the camera, trying to understand it all. She has seen rooms this badly trashed before, quite a few times, but normally it was when unsupervised teenagers and alcohol were involved and normally they had left something standing, but this room is completely wrecked.

Click, she focuses in on the object closest to her. Click. It's a wedding photo in a bent silver frame, broken glass falling out as she picks it up. Click. She takes a long look at the picture of the crumpled newlyweds. Click. She takes a photo of the faintly smiling, newly married couple. Click. Already hating the sight of the groom. Here is the point of impact where it must have collided into the wall. Click. Taking a small chunk of stripy wallpaper and plaster with it. Then she moves on to photograph the alarm clock, which will never wake anyone up again. It only just missed the dirty window. Click. She moves across to look outside. She has to be careful not to step on the broken fragments of light bulb or the remains of the lamp. Click. Moving aside another voile curtain, she can see an overview of the garden. It is as she expects, overgrown grass, a forlorn washing line and a rusty barbecue set in the corner. She turns back to the room, photographing a bedside novel, *How to Love Again*, which has been trodden on, its spine for ever broken, a droplet of blood adding to its cover. Click. The wardrobes, not destroyed, being too heavy to throw. Click. There is little point in throwing pillows but they had been thrown anyway. A bent comb. Colvin scans the wreckage carefully but can see no trail of blood drops in here, just a couple of random drops. A connecting en suite had been spared the onslaught. Colvin notes the single toothbrush and toothpaste next to a dirty sink and the toilet seat firmly up. Nothing seems out of place in this small en suite, no blood spots or splats. She moves on.

A garish green bathroom is next. She peers into and

photographs a dirty shower and a cheap bottle of shampoo. Apple scent. The forensic team had the unpleasant job of documenting the toilet, which is flaked with vomit and smeared with blood. Colvin takes a few quick photos then rapidly moves away. The blood spots in here indicate that the bleeder came in, then they stayed in front of the toilet, being sick, smearing blood around the toilet. The evidence indicates only one person came in here, by the look of the spots, and they walked in and eventually walked out again, they weren't running or trying to hide. Interesting. Some of the blood smears are at a height that suggests a hand may have leant on the walls for support as they came in. She thinks this bleeder is the same person as the victim but is unsure. She follows the blood tracks out of the bathroom and into the last room, maybe she will find more answers in there.

The last room feels like a suicide note laid bare. It has been decorated in depression, intertwined with gloominess, the heavy scent of alcohol, dust, body odour and urine. The room is lit only by one bare overhanging bulb, still turned on. The light from the room's only window has been completely shut out by dusty blinds, curiously framed by curtains with a childish blue elephant motif. These curtains now hang limp, almost completely pulled off their rings by a bloody hand.

Glass shards, representations from all of the major spirits bottles, border the room's floor, having been thrown with some force into the dented walls. Everywhere Colvin looks is glass, glass and more bloody glass. Colvin is feeling slightly tipsy just breathing in the alcohol fumes. A surviving empty bottle lies half in, half out of a kicked over bin, complete with a bloody footprint. Colvin moves closer to the bed, glass crunching under her feet. The bed is crumpled and stained, with a smell so strong that Colvin has to check that someone isn't still sleeping there. Just in case.

Curiously, like the elephant curtains, the dirty duvet has a faded pink polka dot motif, another thing that felt childish and out of place. Next to the bed is a splintered, overturned bedside table, haloed by spilt pills and more broken glass. Colvin picks up one of the pills, paracetamol judging by the stamp. Colvin turns, finally noticing the writing on the wall. A wobbly hand had written *Fuck you Daniel* on the chipped, baby-blue walls with a marker pen, then hand stamped it with more blood.

In the centre of a room stands a mostly empty tequila bottle, its lid off, looking as if someone has left it and will come back for it at any moment, another full bottle of vodka also faithfully waiting close by. Judging by the numerous blood spots on the wooden floor and the blood smears on the tequila bottles, she thinks someone sat here for a while, just drinking or possibly they had continued throwing the empty bottles at the walls, or even emptying any remaining bottles and then throwing them at the walls. It is hard to tell but either the two rooms were wrecked by two different people or the person started in the first bedroom, then came into this one. The drops and smears on the floor suggest that they moved around a lot in this room, cutting open feet and hands on the glass shards as they operated. The alcohol would explain why they continued smashing despite their injuries. It will be a nightmare waiting for all those samples of blood to come back.

Colvin finds it hard to believe that this is it, that there is nothing else to show that in this house lived two married people, loving each other. Everything in this house feels lonely and separated, hinting at people barely there. This was a house, not a home, for the Mills, and to her this felt like long-term abuse and neglect, and not just to the house. What she has seen so far has only made things more complicated: someone or some people had been drinking heavily in this house, and an accident could have happened today resulting in the victim's death, but the *Fuck you Daniel* in here and the smashed ornaments in the main bedroom, they all suggest a fight, a very angry fight, a possible motif for murder. Then the smaller bedroom just screamed of suicide and despair. Something had been building for a while in this house. Either way the survivor has a lot of explaining to do.

Downstairs, the front door loudly swings open, intruding on the concentrated silence. "Sam?" a voice calls.

Colvin takes one last look then carefully treads back downstairs to meet her partner, DCI Nicolas Grimm.

If Anne-Marie could still smell, she would smell the sharp scent of cleaning fluid, barely masking other rotting smells, including herself. The kind of smells we are normally forbidden to mention in polite conversation. If she could still see, she would think she is in another hospital, but she is not. Thankfully she can no longer feel, because she is not going to like what happens next.

The staff confirm her identity then carefully strip away her clothes, bundling the dirty garments into waiting bags, carefully labelled by police officers. The forensic pathologist begins the arduous task of photographing, examining and swabbing every single one of her bruises, abrasions and lacerations. The pathologist carefully notes the size and shape of each wound, then swabs it, looking for fibres, flecks of paint and other evidence. They find quite a lot of glass, clear glass, green glass, brown glass, even a shard of blue glass. The glass shards are lodged in a number of wounds and to their horror, these wounds are definitely pre-mortem. They brush her knotty short hair very carefully, wincing as even more glass falls down into awaiting containers. Then from beneath Anne-Marie's fingernails, small traces of flesh are removed. The autopsy is going to take a few more hours and the analysis and testing a few weeks.

Questions are asked. Did she put her hands out as she fell or was she already dead? It is not dinner conversation, the present officers never talk to their families about how to spot the difference between the marks on someone who has fallen whilst alive against someone pushed when already dead. It is sickening what some people will do for insurance money. This body is difficult because of the scale of the wounds. The questions have become harder – does that head wound suggest she had been hit by anything except the stairs? And most importantly, what has caused those circular dark bruises around her wrists?

"You should return tomorrow, when the lividity has settled. Sometimes then, we see even more bruising, especially if they were caused just before death," one of the mortuary technicians tells the police officers. "These bruises," she gestures to the wrists, "all show signs of inflammation, meaning that they were inflicted before she died."

The police officers nod, taking even more meticulous notes. The technician is thinking of a similar case, another frail lady, another tragic "accident". They had almost signed it off as such, but decided to do one last check before releasing the body. To their horror and disgust, they had found ten very distinctive finger-sized bruises, inflicted just before death, on the victim's back. Bruises the partner had no explanation for.

One thing they could be sure of, judging by the smell on her clothes, judging by the faint, sickly sweet odour that wafts as they cut open her internal organs, Anne-Marie had been wearing the smell of alcohol like a cheap perfume. When she had died, she had definitely been pickled.

CHAPTER SEVEN

Daniel can barely think straight. His wife is dead, that's something he didn't expect, not today, not ever, despite his hopes and fantasies. He expected her to be the thorn in his side for a lifetime, just to spite him. The world could end and she would still be at his side, screeching for a beer. No matter what happened, she would be there.

But suddenly she is gone and he doesn't know how to feel, he has forgotten how to feel anything, other than empty. He has felt nothing since he found her, lying at the bottom of the stairs, just like before, except this time she wasn't screaming for a plaster. She wasn't gripping him tightly in her claws, shrieking. She was quiet, serene, bloody and very dead. It was all his fault. It wasn't his fault.

He doesn't feel sad, doesn't even feel the occasional flashes of anger that have been a constant norm in the last year. He knows he should be feeling a little humiliated but doesn't. When he arrived at the police station, hours ago, the officer unemotionally ordered him to stand on a large sheet of paper, then made him remove his shoes and then his clothes. The officer took everything away "for processing". Gone were his favourite jeans and shirt. Gone were his socks with the pizza motif. In return he has been given a pair of *custody* shoes and clothes. The custody clothes don't feel right and the shoes are plimsolls. Plimsolls, the last time he wore plimsolls was at school. Any other time these plimsolls would have reignited the old feelings of shame and humiliation, but right now he is a worm and life is a bird.

He suspects that the police are laughing at him right now. Isn't that what police do? On crime shows, the detectives were always making wisecracks about their victims and the murderers. No doubt they were holding up his favourite jeans and making some wise-ass remark about his weight. Fuckers. They had probably been in his house too, criticising the décor, his wife, his everything. Judging him. Finally a flash of anger cuts through the nothingness, overwhelming him. They should leave him alone; he just wants to punch all those fuckers and scream that he didn't do anything wrong.

He can't keep control of his anger today, the argument opened up a whole vault of his repressed anger. The anger that has been building up for years keeps gushing out, like a nosebleed on a hot day. His stomach rumbles. The argument meant that he missed lunch, and now Anne-Marie is making him miss dinner. Her last laugh. He doesn't expect anyone here to offer him food, despite the fact he pays their salary. They could use some of his taxes to get him a sandwich, couldn't they, just one measly sandwich? Not that he feels hungry or could eat, but the gesture would be nice, someone acknowledging he was there and actually treating him like a human being would be nice.

What is taking them so long?

He has seen no one for the past hour. The last person was some sour-faced officer offering him the chance to call his lawyer. His lawyer! Like he could afford his own personal lawyer and had them on speed dial! What does he need a lawyer for anyway? That's what the guilty ones do, isn't it? They immediately start calling their lawyers. Because lawyers aren't expensive and he is just so rich, he can afford anything he wants. When their questions start, they will just be prodding him, waiting for him to say, "I want my lawyer." Then they will know that they have hit a nerve and to keep probing. No, he isn't going to waste good money on a lawyer. He can prove he is innocent without one. It is just a case of saying the right thing, at the right time. He can do that.

Deep breath, what is taking them so fucking long? Another deep breath to stay calm, he needs to appear calm, co-operative, as co-operative as possible. It's not like he wants to go home. Home is never going to feel like home again. Not that it has felt like home in a long time.

Outside the room, Colvin and Grimm are watching him. They have already decided that Grimm should lead on the interview. Grimm is of a similar age to Daniel and might be able to create an *us-lads-together* vibe; it might make him relax a little, and if they get lucky, slip his guard occasionally. Colvin is going to observe and take notes – she will watch Daniel's facial expressions and movements carefully, writing down any questions that Grimm might miss. She will ask a couple of questions, just to see how Daniel reacts to talking to her – will he sneer at her? Will he be dismissive? Or treat her indifferently? Or perhaps he will respond more positively to her. In which case, she will take over the questions. Grimm and Colvin have been partners for over a year now, there is no longer a power struggle between them... most of the time.

"Give me a sec," Grimm says before vanishing down the corridor, leaving Colvin alone to stare intently at Mr Daniel

Mills. Mr Mills, Colvin decides, is the type of person she would expect to see in here as a victim, not as a person of interest or a prisoner-defendant. He has the characteristics of a duped John or a mugging victim. In her opinion, he looks like an owlish teacher, middle-aged, chubbing more around the sides as he loses on top. If she got on his bad side, she would expect him to retaliate with a strongly written letter, the type who hides behind letters and rules, not the type to attack outright. Not a physical aggressor by nature, but then she is well aware anything can happen in the heat of the moment. He does look tired and stressed, that is a good start, tired people can't always think straight, sometimes they break more easily. His hands are already trembling, nerves have hit him hard. He looks the type that will talk, the *I-will-confess-all-in-exchange-for-leniency* type. The *it was an accident!* type.

Mr Mills can't deny that he had been in some kind of fight today. You didn't have to be a detective to know that, looking at the three bright red scratches running down his face. Something, like a certain lady's fingernails perhaps, had dug in deep at his forehead, tearing down at his meaty cheeks, the lines breaking only at his glasses. Not deep enough to be the source of the bloody mess in his house, but deep enough to contribute a few drops of blood. Now the real question is, who or what caused those scratches, was it the same thing that has caused the small swelling to form on his bottom lip? Something that happened as she was falling? Or what led to the push? Colvin takes a deep breath and cautions herself about jumping to conclusions. Mr Mills could have had an encounter with an angry cat or got into a fight with a stripper. He could have a reasonable explanation about why he and his wife lived in squalor and neglect.

Daniel looks down at the table as they enter the room. Colvin thinks she sees a scowl cross his chubby face. She sits down as Grimm starts setting up the tapes.

Daniel doesn't want to talk to them, he doesn't want to talk to anyone. He has been waiting so long for someone to come in and now he just wants them to go away again. He suspects that Peter isn't getting treated like this. Peter was probably allowed to go home hours ago. Peter has always been good at talking his way out of a situation, just like his sister. Peter is probably at home, laughing at him. These officers are probably just the beginning. Daniel imagines that they are the first in a long line of officers just waiting for their chance to laugh at the loser. Anne-Marie undoubtedly had planned this all along. She wasn't really dead, she is backstage, somewhere out of sight, laughing along with Sherri. It's just a game, the first episode in a new TV show, *How to Humiliate your Husband* or something equally stupid. It's all just a joke, a big, unfunny joke. They have really got him, ha ha, those special effects really fooled him into thinking his wife is dead. He holds his breath, waiting for the presenter of the show to show up and announce the joke. He is ready to laugh it off and say something like, "You really scared me there, honey" or something equally macho.

That blood had looked so realistic. The paramedics had been good actors, he has to admit, really authentic. They had him worried for a while but now he has figured it all out. He is poised, ready to laugh a fake laugh. *Oh you guys got me good this time.* They can't drag this out much more. Any minute now. It's going to be such a relief. Any minute now.

In front of him, Grimm is busy unwrapping tapes and explaining the recording equipment. Daniel isn't really paying attention. He is purposely avoiding eye contact with the other officer, who is staring intently at him. She is probably on Anne-Marie's side, savouring the joke.

"This is DCI Nicolas Grimm and DCI Sam Colvin interviewing..." one officer announces to the machine. This has definitely got to be a stunt, no one would have a name as ridiculous as that in real life, Daniel thinks, as Grimm states the date and time to the recording equipment. They are really playing this joke to the death, aren't they?

"Please state your full name."

Daniel hopes all the questions will be this easy.

"Daniel Ian Mills." God, how cruel his parents were. The officers will have a good laugh at that too, everyone else did.

"Please state your full address."

Daniel states his address in a low voice, he doesn't want to think of home right now.

"Please state your date of birth." Why do they need him to state this? Surely they would already know. This interview is going to take for ever if they keep asking pointless questions, but Daniel begrudgingly complies. The female cop seems to be scribbling something intently, whilst peeking glances at him. Daniel wishes he could grab the notepad, yell at her that this joke is not funny anymore, but he knows he needs to keep playing along.

"At the moment, there is no lawyer present, are you sure you wish to proceed without one?"

"Yes."

"You have the right to free and independent advice either in person or over the phone. If at any point you wish to seek legal advice, please tell me and I can stop the interview to allow you to contact a representative." Grimm is good at being polite and calm, he has to be; one rude word, one impolite gesture can throw the whole interview.

Daniel doesn't appreciate his politeness; he just wishes they would shut up about the damn lawyer already.

"I now need to caution you," Grimm continues. *Oh my God,*

here we go, thinks Daniel. "It is important that you understand, you do not have to say anything..." *But anything you do say, yadda yadda, come on hurry up, I want to go.* "It may harm your defence if you don't mention, when questioned, something which you may later have to rely on in court." *Court? Court? They are really taking this joke too far now.* "Do you understand?" *This isn't real, is it?* "Do you understand?"

"Yes, I understand," Daniel hears himself mumble.

"This is your opportunity to explain what happened today." *I don't know what's going on anymore.* "You are not currently under arrest." *But if I try to leave the room, I will be, won't I? That female officer looks like she is dying to get her handcuffs out, and not in a good way either.*

Colvin notes that Mr Mills is visibly uncomfortable, he is leaning away from the table, distancing himself from the officers. She thinks he will be unwilling to trust them or even to tell the complete truth. He is only here because he thinks he has to be. People these days feel they have to play a certain role or act in a certain way at interviews, sometimes this works to their advantage. She supposes they just don't know what to do or say, so they take cues from what they have seen on television. It is true that Daniel can leave at any time, but they will soon have him back again if he does.

"Would you like a drink or anything to eat before we start?" Grimm is the good cop after all, his voice has taken on that fatherly tone again.

Daniel mutters "No." He is not falling for that one. Daniel is still hoping that this is a joke, a stupid stunt, but that is starting to feel like a foolish hope, just like the possibility his wife is still alive.

"Do you have any questions before we start?"

Another muttered "No."

Colvin thinks this interview is going to be slow, painful and of no use to anyone. They have to go through all the motions, jump through the right hoops. Where will Grimm start? "Mr Mills, did you murder your wife?" is direct at least, but maybe too blunt. Murder is a nasty word, people prefer to use words like accidents, incidents. She needs to be fair, there might be a good explanation behind Mrs Mills' death. But an honest answer to that question would save them days and days of mind numbing, exhaustive backbreaking work. Especially as Colvin thinks she knows the answer to this question. So does Grimm.

"What do you do for a living, Mr Mills?"

"I am an accountant," Daniel mutters. He is a desk jockey, a drone, it's nothing of interest. He is coming to a sinking realisation that the police are likely to interview everyone he knows, not just Peter but Sherri, and probably his boss, his co-workers, his neighbours, so many people who didn't like him because of Anne-Marie, so many people who will relish in the opportunity to drag his name through the mud and deeper.

"Did you go to work today?"

"No."

"Why didn't you go to work today?"

"I have some holiday I am using up." A holiday at home because Anne-Marie didn't want to go anywhere. Daniel had desperately wanted a week away in the sun, but there never seemed a right time to talk about it. He would have even paid for an all-inclusive just to keep her supplied, but every time he tried to bring up the subject, she ignored him. They couldn't really afford it anyway and it probably wouldn't have been worth it.

"How long have you been on holiday for?"

"Three days." Three miserable, television-filled days, chugging weak beer and wishing he was back at work. No wonder he had snapped. He was supposed to be off for another week and a half, but had been considering going back early. Cancelling his leave until Anne-Marie was better.

Colvin notices the flash of anger sprinting across Daniel's face. She thinks her earlier impression of the owlish teacher may be wrong. Daniel Mills is not as harmless as he appears to be.

"So, starting from this morning, what did you do today?"

"I got up, ate breakfast, watched the news." The morning seems so long ago now. He had woken up alone and tired. Anne-Marie had started drunkenly singing last night, at God knows what time, before loudly crashing into the bathroom and slamming the door. Anne-Marie didn't get out of bed until midday today and she was already drunk. Should he tell the officers that? That his wife was drunk before she even got out of bed? He doesn't even know if she did go to bed last night, she might have just passed out on the floor. He has to give them something more, he knows that, something to make them see how difficult she was being, but he just doesn't know what to say. What do they want from him?

"Then what happened?"

There is a long pause; both officers can see that Daniel is closed up, not wanting to talk. Grimm knows this isn't necessarily a sign that he is guilty. From experience Grimm knows that sometimes the chatterboxes, the ones who try to smoke screen their way through, the ones who think they can lead the interview, the ones who try too hard to appear as the good guy, they are the ones you should be suspicious of. The important thing to do, he reminds himself, is stay calm and appear in charge. He thinks Daniel might respond well to a sympathetic ear, he knows already the Mills did not have a happy marriage. What they need to know is how unhappy it was.

"I just want to hear your side of the story, Mr Mills," Grimm says in a slightly sympathetic tone. Well, it's not like they are going to hear Mrs Mills side.

There is an audible sigh, Daniel drops his head, exhausted. He doesn't want to be here, he doesn't want to go to home either, or anywhere else. He wishes he could be someone else. He regrets every choice in his life, everything that led him to Anne-Marie's arms and kept him there.

"Anne-Marie got up about twelve-ish." Daniel had been getting ready to leave house, contemplating where to treat himself to a lunch, alone. He was just looking for his wallet when she appeared. If only she had got up ten minutes later or if he had made his mind up sooner. "I was just about to leave." What does he tell them now? Does he say, I was going to meet a friend for lunch, so he doesn't sound like a complete loser, but then they would want to know who the friend was. Or does he say, I was about to leave for lunch, without Anne-Marie, because that's how shit our marriage had become. "I was going food shopping." Daniel can feel his cheeks flush and ducks his head a little more. He is a bad liar, now they will all think he is lying for a different reason. Might as well come out with it all now. They already know what a loser he is. "She was already drunk when she got up." Not a happy drunk either. *"Where the fuck are you going?"* had been her first slur.

Something inside Daniel had snapped. Why did he have to put up with this shit? It wasn't fair. "Don't you talk to me like that", or something along those lines, is what he snarled in response. He may or may not have added the word bitch in the heat of the moment, his mouth had said words without thought.

"We started fighting and I left the house."

"What were you fighting about?"

Daniel really doesn't want to answer this question. Everything, they were fighting about everything these days, neither of them willing to back down. Money or the lack of it.

Alcohol. Food. The arguments were easier to cope with than the constant silent treatment, which had also been his mother's weapon of choice.

"Oh, just something really petty."

Grimm stays silent, waiting for Daniel to expand on his answer. Daniel has closed his eyes, he is trying to block out the police officers, the interview room, Anne-Marie, everything. In his mind, Daniel is trying to reach a happy place, a deserted island somewhere warm.

"She saw I was leaving and she didn't want me to leave." It was a continuation of a previous fight. They had fought the night before: their fifth wedding anniversary was in three days, and he wanted to do something special, something to try and help them to remember that they loved each other. She wanted to get drunk. They had fought, he had retreated to the TV, she had retreated to the bottle. It's probably why she had woken him with her singing, just out of pure spite. He had gone to bed angry, had been woken up repeatedly during the night, then woke up mid-morning still angry. He had then exploded when he saw her already drunk early in the afternoon. Really, why was he even trying anymore?

"I didn't tell her I was only going out for some food. She thought I was really leaving." He had wanted to upset her. He was so angry with her, part of it was spite but it was also to help her, well that is what he will tell himself later. Over and over. He just thought if he could make her see how much she was hurting him and herself. Maybe if she thought she was going to lose him for good this time, he had rationalised, maybe she would finally agree to get help. It was a shitty plan but he didn't know what else to do. In his mind, when he fantasised about this plan, she had fallen to her knees, begging him not to leave and she would do anything. He would drop her off at some rehab clinic, and she would emerge a few months later, marriage saved. He never expected her to lunge at him, screaming.

Silence.

"Then we started fighting," he mumbles. The police officers probably just think he is a pussy. He can't tell them everything, they won't understand.

"When you fought with your wife, did the fight turn physical?" Colvin doesn't know how Grimm is able to ask that without a hint of a smirk, of course it turned physical; Mr Mills had no other explanation for the long scratch marks. There was no way Mr Mills could deny it. Of course he wasn't going to admit to everything, not straight away, they always start with a lie, then a half truth, whatever they think they could get away with.

Daniel deflates even more, the officers definitely think he is a pussy, he can see it in their eyes. He is tired of making excuses for Anne-Marie, tired of defending her from what people thought. What does he have left to lose now? She took his dignity years ago. Why is he still protecting her? It's an automatic response these days.

"Yes, when I told her I was leaving, she..." He dry swallows, suddenly feeling very thirsty. "She kept trying to scratch my eyes out," he says finally, with a slight gesture towards his face. Not an easy thing to do to a person who wears glasses, but Anne-Marie was drunk and determined. She just wouldn't stop. Daniel thought he had seen all of Anne-Marie's bad side, but he had never seen her like this... ferocious. He thought she was going to kill him with her bare hands. Was she trying to stop him from leaving or just put him off ever coming back? Or did she just want him dead?

"What did you do?"

"I tried to hold her back. She just wouldn't stop... She

started screaming at me... telling me she hated me, I couldn't make her stop."

"How were you restraining her?"

"I was holding her wrists. She then started trying to stomp on my feet." The officer who had taken his clothes earlier had remarked with astonishment at the bruises on his feet, then insisted on taking a photo. She tried biting him too, she was an angry, drunk mess. "I couldn't control her."

"Then what happened?" Grimm continues to prod, with a note of sympathy in his voice.

It sounds fake to Daniel. He takes a deep breath, reminds himself that he has nothing to hide. "I pushed her backwards."

It was inevitable that something like this would happen. They were arguing more than ever, she was drinking more than ever, something he didn't think was even possible. In the previous months, she had started lashing out at him more, drunken slaps that she insisted didn't hurt. One of the reasons he took this holiday was to try and figure out what was upsetting her so much, before any of his colleagues saw the bruises she was inflicting.

She had been driving him mad all this week. She was determined to be either drunk or sad, there was no snapping her out of it. She seemed to have an endless supply of alcohol now, and Daniel had no idea where she was getting it from. On his first day off he was determined to use his time to help her, restore their marriage and eat some cookies, no more ignoring the problem. He tried and she wore him out in less than a day. On that first day, he noticed her door open. She was sitting on the bed and barely acknowledged him when he said good morning. She just sat there, staring at nothing. Her room was a mess again, a graveyard of spirit bottles.

"Maybe you should take a shower," he said, trying to be as gentle as possible. He didn't quite know what to say. He was sure, given how badly his wife was reeking, that she would feel much, much better after a shower, she would be easier to talk to, too.

"Yeah, maybe." A pause, she didn't even twitch a muscle.

"Then maybe we could go out." He thought he saw her smile slightly; he took it as encouragement.

"We could go see your brother or go out for lunch, wherever you would like to go." He had been really trying that day, it had something to do with the expression on her face. She looked tired and drained, but there was something else there, something he didn't like. A real expression of sadness.

"Yeah that sounds good."

"So if you get showered and dressed, I will do the vacuuming and then we will go?"

"Yeah."

He didn't want to rush her. Didn't want to provoke her. No arguments today. He was trying. No raising his voice either but despite his attempts to be kind, she wasn't moving. He went off to vacuum, and twenty minutes later he came back, but she was still sitting there.

"Aren't you going in the shower?"

"Yeah, in a minute."

"I am ready to go when you are."

"Yeah, okay."

"Your brother is expecting us in thirty minutes." That was a lie but he just wanted her to move or even to react. He hadn't even called Peter at that point. He knew Peter would only say it's an attention stunt and to ignore her.

"Yeah, okay." It was something in her voice too. Daniel didn't know what else to do. Give her time, he thought hopefully, but an hour later, she was still just sitting on her bed, staring into space. She hadn't even touched the bottle this morning.

"Do you want a cup of tea?" He tried to change tactics, maybe he should call Peter, ask him to come here.

"Yeah. okay."

The tea went cold, untouched at her side. Peter wasn't answering his phone, Sherri was still on holiday. Daniel didn't know what else to do. He had tried. He had been patient, tried to be kind, but she was annoying him now. It felt like she was playing a game with him but he didn't know the rules of the game. Why wouldn't she talk to him? Why was he wasting his holiday waiting for her to do something?

He thought about calling for medical help, but who was he supposed to call? What was he meant to say? I am worried because my wife won't drink her tea? It all just seemed so ridiculous. When he went to bed that night, she was still just sat there but by morning she was herself again.

Does he tell the officers all of that? It made him seem so uncaring and they want to point fingers anyway. It didn't matter what she did or how crazy she drove him, everyone took her side. The officers stare at him, waiting for him to open his stupid mouth and continue incriminating himself.

"I pushed her backwards, off me. She ran into my bedroom. I told her again that I was leaving. Then I left."

"What was she doing when you left?"

Daniel takes a deep breath and resumed his staring contest with the table. "I could hear her throwing things in my room." She was screaming about how much she hated him. He doesn't want to admit that he yelled back at her, yelled that he hated her too and that she better not be there when he came back. He doesn't think she heard him anyway, he just needed to get out of there, before he did something stupid... Or before she really hurt him – never had he been so afraid of her and so angry at her at the same time.

"What time was this?" They don't believe him, he could tell. No one ever believes him when he talks about Anne-Marie these days. Especially when he talks about how violent she could be.

"About 1 pm." He should have just left her sleeping and gone out to lunch. He should have made sure he left before she got up. He should have done a lot of things differently, not just today.

"What did you do after you left the house?"

"I called Anne-Marie's mother, Sherri, she didn't answer. Then I called her brother Peter. He didn't answer either."

"Why did you call them?"

Silence. Daniel's hands quickly withdraw from his sides, moving to grip the armrests of his chair firmly. Colvin can't quite see but she guesses his feet have also locked around the chair legs. Daniel's body language has gone from comforting himself to restraining himself. It tells Colvin that Daniel is now rather anxious, these questions are unnerving him. Her real interest is why are they disconcerting? Why are they causing such a reaction? Is Daniel upset because he is facing the truth that his marriage was... what? Out of control? Long over? That he had no one to turn to? Was he trying to tell them something? Was he upset because he is looking more and more like the bad guy? That this interview isn't going the way he hoped?

"I wanted..." A gasp, a feeling of weakness chokes in Daniel's throat. "I wanted them to take Anne-Marie away, just for a few days." Daniel won't admit he has failed yet another drunk and if Sherri or these officers hear the voicemail that he left Peter, they would think him weak and pathetic. Who was he kidding, they already knew. Weak and useless, that's what his father used to call him – he can hear his voice echoing, *"Weak and useless."* Daniel hates being made to feel this way, anger starts to bubble again deep in his stomach. "She was out of control; she was destroying everything! I didn't know what else to do." His fists pound against the table, surprising himself. He didn't mean to do that; he didn't mean to do a lot of things today.

"Would you like to take a break?" Grimm offers, trying to sound kind. Third rule of interviewing, don't react, don't be threatening, don't do anything that will turn a court against you, but be patient, and eventually the suspect will dig their own grave. Colvin inwardly sighs, just when they seem to be getting somewhere, Grimm starts to go easy on him.

"No. thank you," Daniel says quietly, trying to swallow back down the cocktail of rage, impotency and shame.

"Are you sure you don't want a lawyer present, Mr Mills?"

"No, please continue." Daniel's body language reverts back to comforting motions, Colvin notices. He probably isn't even aware of what his body is doing.

"When you left the house, which way did you go?"

Daniel closes his eyes, trying to remember. Left? Right? Straight? "Left," he guesses. His voice is hesitant, he can't say for certain, he had been angry, he had just wanted to get away.

"What did you do?"

"I walked around." Colvin notes that they have returned to the minimal communications. Daniel does not want to talk about where he went.

"Where did you go?"

"I just walked; I didn't really look at where I was going." Traces of anger can be heard again in his voice.

"How long did you walk around for?"

"A few hours." Daniel is defensive. He doesn't want to admit that he stormed out the house with just his phone. That he marched around and around becoming more and more hopelessly lost, more irritated with Anne-Marie. He was going to leave her for good this time. It didn't matter what she did now, she wasn't his problem anymore. He was going to divorce her this time. He stormed around in the hot summer heat; the more he stormed, the hotter he became. The hotter he became, the more irritated. The more irritated he became, the faster he marched, and the more his thighs chafed, the more sweat poured down his skin, making him hotter and angrier.

"You just walked around for a few hours?"

There is another embarrassed pause. "I got lost. I wasn't really looking at where I was going." Daniel had stormed round and round, inwardly promising himself that this was the last time he was putting up with this shit, outwardly not noticing a single thing. He couldn't say where he walked or what he saw. He eventually found himself at a park, not a place he recognised. He continued walking, too angry to notice people whispering and pointing at him. He was too busy inwardly ranting to himself about his misfortune to be stuck with such a wife, such in-laws, such a shitty job, reassuring himself that he deserved so much better to notice such petty details around him. Finally, he found an unoccupied bench and sat down, slowly deflating himself in defeated submission. He then spent around an hour sitting on the bench, watching all the happy young and old couples pass him by. They seemed to bounce in the heat, radiate the annoying happiness of those in love. Daniel, in contrast, felt like he had melted into a slug, leaving only a trail of sweat and sorrow wherever he slithered. "I sat for a while in the park... you know... to calm down."

"Mmm." Grimm makes a sound to show he is still listening, indicating that Daniel is to continue. They all know Daniel needs to say more.

"I didn't really know what to do. I just needed to get away from her." Before something bad happened. Daniel knew if he had stayed in the house, they would be having a different conversation. He might even be the one on the autopsy table and Anne-Marie the one sitting here, with some explaining to do. He wishes that had happened instead, at least he would get some peace. He wonders idly what Anne-Marie would have done if he had left before she woke up.

"Then what happened?"

"Peter rang me." The phone call caught him by surprise, Daniel didn't realise that it was already past four. "I told him that Anne-Marie and I had a fight and I asked him to pick me up." Daniel doesn't know why Peter even agreed to pick him up. Sherri would have just left him there to melt. "I gave him the park name and he picked me up about fifteen minutes later."

"What time did Peter collect you?"

"Around four thirty-ish, I think."

Colvin thinks Daniel had enough time to leave the house at midday, wander around, go back and have another argument with his wife, push her down the stairs and still have enough time to go back to the park for 4.30, that would explain why he is being so elusive about where he went. That's if what he is saying about leaving the house at midday is true. It would explain why Anne-Marie had the time and the inclination to trash both rooms before her death.

"Then what happened?"

"Peter drove me home." Daniel saw the scratches on his face for the first time as Peter was driving him home. He had been oblivious to the pain whilst he was marching around, but when he finally unclenched his jaw, his whole face throbbed; his feet throbbed too. Things are still throbbing now, in the interview room.

It didn't matter on the drive home. He had seen the look of sympathy in Peter's eyes. He was elated. Peter had finally agreed to take Anne-Marie away with him. Peter agreed that he would help Daniel convince Anne-Marie to seek treatment.

Sectioning had also been mentioned. Daniel had been so happy on that brief drive, things were finally going to get better. What a fool he had been.

"We got home and Peter went into the house first to talk to Anne-Marie." To make sure she wasn't still an angry threat. Daniel isn't going to mention that he had refused to get out the car until Peter agreed to check on his sister first, to make sure it was safe for him to get out of the car. "I noticed Peter had stopped in the doorway and I got out the car to see what was wrong." He had got out the car with resignation, thinking what has Anne-Marie trashed now? He was just expecting to find a mess and her passed out on the floor again. "I saw Anne-Marie lying in the middle of the floor." He looks away, the feelings of guilt and shame are finally making a reappearance. Daniel thought that she was just playing. He didn't feel anything or do anything until Peter screamed at him to call an ambulance. "I called an ambulance."

"Did you touch your wife in any way?"

Daniel could tell, by her eyes, her wide, staring eyes, the angle of her body, the blood, that there was nothing he could do to help. He was too afraid to touch her. Afraid that she was dead. Afraid that she was still alive. It is a blur what happened before the ambulance came, he can't remember what he said on the phone, or where his phone went after he finished the call. His brain went on autopilot and recorded nothing.

"No, I don't know any first aid. I thought it would be better to wait for the ambulance." They came within minutes but there was nothing they could do.

"What did Peter do whilst you were waiting for the ambulance?"

"I don't... I don't remember." He remembers that Peter had also been afraid. Normally Peter is not afraid, he is dismissive of fear. They were both frozen in place, until they heard the ambulance siren. Peter kneeling beside his sister, Daniel standing at the door, both powerless to do anything. Daniel had expected to go back into the house, to have another screaming match with Anne-Marie, for there to be crying and more fighting, or to find Anne-Marie slurring at them from the bottle. He was ready for another fight; he wasn't ready for this... then Peter had looked at him with those accusing eyes. Then the paramedics had shoved him out of the way and the police had ushered him here.

Grimm waits for a few minutes to see if Daniel wants to volunteer any other information. He and Colvin both note that Daniel isn't displaying any emotion, he seems to accept that his wife is dead. No regrets, no depression or sadness, just the occasional waves of anger and guilt.

"You say Peter went in the house first? Did he have a key?"

Daniel paused. Anne-Marie had lost her key and then she had taken the spare key and lost that too. Daniel didn't want to bother with the expense of changing the locks. It's not like they had anything worth stealing, except the television.

"No, Peter doesn't have a key, the door must have been unlocked."

"Did you leave the door unlocked when you left?"

"I don't remember. I thought I had closed it."

"Is the front door often left unlocked?"

"Yes, my wife keeps losing her key, so sometimes she doesn't bother locking the door." Sometimes she is too drunk to remember to lock the door.

Colvin finds this hard to believe, everyone in this city still locked their door religiously, after a serial killer brutally struck two years ago. Locked, bolted, sometimes even barred. Even she, a relative newcomer to the city, took extra precautions.

"So to clarify, you and your wife started fighting around midday, she had already been drinking and became quite aggressive. The fight turned physical, you tried to restrain her and then you pushed her backwards. She then went into your room and started breaking things. You left the house around 1pm and didn't return until after 4.30pm, when your brother-in-law Peter brought you back? Is that correct?" Colvin asks, slightly too sharply.

"Yes." A barely audible squeak. For it to be put in those terms is embarrassing.

"Is there anything you would like to add or clarify?"

Daniel opens and closes his mouth repeatedly. What does he say? I didn't expect to come home and find her dead? I thought she was just messing around, that women seek revenge in petty ways sometimes? I know what you are thinking and I didn't do it?

"I would never hurt her." Oh, how often the officers have heard that one. Daniel doesn't add how often she would hurt him but he would never hurt her, except in self-defence. He would never hit a woman. His mother had been adamant in teaching him that.

Colvin notes that Daniel seems agitated now, almost desperate.

"Have you and your wife fought like this before?"

Daniel's eyelids flutter rapidly, and he places his hands down and across himself, giving the impression he is hugging himself. Both officers note that this is another question that has caused Daniel discomfort.

"We have fought a few times, yes." Nearly every single fucking day. Why didn't he leave? Why didn't she leave? How did it come to this?

"Has the fight turned physical before?"

"A few times." More and more often. Only last month Anne-Marie head-butted him right in the nose and he still hasn't forgiven her for it. It was a blow without warning, and then, as blood trickled down his face, she had just laughed, laughed and laughed. The laughter of someone who had completely drunk their mind away. He had left her laughing, to try and stop the bleeding. In fact, it took longer for her to stop laughing than it did for him to stop bleeding. When she asked him, the next day, in front of Sherri, what had happened to his nose, he didn't know what to say. Was she bragging or did she genuinely not remember? In the end he had mumbled something about tripping and changed the subject – oh shit, he has paused too long, they are going to think he was abusing her. Shit, shit, shit! What does he say?

"My wife could be a little aggressive when she was drunk," he finally stammered.

"What was the cause of these fights?"

"Her drinking mostly." Daniel flinches at this question, as he could envision his wife screaming at him from the corner of the room, screaming that he was the cause of the fights, because he was an asshole! A stick in the mud! Stuck-up shit-head!

"Were you going to leave your wife?"

Oh, how often he had come so close to leaving, despite everyone telling him that she needed his help, that she needed him. The last time, he had packed an overnight bag and paused, trying to decide where to go. He could hear Anne-Marie singing drunkenly in her room, *"Then I went and fucked it all."* She sang with that sad, defeated tone that agreed, yes, she really had fucked it all this time. Then she started to cry. He made it outside the house but made the mistake of going back inside, to comfort her. Something inside him just wanted to hug her and tell her it was okay. But he was too late, she had passed out before he made it back upstairs: but still, defeated, he unpacked. He had nowhere else to go.

"My wife had some problems, but we were getting..." Daniel had been about to say, we were getting through it, but they all knew that was a lie. What else could he say? "We were getting help" is also an unbelievable lie, but what else could he say? What did they want to hear? Daniel trails off and there are a few moments of silence. "We were staying together," he finally mutters pathetically.

Grimm continues to wait. Don't machine-gun question is rule number four of interviewing. He waits to give Daniel time to elaborate or even confess, he feels that Daniel wants to say something else. The anger, the defences he saw at the start of the interview are crumbling. Either he is afraid of incriminating himself or he is afraid of the truth. Colvin thinks Daniel is sweating guilt.

"I noticed from our records that your wife had a similar incident a few months ago, back in January. What happened then?"

A gentle prod.

Daniel looks shocked for a moment before he shrugs. Grimm can't decide if he genuinely doesn't know or if he is trying to be evasive. He hadn't been expecting them to know about that incident, that's for sure.

"You rang for an ambulance at four in the morning, after your wife 'fell' down the stairs after a heavy drinking session?"

"That wasn't my fault." It wasn't looking good for him before, now it's looking very bad. He had said that like a clichéd fool, implying that this fall was his fault. They all thought that it was anyway, everyone. Peter, the paramedics, the other police officers, all of them kept staring at him with eyes devoid of emotion; those stares are scalpels, slicing deep inside him, exposing his guilt. He can't afford to let that guilt show again.

"No one is blaming you. I just want to hear your side of the story."

Daniel is still non-committal. He won't make eye contact

with the officers. He has gone back to rocking himself slightly, unknowingly hugging himself again, the comforting motions.

The now unsympathetic Grimm continues to prod. "Tell me, what really did happen the night your wife was hospitalised?"

"Do we really have to talk about this?" Why did they have to bring up this one? Well, it's not like they can bring up the other incidents, those that didn't require hospitalisation. No one else knows about those.

"I am only trying to understand, Mr Mills."

No one understands.

"I don't really know what happened. I was asleep. She woke me up at 4am, crying my name." He still wakes up sometimes, in the early hours, convinced something is wrong. "Daannnny... Dannnny." He hates being called that. A couple of times, afterwards, in the early hours of the morning, she would stand, whispering "Danny, Danny" outside his door, just for the hell of it. She thought it was funny.

"I told her to go back to sleep, but she kept yelling. I got up and found her at the bottom of the stairs," Daniel finally finishes, sullenly. When Sherri found out about the accident, she had screamed at him for nearly an hour for not looking after her baby properly. She wouldn't speak to him directly for nearly a fortnight, and instead of calling him Daniel, his name was now the Toad. Oh shit, Sherri! Daniel doesn't want to be in the same building as Sherri when she finds out about this. She is going to come up with a worse name for him now, worse than the Toad or Turnip Head.

"She wasn't badly hurt, just a bit... She kept saying that she just wanted a plaster. I called an ambulance."

"What was your wife's state of mind prior to the incident?"

Grimm gives Daniel a few moments to answer: instant answers are usually a good sign that the person is lying; if they are telling the truth, it will take them a few moments to remember the truth. Daniel is trying to choose his words carefully.

"She was... moody... It depended on how much she had to drink and how much sleep she had."

"How did she act when she was taken to hospital?"

"She was very drunk and upset. It took the nurses a while to calm her down." They were just reaching the physical restraints point when Anne-Marie finally gave in and let them place their needles in her arm.

"Do you think she fell?" There is a look in Daniel's eyes. A startled look. A deer in the headlights look.

"She said she fell and I believe her."

"What happened after the incident, when your wife was released from hospital?"

"When she first got out, she was better, she stopped drinking and started applying for jobs."

"Your wife was unemployed?"

A flicker of pain crosses Daniel's face. He nods.

"How long had she been unemployed for?"

"My wife quit her job nearly a year and a half ago. We were going to have a baby..." Daniel pauses, but then continues, knowing they would ask anyway. "She lost the baby. We thought it was best to give her time, there was no pressure for her to return to work."

"I am sorry to hear that."

Daniel grunts, he had felt nothing when his mother died, when he was fifteen. Nothing but relief when his father died, when he was sixteen. But his baby, his baby's death evokes an unfamiliar pain, something he can never talk about. The end of the dream.

Anne-Marie had tried when she came home after the fall. She had really tried. She managed to stay sober for fourteen days straight, which was a new record that year. She said she was applying for jobs and he just wanted to believe her. They played pretend for all that week, let's pretend that everything was okay, pretend they love each other, pretend she could cope with being sober. But she couldn't cope anymore. It got worse when her pain medication finished. She didn't know what to do or how to act or what to do with her hands. Sober meant feeling things again, which meant if she wasn't crying, she was frustrated, sad or bored. She would be constantly around him, something that he couldn't cope with, now he was used to being alone. Always expecting Daniel to provide some kind of entertainment, but not wanting to do anything he suggested. So bored and irritable and, my God, was she irritable. One minute they would be awkwardly talking, the next she would be snapping at him to shut up, then snapping at him for being too quiet. It didn't help that she couldn't sleep either, nor would she let him sleep. She wasn't in the mood to do anything fun, no, 3am was "talk" time. He tried to be as supportive as he could but he needed sleep. It was always the same old conversation over and over again, as if they were rehearsing for a play. He was sure she didn't listen to a word he said anyway.

Things got very tense, neither of them were able to relax anymore. If he tried to watch TV, she would be there endlessly asking questions; if he tried to involve her, she would want alone time. If he cooked, she wasn't hungry. If he ordered in food, then she was sick of take-aways. If something was left lying around, it wasn't anything to do with her. If he tidied something away, she was using that, THANK you. Everything he did or said was wrong. Then he made the mistake of having a beer. He just wanted to turn off a little, it had been a hard day at work and he was very tired. He had tried to do it in secret but she had caught him. You would have thought he was hiding the crown jewels from her, the way she started. Then she wanted one. Just one. What was wrong with one drink? He had tried to stop her, but she wore him down to agreeing to just one.

Then one more, you fucking killjoy.

But at least they both finally slept that night. Daniel knew it was over then, that she had stopped trying. But they kept playing let's pretend.

Then she took the game to the next level.

She had taken an interest in showering regularly again, and then she started talking, unprompted, about how much weight she had lost, how much better she was feeling, how badly she needed a haircut and new clothes, especially if she was going to start interviewing again. Daniel, wanting to encourage her and feeling still guilty about the beer, offered a credit card and to accompany her on a shopping trip. She had taken the card but refused the company, saying she was going with her mother. Daniel, like the fool he was, believed her.

When he got home that night, she gave him his card back and just said that she couldn't face going outside just yet. She had been struggling to get a brush through her hair, that was her reason for not leaving the house. Daniel had expected this and generously gave her a hundred pounds in cash as an early Valentine's present. He told her to get her hair done professionally and maybe treat her mother to lunch with the change. He had left his wife that morning with a mane of knotty hair, shoulder length, and had gone home to a wife with a neat little bob cut, sitting drinking tea with her mother. "You look nice." That's all he had said.

Unprovoked, Sherri had looked at him like he was a piece of shit and snarled, "No thanks to you." Anne-Marie had looked down, a rare flash of guilt crossing her face. He had been too shocked to say anything at the time. It wasn't until later, when he noticed the hair in the bathroom sink, that he realised what had happened. She didn't give him his money back, or say so much as a thank you. Daniel later found out, when he got his credit card statement, that she had gone out shopping, just not for clothes. She had spent over £200 on his card and had hidden the evidence all over the house. By then, it just didn't seem worth fighting over.

It started again, the swaying motions, the drunken laugh, the dark circles started to reappear again under her eyes. But still they played let's pretend. Let's pretend it's not serious. Let's pretend Anne-Marie can handle it, that it's under control. Let's pretend that it's not a relief, let's pretend that Daniel doesn't prefer drunk Anne-Marie, just because she was usually happier to see him.

"Was your wife encouraged to seek help about her drinking?"

"She didn't want help."

Anne-Marie had received some counselling after losing the baby. Daniel hadn't. She never spoke about what happened in the sessions but afterwards she said she was never seeing "another Goddamn sicko psycho quacko". She repeatedly insisted she was fine. Daniel lied and said he was fine too. They both drank heavily in that first dark month. Neither of them wanted to talk about it. The baby they used to love talking about became a taboo subject. "Just give her time," people urged before quietly abandoning them. Give her time? No one ever gave him time, he had to get over it for her sake.

A resentful feeling grew in his stomach. It had rooted when the baby was lost, slowly growing a little more each day, then when he picked Anne-Marie up from the hospital, after that first "fall", it seeded. He felt like he was being played; she had sauntered out of the hospital, grinning like a Cheshire cat, pausing only to stuff a leaflet in the closest bin. She was happy because she had managed to fool those "stupid doctors and shrinks" into letting her go. Daniel wasn't happy, he thought it was all a game to her, that she played the lie game with everyone, seeing what she could get away with. Milking their pity and guilt for all she could get. He could never prove it, never quite managed to catch her out, never dared to air a suspicion. But he started wondering about what games she played with him; he had a new forbidden suspicion about the "baby" then. He didn't dare risk the wrath of Sherri by mentioning it though, just tried to forget it, convince himself that he was wrong. She wouldn't have gone that far, she wouldn't have.

Anne-Marie didn't fool those stupid shrinks as well as she thought. They had also met with Daniel afterwards, voiced their concerns, and he voiced his concerns, but they couldn't quite agree on how badly she was fooling them. One thought she was in denial, but it wasn't too serious yet. The other thought she did need treatment, but treatment would not be effective until she admitted there was a problem. They all agreed then that the fall had been an accident, not a cry for help. They talked about sectioning her but since she wasn't seen as a serious danger to herself or other people, she could not be sectioned. That was Daniel's fault, for helping hide her lies, for not telling them the truth about how bad it was. Daniel knew Sherri would destroy him if he dared to agree to sectioning her precious baby. He also had been warned that whilst Anne-Marie was this resistant to treatment, there was no helping her. Maybe he could convince her otherwise, they had suggested.

He had tried and tried but Anne-Marie never uttered those words that Daniel longed to hear: "I need help." Maybe things would have been different if he had tried harder, if she wasn't so stubborn, if he hadn't lost their number.

Daniel is looking more relieved now, he thinks that the interview is nearly over, not knowing that Grimm and Colvin have only just started. They both know how easy it is to tell the lies on the first time round. Let the suspect get the full story out, don't rush the liar, let them think they are fooling you, get everything down and then start again. See how well they remember their lies on the second and third round. Keep going over and over, until you can catch them out.

Now was time for the second round, time for the *"I am sorry, Mr Mills, but I didn't quite understand..."* *"So you say she did this, can you describe..."* *"What was Anne-Marie doing when you..."* *"What makes you sure of the time when she..."* *"Is there anything you would like to add or clarify about this...?"*

The more questions they ask, the more they repeat, the more Daniel Mills has to remember what he said previously, and the more lies he has to juggle in his mind. They are just waiting to catch him out on those little inconsistent details. Then when Mr Mills thinks it's finally over this time, they will take a little break whilst they interview friends, family and neighbours for more details, view the autopsy notes and also review their video footage of the interview, checking for anything that hints that something has not been said. Then they will start another interview with Mr Mills, starting everything all over again, and then again and again, focusing in on those areas. *"I am sorry, we just wanted to check..."* *"Please explain."* Until they finally wore the bastard down.

CHAPTER EIGHT

"Please state your full name."

"Peter Fowler."

Peter *Too-Fucking-Tired-For-This-Shit* Fowler.

Peter doesn't care anymore. How bad does that sound? His sister is dead and he is too tired to care. He has spent months being angry at Anne-Marie, wishing he was an only child, wishing his mother wasn't so blind to her stunts, wishing Anne-Marie was dead – and now she is.

She had called him, drunk out of her mind, at 3am this morning, she muttered some things he didn't understand then refused to talk to him. He finally lost his temper, told her to go to fucking sleep. She told him to fuck off and hung up on him. Peter envies anyone who can go back to sleep after a conversation like that. No, he couldn't go back to sleep. He then spent the next four hours tossing and inwardly ranting. He tried calling Anne-Marie back, just to be childish, teach her how it feels for a change, but she didn't answer. The lucky bitch had probably passed out, it was all right for her, she could sleep till noon and no one would care. But he had to get up at seven, to work an eight till four shift. He tried to calm down, close his eyes, drift away but it felt like he had only blinked when his alarm began bleeping. Right now Peter feels like he could just rest his head against the table, despite the uncomfy chair, and just sleep, no matter what the two officers across from him might think.

"At what time did you receive a phone call from Daniel Mills?" the male officer asks, a tad irritably. From the expression on their faces, this is the second or third time they have asked this.

Peter is too tired to lie. The adrenaline has worn away and he can't think. *I don't know what happened or what fucking time it was, what does it matter?* he wants to yell but instead he answers, "It was some time around..." Another yawn, he just can't help it, before finishing, "...one?" Peter had just been finishing his lunch break at the time when he saw he had an incoming call from Daniel and he decided to ignore it. He knew Daniel would only be calling to complain and he just didn't want to hear it. With another yawn, Peter fishes his phone out of his pocket. "I can show you the time on here. He left a voicemail too... but I, um... I deleted it."

He didn't even listen to it, he just pressed delete, without a second thought. Voicemails like this were becoming all too frequent and he stopped listening to them weeks ago. *What do you want me to do?* he had wanted to shout at Daniel, *I can't cope with her either.* He especially didn't want to be fucking near her after last night.

"Do you remember what the voicemail said?"

"I didn't listen to it." Peter is too tired to explain, he just hopes they will shut up soon and let him go home.

The female officer is carefully looking over the call logs on the phone, making notes. She points out to Grimm what time Peter responded to that phone call and also that Daniel has made over eighteen phone calls to this phone recently. She also notes the frequency of calls from someone named "Bitch", the last call being received at 3am that day.

"And you called him back just after four?"

A feeling of dread made him call, what had the bitch done now? He had hoped whatever it was had passed, but no.

"Yeah, just when I finished work."

"What state was he in when you called?"

"He was agitated, he said he was lost. We spent most of the call figuring out where he was." Peter had little patience for bumbling Daniel, but agreed to pick him up. He immediately regretted the offer because it turned into another headache as they tried to figure out where Daniel was. All Daniel would say was that he was in a park, in a dazed voice that just made Peter want to slap him. It took ten minutes for Daniel to figure out that it was King's Park. Peter had been so close to hanging up and leaving him to deal with his own shit, the only reason he even agreed to collect him was because he was going to get the pair of them together and make it very, very clear to both of them that they were not to call him again, no matter what the reason. Something had to be done before... before...

"I picked him up from King's Park about twenty to thirty minutes later."

Daniel had looked as tired and as angry as Peter felt. Peter took one look at the bright red scratches on Daniel's beefy face and realised that this wasn't the same old shit again, something had really happened this time. He tried to listen as Daniel babbled on and on, an endless loop of anger. "She has gone too far this time." He kept repeating: "I want her gone."

"We are going to sit down and talk through this together," Peter had said through gritted teeth, whilst trying to navigate the traffic. He was so tired he could barely remember how to drive.

"I am tired of talking! I want her gone!"

Peter had nearly thrown Daniel out of his car at that point, despising the man-child. Why was he even getting involved? After last night's, or rather this morning's, phone call, he had spent the day telling himself that he was wiping his hands of the pair of them, for good this time. No more stunts. No more phone calls. No more whining from either of them. He was done.

"So you collected Daniel from King's and drove straight to his house?"

"Yes." Another yawn.

"Did Daniel say anything during the drive?"

"He muttered a lot; I didn't really listen."

Daniel never shut up for the whole fifteen-minute drive. Peter had finally agreed to "take her away" just to shut him up but it didn't even slow Daniel's ranting. Peter just tuned him out. The face scratches had made him feel a little sorry for Daniel, but not sympathetic enough to take Anne-Marie in himself, oh no, he was never going to do that again. No, he was going to take her straight to Sherri. His mother had made Anne-Marie like this, she should deal with the consequences.

"What time did you arrive back at the house?"

"It was about ten to five."

"And then what happened?"

"Daniel originally didn't want to get out the car." This little detail of Daniel's cowardice suddenly seemed important. "He was afraid of what Anne-Marie might be doing. He waited in the car as I went to the door. I couldn't hear anything so I went into the house." She was there, waiting for them to come home, right by the front door, waiting more patiently in death than she had ever waited in life. Peter had stood frozen for a moment, staring with cold relief. "I told Daniel to call an ambulance."

There is a long silence, the officers watch and wait.

Peter closes his eyes, remembering the crumpled body, her

hand outstretched in one last plea for help, the blood, the open, pleading eyes. "She was already... she... she..."

"Do you need a minute?"

Peter nods, trying to control his emotions. He is not going to cry here. It's only because he is so tired that he can't... He won't cry here. Not for her.

"Would you like something to drink?"

Peter shakes his head no, angrily rubs his eyes and leans forward, in an *I-am-ready* gesture.

"You said you pushed open the door? It wasn't locked?"

"No. My sister... she usually leaves the door unlocked." Another cause of the endless arguments.

"She often left the door unlocked?" The officer parrots in slight surprise. Are they wondering why Peter thinks his sister left the door unlocked if Daniel had been the last one to leave?

"Well it's not like anyone is going to steal their shit." Peter without thinking mimics his mother, to no one's amusement.

"Did you move your sister in any way?"

"No." Peter knew she was dead, but still had to touch her, just slightly. She was still warm. He rubs his fingers against the stubble on his chin, trying to get rid of the feeling still lingering in his fingers. The feeling of her warm skin won't leave him, neither will the smell of the blood. This shouldn't be how he remembers his sister. "Fuck off" shouldn't be the last words that you hear from anyone.

"Did Daniel move her in any way?"

"No."

Daniel had deflated on seeing her and been utterly useless. His only contribution had been to stammer over the phone to the emergency services, then they had both waited in silence, staring, finally united with a sense of guilt.

The officers stare at Peter, waiting for him to say more.

"Did Daniel say anything?"

"No, he called for an ambulance, but I don't remember him saying anything else." *What do they think he said?* You grab her legs and I will get her arms? Trash day is tomorrow? *It's not like they tried to hide her. They did nothing, said nothing. What do these officers want him to say?*

"What kind of relationship did Anne-Marie and Daniel have?"

The realisation hits through the sleepy fog, they think Daniel had something to do with Anne-Marie's death. The thought had never even crossed Peter's mind, he thought his brother-in-law was far too much of a coward to do such a thing. He just thought his sister had done something stupid, again, but only this time she was paying the consequences.

"My sister was working through some problems; it was affecting their relationship a bit." Sometimes Anne-Marie was going to leave Daniel, sometimes Daniel swore he was going to leave Anne-Marie, but it was always just talk. Sometimes Peter wished one of them would leave just to change the conversation, but he knew if one of them ever did the other one would never shut up about it. Without each other, they would both still be boring and miserable. They would still be doing all they could to make everyone else miserable too.

"When did you last speak to your sister?" They have seen his phone, they already know the answer to this one, Peter thinks irritably, forgetting that he had changed his sister's name to Bitch on his phone, in a fit of anger.

"Anne-Marie called me at three this morning. When I asked her what was wrong, she said that I wouldn't understand and hung up on me. She likes to do things like that for attention sometimes, I don't take her seriously."

Now he sounds like an asshole. How do you explain Anne-Marie and Daniel? And their relationship? They were unhappy and they liked to make everyone around them unhappy, they were united in self-pity? That they deserved each other? They were the reason he rarely got a full night's sleep or any enjoyment out of life? Peter wishes that the officers would just leave him alone, let him sleep. He could answer their questions later, when he could make sense of everything. He could be more articulate, actually think of examples to give them, but right now he really can't think straight. Everything he says comes out wrong. What should he say? He was a sounding board to both of them but neither of them ever said anything worth recording.

"Anne-Marie had a previous incident in January. Do you know what happened?"

"I don't really... she fell. She was drunk and she tripped down the stairs."

"Is that what Anne-Marie told you?"

"No, Daniel did. Anne-Marie didn't really want to talk about it." His sister's voice echoes in his mind. *"I should have said he pushed me,"* that's what she said. She had been drunk at the time and furious with Daniel for some petty reason. She was in a paranoid stage at the time, convinced that everyone was out to get her. But she would have the last laugh, she assured him with a maniacal laugh. Peter, as usual, just dismissed it as stupid drunk talk.

"Were you concerned about Anne-Marie's drinking?"

"She said it was under control." Here he goes again, protecting her with lies. Of course he was concerned at first, wanted her to get help when it first started. Didn't want her turning into his mother, but Sherri insisted Anne-Marie was fine. Then she just got more and more abusive. At that point Peter had to give up, for his own sanity's sake, give up on his sister and leave her for dead.

Sherri Fowler doesn't know what the fuck is going on. She needs to see her daughter, she knows that much, if everyone would just piss off out of her way. First that worthless twat Dummy Danny kept calling her. You would think the fact she won't answer would give him a hint, but no. He has called twice today and that is two times too many.

Then Peter called and babbled a lot of things that didn't make sense, some nonsense that Anne-Marie has had an accident and that the police needed to see her. She told him he was too old for these kind of stupid pranks and to grow the fuck up. He insisted over and over, daring to raise his voice at her! And then finally he yelled that Anne-Marie was dead. She had an accident and she was dead. When she asked him what kind of accident, he was snappish and didn't want to give details – a sure sign he was lying. But then he told her that Anne-Marie may have killed herself. Which was utter bollocks! Her daughter would never do such a thing. Peter had cowardly backtracked to babbling again about how Anne-Marie had an accident, that Sherri needed to come down to the police station, that the police wanted to talk to her about Anne-Marie. No, he couldn't pick her up, he wasn't allowed to leave the police station. A likely fucking story.

Sherri somehow made it into her car, while in her mind she is driving to pick up her baby girl, take her home, away from that asshole of a husband. She knows Peter is lying, she can't be dead. She might be in trouble, people were always out to get her baby, the police should know better than to play along. He is lying, lying, LYING. She couldn't be dead. She is still so young, she had made some stupid mistakes, like marrying the king of idiots, but she still has time to fix her mistakes, she still had time. Sherri had told her daughter over and over not to marry someone who promised her the world, but to marry someone who actually gave her the world; she shouldn't marry anyone even slightly like Anne-Marie's own cowardly louse of a father. Anne-Marie typically refused to listen to Sherri's worldly wisdom.

"Now look what you have got yourself into!" she bellows to an empty car seat.

Anne-Marie never listened to her. (Peter didn't either but that is because he is an idiot.) Anne-Marie had no confidence. That was her biggest problem, she could never believe that she could have done much better, certainly better than Daniel. She was too much like her father, despite Sherri's best efforts. Sherri tries to concentrate on the road, every fucking idiot seems to be on the road and in her way.

"Fuck you!" she screams over and over, as they honk horns and gesture. Don't they know her daughter needs her? "Eat shit!" she screams at an elderly lady who is trying to cross the road at the wrong moment. She parks, taking up two spaces in the police station car park, and stands outside, furiously smoking cigarette after cigarette in an effort to calm down, refusing to allow even one tear to fall from her eye.

She gives her name to the gormless twat on the reception desk and is ushered quickly into an interview room, bringing her own smokescreen with her. Sherri badly wants another cigarette, anything to help stop her fingers from trembling, to stop the shaking palpitations coming from her heart. She needs the assurance that only comes from setting something on fire and inhaling it. Her grief makes her feel weak and Sherri despises the weak. Sherri is usually the one to prey on the weak. You wouldn't think to look at her that she was capable of being mean – demure, with little grey curls and granny glasses. You wouldn't suspect her catchphrase is *"I expected better"*, or that she often ends conversations with, *"We are done here."* Nor does she believe in using *"please or thank you"*.

Sherri has been in the interview room for only a few

minutes but already knows that these officers are useless. She can tell just by looking at their gormless faces. She doesn't understand why she is even being interviewed. The female officer Colvin looks like she has just graduated and the older one Grimm? Well, who can expect any kind of competence from someone with a name as ridiculous as that! He looks as idiotic as his name suggests. Where is her useless son? And where are they hiding that bumbling cockwaffle, Daniel? He has some explaining to do! She doesn't have time for this shit.

"...and I know this must be hard for you right now, but we need to ask you a few questions to help us understand what happened to your daughter."

Sherri understands that her daughter is dead and that her daughter shouldn't be dead. She doesn't understand why she is dead or what happened but she is starting to guess what or who might be to blame. The officer continues asking questions: "Where she has been today?" "Did she receive a phone call from anyone today?" "And what time?"

They seemed particularly interested in what time she received those calls from Daniel. But that was nothing out of the ordinary, the Toad never stopped calling her. She was always there if her daughter needed her, that's what was important.

Now they are asking even stupider questions. "What kind of relationship did Anne-Marie and Daniel have?"

A shitty one, obviously. She has to hide her face in a tissue so the officers won't see her expression. What should she say? *I don't know why my daughter insisted on staying with that warthog?* That Sherri had offered plenty of times to take Anne-Marie away from that stupid fucking idiot, and her daughter always insisted on staying because she loved him. It was bloody revolting. Why won't they tell her what happened?

"I kept telling her to leave him but she wouldn't leave him." The police need to know the truth after all.

"Why would she want to leave him?"

Sherri thinks quickly, what answer will get Daniel into the most trouble? Because he is a greedy pig? Stingy too, never gave her daughter anything she needed. Sherri had to privately slip her daughter money for essentials every time she saw her.

"We thought Daniel was having an affair. She would call me in tears sometimes." Sherri would always go round after these calls, her daughter always looking tired and thin. She would be wearing ratty clothes despite the money Sherri gave her for new ones. All of her money must have gone on the ever-increasing swill bill for the pig. But at least Anne-Marie's eyes always lit up at the sight of her mother and they would sit and drink the wine Sherri had brought. They would talk for ages over her suspicions. The wine would always go down too fast, even when Sherri brought two bottles. When it was gone, they still had so much left to cover so Sherri would buy food and more alcohol from the mousy woman in the corner shop, whilst Anne-Marie had a shower.

"Was there any evidence of an affair or do you know who with?" The officers are making careful notes now. She hopes they will find out who Daniel had been seeing, she would like a little word with them.

"No, we were trying to find out more." It is hard to believe that there were two women in the world stupid enough to even kiss Daniel. Anne-Marie would never let Sherri confront Daniel. Made her swear on her life. Sherri sees now that she should have ignored her daughter, for her own good. She should have confronted the pig outright. Just wait until she sees that bastard.

"When did you last speak to your daughter?"

"I have been on holiday for the last two weeks. I came back on Tuesday. I didn't speak to her before I left." Sherri had been looking forward to sitting down and telling Anne-Marie about all the dreadful people on her holiday, the disappointing rooms and disgusting food. Now she will never speak to her again. A sob threatens; no, not here. She will cry later. "I haven't spoken to her since the beginning of June. She had been a bit down. I think she was hoping Daniel would be taking her on holiday too."

"Oh?"

"He is too tight to take her anywhere nice." Miserable sod. Sherri had slipped her daughter the usual cash and promised to take her away somewhere nice when she got back.

Sherri sees now that she should have taken her daughter away when they first suspected an affair. Sure, he tried to pretend it was just one drunken kiss at that party Anne-Marie hadn't been invited to and he had no business being there in the first place. They all knew it had been more than just one kiss. He was doing things he shouldn't.

Why did she agree not to talk about it? Now she is suspicious. Just why had her daughter begged her not to say anything? Why are these officers asking these questions? Just what has that bastard been doing to her?

"Your daughter had an incident back in January. Do you know what happened?"

"She tripped down the stairs." Peter had only told her that Anne-Marie had an accident and that was after Anne-Marie was released from hospital. No one had told Sherri that Anne-Marie had been drunk out of her mind at the time. Sherri didn't speak to her son for a month for not telling her sooner. She had rushed to see her daughter, bearing flowers, chocolates and wine. It was a good job she had too! Her daughter looked at her with an expression of sheer joy and relief. The room she was in wasn't helping either, Anne-Marie had moved into the spare room to escape Daniel's snoring or just, Sherri suspects, to escape Daniel. The spare room was sparse, nothing in there to make it homey or welcoming. No wonder her daughter felt down. Only a faint waft of something unpleasant in the air, mostly masked by the smell of the flowers, gave any hint of how the room had previously been. But Sherri had not noticed the smell, she was too busy fussing over her daughter. Anne-Marie repeatedly assured her mother that it had been a silly accident, that she had tripped down the stairs, nothing to be concerned over. Sherri sees now that she was just putting on a brave face. The same stupid brave face she put on when Sherri told her it was time to take down those stupid babyish elephant curtains. Her daughter was too sweet for this world.

"Did she say any more about the incident or why she fell?"

"No, she just told me it was an accident." What did the officers know? What are they not telling her? "After the accident, a few weeks after, Anne-Marie called me in tears."

The officers lean forward slightly, oh finally they are interested! "Oh?"

If you say "Oh" like that again, you stupid man, you will regret it, Sherri thinks, trying hard not to let her anger show on her face.

"Daniel refused to give her some money for a haircut, told her to do it herself. And stupidly, she did. I had to help her out." Anne-Marie had tried, bless her, but she was not a gifted hairdresser. Sherri took one look at the brutal cut and ordered her daughter into her car. She had bullied her own regular stylist until she agreed to fix Anne-Marie's hair, calling it an "emergency appointment". Then after Sherri had paid, she treated her daughter to a bite to eat and drinks to get over the upset. It had taken quite a few drinks too, just to see her daughter smile. Sherri even slipped her daughter more money for new clothes. Sherri was just having a cup of tea with her daughter, when the pig came home, and he dared to say that Anne-Marie looked nice! No wonder her daughter was always so thin, with that man taking everything and not looking after her properly. Sherri hated seeing her daughter cry and hated him for making her cry. She will get him for this. He won't get away with this.

"Were you concerned about your daughter's drinking?"

"Well, anyone who was married to Daniel would need a drink every now and again, but my daughter did not have a drinking problem."

Colvin thinks of the Anne-Marie she saw in the crime scene photographs, the remains she saw in the house, everything they have seen so far is conclusive of long-term alcohol abuse. Anne-Marie's body screamed clear signs of malnourishment and personal neglect over a long period of time. Was this woman really that blind to her daughter?

Colvin is looking at Sherri in a way she doesn't like. Colvin is the stupid one here, not her, she decides. Sherri has had enough of this and finally asks the officers for what she came here for.

"Can I see my daughter now?"

The only thing the police would tell Sherri was that there had been an "incident". Whatever that fucking meant! They had confirmed that her daughter was dead as nicely as they could, and she just wanted to punch them in the face for being so condescending. Then they wasted even more of her time by asking her stupid questions. Questions that hinted she had been missing something, insinuating that they knew something about her daughter or the dork that she didn't.

They had told her it was best that she didn't see her daughter, but she insisted. She is glad she insisted. Even though it meant she had to wait for two hours, whilst they messed around. If she hadn't, then she would have believed them when they said her daughter had had an incident. She would also have believed them when they told her that Anne-Marie didn't suffer, didn't feel a thing.

Her baby was bruised, battered. In death she looked neglected and half-starved. So small and still so young. She didn't look like her daughter, this was a stranger in a hospital gown, a stranger with her daughter's face. The nurses had carefully covered Anne-Marie's legs and feet, hiding some of the worst of the damage; they had even gone as far as to seal Anne-Marie's large head wound but couldn't hide it completely, and they couldn't hide all of the bruises either.

Sherri's hand reaches out and grabs a small tuft of Anne-Marie's shorn hair, it feels greasy and cold. She remembers stroking baby Anne-Marie's curls, plaiting her play-school hair. So many times she had stroked this hair in comfort and now it's just this, the tainted memories of a butchered haircut and nothing more. Sherri grips the hair tightly as she leans down, promising silently to her daughter that bastard wasn't going to get away with this. She seals the promise by planting one last tender kiss on her daughter's cold forehead.

There was nothing accidental about this.

Grimm is in a grim mood. His new shoes are too tight, causing a throbbing blister to form on his right foot. Normally this wouldn't be much of a problem but today he is conducting door-to-door interviews of the Mills' neighbourhood with Colvin, a job that involves walking around, standing around and looking polite. A job that needs to be done quickly, before people forget important details. They have left Mr Mills at the police station. He is not under lock and key, nothing and no one is holding him, but Daniel has consented to stay longer under their protection, providing breakfast is provided.

It's a weekday morning; they are expecting most of the neighbourhood to be at work, but still they have to be seen making an effort. They start at the top of the road. Grimm makes sure that Colvin walks on his left side, so she doesn't see his slight limp. There is no answer at the first house. They both notice the expensive security features, along with the look of abandonment. The second house looks more derelict, a long-standing *For Sale* sign planted firmly in the overgrown front garden. They try the doorbell anyway but no answer. Grimm is starting to think this will be quick and easy. The next house on the row is firmly marked with *DO NOT CROSS* tape. Not that the neighbourhood needed any warning not to cross Anne-Marie's doorstep. Maybe it is because she has been inside but Colvin feels a chill sweep down her spine despite the sweltering heat. She looks up expecting to see Anne-Marie's face scowling down at her, but nothing.

At the neighbouring house they walk down a small path, edged with carefully manicured flowers and lovingly fixed garden gnomes. A considerate amount of time and effort has been made into making this garden look pretty, such a huge contrast to the previous homes. Loud, cheerful chimes emit from behind the door as Grimm presses the doorbell, and Colvin suspects that someone slightly hard of hearing lives in this house.

An elderly woman with a tightly drawn face answers the door and fixes them both with an unforgiving stare. "Can I help you?"

"Good morning, Madam, I am DCI Grimm. Are you free to talk to us for a few minutes?"

There are a few moments' hesitation, the lady is not responding well to Grimm's boyish grin. Colvin gets the feeling that if they weren't police officers, they would have been told politely but firmly to bugger off. Reluctantly, the door opens wide enough to let them both in but closes quickly again. The house is a mirror image of the Mills' house but it couldn't be more different. The Mills had favoured bare walls, dirt and minimalism, this lady has patterned, faded wallpaper and ornaments, so many ornaments, and each one positioned in its own special place. Knick-knacks from holidays in Hawaii, York and Africa anoint the walls, giving the house a more welcoming vibe than its occupant.

They sit down and the lady sits opposite them, neatly smoothing the creases in her beige skirt as she sits.

"Can I take your name, please?"

"Mrs Ludmilla Bryski."

Ludmilla in the good old days would have offered the officers a cup of tea or a piece of home-made cake, but her goodwill has long gone. She stares at them wearily. She doesn't even ask them why they are here. She seems to have been expecting them and just wants to get this over with. She nods expectantly whilst Grimm explains that they have questions regarding her neighbour, Anne-Marie Mills. Colvin has already noted that Mrs Bryski had made quite a few official complaints against her neighbour. There were a number of official complaints listed for this area, not all of them regarding Anne-Marie Mills. Whilst Ludmilla Bryski does seem genuinely shocked to hear that Anne-Marie is dead, Colvin also notes a tiny flash of guilty relief.

"...we just wanted to know if you heard anything out of the ordinary yesterday," Grimm finishes.

"I heard her yelling and screaming again yesterday. Once she starts that, I turn the radio up to block her out." But not too loud, too loud would mean Anne-Marie hammering her door, screaming for her to turn it down, "you old bat".

"Do you hear her yelling often?"

"More often than I can stand," Ludmilla snaps, shocking herself with her own bitterness. She continues more softly: "They have been fighting a lot more recently... it's starting to get to me... I call you and call you but no one stops her." Both officers have the grace to look away in mock or genuine guilt. It wasn't just Daniel Mills who had been brought to the breaking point by Anne-Marie. There have been several meetings between the neighbours and their lawyers discussing the "problem" and how to get rid of it, legally. The last piece of useless advice was "to document Anne-Marie Mills' behaviour, then in a few weeks..." BUT they needed a solution faster than that.

"I am sorry to hear that," Grimm says. "Did you hear what she was yelling?"

Ludmilla shakes her head.

"Do you remember what time you heard the yelling?"

"I don't know, sometime around half-twelve." Ludmilla closes her eyes and leans slightly back. "During the one o'clock news I heard the front door slam and I thought I saw Daniel going past. I could hear her screaming and smashing things. Then it was quiet for a while. Then she started smashing again so I turned the radio up again." Ludmilla omits to mention that she heard Anne-Marie crying whilst she was smashing. It seemed heartless to say that now. She didn't want to explain what happened the last time she showed Anne-Marie pity.

"Do you remember what time you heard the second lot of smashing?"

"Two thirty," Ludmilla replies bitterly. It had been right in the middle of her favourite radio programme, so she is definitely sure of the time. Ludmilla remembers remarking to her husband Paul that she couldn't even enjoy the programme anymore because of next door. Not that Anne-Marie ever bothered Paul. Paul is too deaf to hear any of Anne-Marie's antics. The only time Paul has ever really been shaken by Anne-Marie was when she was screaming in their faces that she would smash their heads in if they called the fucking police again.

On Daniel's prompting, the next day Anne-Marie had brought them a bunch of wilted flowers and a muttered apology and, in Paul's opinion, that made everything quite all right. "Just ignore her, dear Ludmilly," was Paul's usual response, along with "She is harmless." or "She is just drunk again, Ludmilly, we all do stupid things when we are drunk."

Not Ludmilla, Ludmilla doesn't drink and, unlike some people, has never been drunk. She had become quite suspicious of Paul's pre-retirement "working lates" and post-retirement trips to see the lads. "She is just blowing off steam, Ludmilly," Paul had said when Anne-Marie had started a screaming match at three in the morning. Ludmilla couldn't understand why her husband was so forgiving towards Anne-Marie. Perhaps she should have believed Lying Penny when she said that Paul and Anne-Marie were occasionally drinking partners, occasionally another kind of partner too. She didn't want to believe that Paul was capable of such things. No, Lying Penny is a liar, a liar who knows which lies will get the most attention. Ludmilla has promised herself not to fall again for her lies. Ludmilla had caught Anne-Marie and Paul discussing something earnestly in private. Anne-Marie scowled at the sight of her and quickly stormed off. Paul had only chuckled when she asked him what was going on.

"Just doing her a favour, my dear Luddy." When she had tried to probe him for more information, he had changed the subject and infuriated her by saying: "You know she is not a bad gal, Luddy, you really should apologise to her."

"Did you hear or see anything else?" Grimm asks, interrupting her memories.

Ludmilla isn't sure if she had heard a scream later on or if it had been the radio. At the time she told herself it was the radio. She doesn't want to mislead the officers. It probably was the radio. She shakes her head, no.

"How long have you been neighbours with the Mills?"

Too damn long is the answer she wants to give, but Ludmilla doesn't use such uncouth words. "Four years." She hasn't had a regular good night's sleep in over three years.

The Mills had seemed like such a nice couple when they first moved in. How badly she was fooled by them. Oh, how she misses her old neighbours, never heard as much as a bleep out of them.

"What kind of marriage do you think the Mills had?"

Ludmilla feels like she has already answered this question, repeatedly. She sighs wearily. "I think they made each other miserable and they enjoyed being miserable. I don't know how Daniel coped living with that woman." He loved her and she loved gin. She loved him for the alcohol he gave her, and Ludmilla had no doubt she loved any other man who bought her alcohol. Ludmilla thinks again of Paul's tolerance for Anne-Marie and shudders slightly.

As if Grimm knows what she is thinking, he asks, "Have you had any suspicions or seen any evidence that either of them were having an affair?"

Does she say what she is thinking? No, this is silly, too many ridiculous crime programmes that Paul just won't stop watching. Paul is not and never has been unfaithful. Whilst she has her suspicions of Anne-Marie, she has never seen anything.

"Daniel, I think, is too cowardly to have an affair." Wouldn't say boo to a goose, no wonder he had ended up with Anne-Marie. Ludmilla sees Grimm fiddling with a prized ornament, which nervously distracts her from the question. She forgets to tell the police officer about the strange car she sometimes sees parked in the middle of the day. But judging by the bored expression on the female officer's face, they wouldn't be interested anyway. Just like Paul, they think she is a nosey old woman, with too little to do. Paul insisted that it is probably just someone visiting the Nobles or the Hutchings. "People are allowed to have friends and visitors, Ludmilly," he had chuckled.

She can't make them understand what it was really like living next door to Anne-Marie Mills. The fear Anne-Marie threw into Ludmilla, with the same force she threw the cans and bottles into Ludmilla's garden, always with a loud, satisfied, "Here's another for you, Lady Bitchski." How on the bad days, Ludmilla was afraid of every bang, crash and swear word.

Grimm asks, "Is there anything else you wish to tell or ask us?"

Ludmilla doesn't think anything else really matters now. She is starting to feel better. Joyful even. Anne-Marie is dead, really, actually dead. She had seen the ambulance arrive yesterday but thought the bitch would come back, just like last time. Ludmilla excuses herself saying she is a little tired and can't think of anything else.

Everyone the officers talk to say they are tired, all for the same reason. Grimm asks Ludmilla a few more questions about the neighbourhood and then gives her his card, telling her to call if she thinks of anything else.

Colvin smiles politely and says nothing until they are out of earshot. "There is something she is not telling us."

"That, my dear, is why we have repeat visits."

"She really didn't like you touching her ornaments."

Grimm flashes her a cheeky boy's grin. "Why do you think I was touching them?"

At the next house, across from the Mills, a headless doll lies abandoned in the middle of the path. Another set of doll's legs can be seen peeking out from beneath a bush. The grass is overgrown and weedy, with glittering crisp packets in the place of flowers.

Grimm rings the doorbell and a small girl answers. She looks at the police uniforms, Grimm's smiling face and Colvin's forced smile and takes a deep breath and starts shrieking, "Mummy! Mummy! Mummy!"

"Oh, for goodness' sake, Lenore! What?" A voice replies

from upstairs. "I have told you a…" A dishevelled woman comes into view. She takes two steps down the stairs before she notices the officers, two more steps before she remembers she is clad only in a stained pink dressing gown. "I umm… can you give me a minute?"

Grimm nods, still smiling, oblivious to the woman's embarrassment.

"Lenore, come here, please," she calls to the little girl.

"Why?"

"Just come here."

"Why, Mummy?"

"Just come here," the woman says desperately. They both disappear upstairs and a faint, "Chante, can you watch your sister for a minute?"

"But Muuuuum!"

Colvin closes the door behind them gently and they stand in the middle of the living room surrounded by a mess of toys. They take in the family pictures, the random stains and abandoned magazines. Three identical houses, three totally different occupants.

In this house, they dare not move. Colvin thinks about the mess in the Mills' house, the neatness of the Bryskis' house and now this chaos. But this is a happy mess, no hate or anger here.

The woman reappears, dressed in denim shorts and a purple-sleeved top. "Sorry about that." Grimm notices, with a slight smile, that several ladybird stickers have been stuck to her top in random places. "How can I help you?"

"I am DCI Nicholas Grimm and this is DCI Sam Colvin, we would like to ask you a few questions."

"Oh! Please sit down. Can I get you a drink?"

"No, thank you."

The woman gestures to a stained sofa and then spends a few

moments fussing over the mess. As she bends over, Grimm catches sight of another ladybird sticker.

The officers perch on the edge of the sofa carefully. "Sorry, I have two young daughters and, well, you know," the woman mumbles and Grimm laughs in agreement.

Unsmiling, Colvin takes out her notepad as Grimm asks, "Can I take your name?" with an almost flirtatious tone.

"Laura Noble." She grins back.

Colvin inwardly rolls her eyes as Grimm explains that they are investigating the death of her neighbour Anne-Marie Mills.

Laura looks shocked. She finally manages to stammer out, "She is dead?"

"Do you know Anne-Marie or Daniel Mills?"

Laura pauses before speaking. "Most people on this street know of them... I don't really know Daniel but I have had a few... encounters with Anne-Marie." We all know who they are and we wanted them to leave, says the expression on her face.

"MUUUMMMMY!" a wild scream comes from upstairs followed by a loud thump.

"Erm, please excuse me a minute." Laura bolts upstairs before Grimm can answer. There is another thump and the officers can hear Laura saying, "Please can you be quiet for a few minutes. Mummy needs to talk to the police."

"Why are they here?"

"The mean lady has had an accident. Why don't you play with this for a few minutes? Mummy will be back soon."

"Does this mean we can play in the garden again?" the older girl's voice asks.

The officers can't hear Laura's reply. A few moments later she comes back downstairs, smoothing down her sleeves with a cheerful, "Now, where were we?"

"Ah, you were saying you had a few encounters with Anne-

Marie." The look on Laura's face suggests that she wishes they had forgotten she said that.

"We have had a few... upsets. Chante and Lenore have upset her a few times but we don't really know her that well."

"Upset her?"

"She gets upset if she hears them playing in the garden. Lenore can be a bit... screamy. We had to stop the girls from playing outside."

If Anne-Marie even heard a child whispering, she got upset. She would start screaming out the window for them to shut the fuck up. The young girls had learnt several words that children of their age shouldn't know. Any sound of children caused Anne-Marie to hammer on Laura's door, demanding that Laura keep those brats under control. Laura had on one occasion screamed back that she was the only one out of control. There is still a large dent in the Noble's front door to prove it. But Laura doesn't explain this to the officers, she hasn't even told her friends why their children aren't allowed to visit her house. She doesn't want to talk about it to anyone.

Grimm pauses, waiting for Laura to explain more but she doesn't.

"I see, that must have been difficult to live with."

"Derrick, that's my husband, he has been wanting to sell but it is not that big a deal. I take the girls to the park instead. They like it there. It's a good neighbourhood, otherwise, and we are close to Chante's school."

"I see, and what were you doing on Thursday 18th July?"

"Thursday? Oh, I don't know, the days all blur into one, don't they? Oh! That was yesterday!" She gives a nervous laugh. "Lenore has playgroup in the afternoon. I took her swimming in the morning, then I did some food shopping and then I came home to catch up on the housework."

"Did you hear any disturbances during the day?"

"Oh, I was vacuuming most of the time. I don't remember hearing anything." Another nervous laugh. Grimm stares at her. She looks down quickly. "It's a really loud vacuum cleaner. I don't hear the phone ringing when I am using it, it's that loud."

Colvin looks pointedly down at the carpet and wonders where she had been vacuuming.

"Nothing at all?"

"Well... I thought I heard Daniel yelling something at one point. I couldn't make out what he was saying but he sounded really angry, then a door slamming shut."

"Do you remember what time?"

"Around one-ish. I am not sure. I tend to tune them out whenever I hear them now."

"You have heard them fighting before?"

"A few times, we just turn up the TV now so we can't hear them." Or her.

A loud scream comes from upstairs. "Mum! Lenore won't leave me alone."

"Okay, I think we are finished here, Mrs Noble. Is there anything you wish to add before we go?" Grimm asks, seizing the opportunity to leave.

"Erm, I probably shouldn't say this, but erm..." Another nervous laugh. "Are you interviewing everyone on this road?"

Grimm nods.

"When you get to number ten, Penny... erm, she doesn't always tell the truth. She is a little... well... not right." Laura gives yet another irritating nervous laugh. "We all call her Lying Penny."

"MMMMMUUUUUUUUUUUUUUM-MMMMMMMMMM!"

"Thank you for your time, Mrs Noble," Grimm says firmly.

"Do you think anyone will tell us the truth on this street?" Grimm asks Colvin quietly, as they stare at door number ten, Penny Cooper's house, Laura Noble's warning echoing in their mind.

"Doubt it," Colvin mutters back and presses the doorbell. They wait a few more minutes before Grimm puts his calling card through the letterbox.

Colvin is disappointed that she didn't get to meet the one they call Lying Penny. The complaints made from this house to the police had made for some interesting reading. She thinks she sees the curtains twitching slightly as they leave.

The next house also looks abandoned. The windows are covered with taped newspaper. The front garden is overgrown with weeds. They try the door anyway and to their surprise, it is opened a few moments later by a sleepy, middle-aged man. Grimm introduces them and asks if they can come in for a few minutes. The guy blinks repeatedly for a few moments, before regaining himself. "Yeah, yeah, sure, come on in."

His house is bare, completely bare. The living room has nothing, not even anywhere for them to sit, so they stand awkwardly. Colvin can see the kitchen is just as bare, a few utensils on display and a lone chair perched next to a cooking surface.

"Sorry, I have only just moved in. I am not staying here that long."

"Oh?"

"Yeah, I am renting this place from a friend, just while I sort some things out."

"I see. Can I take your name, please?" Grimm asks.

"David Clark." Grimm decides to take a slightly different approach with this guy. He is the first person in the neighbourhood who doesn't seem as though he was expecting them.

"How long have you lived here, Mr Clark?"

"Oh, erm nearly two months now."

"And how are you finding it so far?"

"S'okay, I work nights so I haven't really seen much of it."

"No disturbances?"

"Honestly? I don't know. If I am not at work then I am asleep."

David must have noted their slightly surprised glances and continues. "I know there is a woman in this neighbourhood, who has been causing problems. Like I said, I am renting this place from a friend. He has been struggling to rent it because of her. Anna-something. Is she why you are here?"

"Yes, have you met her?"

"No." David has seen a woman whom he suspects is Anne-Marie a couple of times. Always in the corner shop, always clutching a few bottles as if her life depended on them, a don't fuck with me look in her eyes. His friend repeatedly warned him that if he saw any female who looked even slightly drunk ringing his doorbell, for the love of God, do not answer the door! His friend had told him a few other things about the neighbourhood too. David thought it was best not to get involved and just avoid everyone. But, thanks to Anne-Marie Mills, he is renting this house at half the usual price!

"Has something happened to her?" he asks with a slight hint of concern.

"She had a fatal incident. That is what we are investigating."

"Oh." There is a slight note of disappointment in his voice, there goes the half-price rent. Ah well, he wasn't going to be here much longer anyway. Then David remembers himself and adds, "I am sorry to hear that."

"What were you doing on Thursday 18th July?"

There is a pause as David tries to separate days in his mind. "Umm, was that... yesterday?"

Colvin nods.

"I finished work at 2am. Then I got home and slept till noon, then had something to eat, a shower, got some groceries. I start work again at four, so I left here at about three fifteen."

"Did you hear anything unusual from noon till three?"

David rubs his face tiredly, trying to think. "I thought I heard a scream when I was leaving, but I was running a bit late. Really can't be sure."

"About three fifteen?"

"Three twenty, I was rushing so really can't be sure."

"Did you see anything unusual as you were leaving?"

"I noticed a couple of houses had their front doors open as I drove past. Figured I was probably hearing their TV or something."

"Do you remember which houses?"

"Nah, sorry, mate."

"Do you remember seeing anyone in the street?"

"No." David says this with certainty in his voice.

Colvin makes a careful note of this and also of the fact that David is at the end of this cul-de-sac and would have had to drive past all the houses to get to the main road.

"Out of interest, how well do you know the people on this street? Have you met most of them?"

"Nah, not well. I have only really met next door. Penny. She has been telling me a lot of interesting things though," he says with a chuckle and then a yawn.

"Like what?"

"Apparently the bloke at number six has a whole second family, on the sly, yeah? But they all live in the attic, that's why the girls have to make so much noise, so their mum doesn't hear them. Not that she has time to hear them, as she is running her own..." David raises his eyebrows and says in a low voice, "... private business in the house, with many a young gentleman." He chuckles again. "Number five have their own distillery in their garden, and number eight... well, I shouldn't say in front of the lady." He gives Colvin a wink. "She is absolutely barking, have you met her?"

"Not yet."

David began to yawn, and it became clear he had nothing else to say on Anne-Marie Mills or her neighbourhood.

Out of the ten houses in the cul-de-sac, they have interviewed three occupants, four if you count Daniel Mills. Colvin doesn't think that anyone has told them the truth, not the complete truth, something was being held back. Maybe they were ashamed of how they treated Anne-Marie or ashamed of ignoring her screams. Maybe they were protecting Daniel Mills, maybe they were protecting themselves. In Colvin's experience, people usually lie first, then if they are caught out, they might admit half the truth. They have to be really pushed to admit the whole truth. Colvin doesn't feel that Grimm is quite pushing them enough, he is playing the role of the good cop too well.

She waits until they are back in the car, where no one like Lying Penny can accidentally overhear them. Wouldn't it be ironic, Colvin thinks to herself, if Lying Penny was the only person to tell them the truth.

She doesn't share this thought with Grimm, instead she asks, "What do you think happened?"

Grimm inhales loudly, a sure sign that he hasn't got a clue.

"Let's go through the possibilities," he says finally.

They know now how she died, a subdural haematoma, but the manner of her death? The manner could be one of five categories; it could be either natural, accidental, suicide, homicide or undetermined. The only category that they can immediately rule out is natural. There are currently too many *she could have* and *what ifs* and *maybes* to rule out anything else. They know that the majority of her injuries were caused by her going down the stairs, but evidence suggests that she could have tripped, jumped or she could have been pushed. They think she may have fallen forward but can't be sure because her body might have been moved by her husband or by her brother, despite what they say – or she could have been moved by someone else.

The accidental evidence is backed by some of the blood swirls and hand prints in the hallway. If they were caused by Anne-Marie Mills, they suggest that she was having difficulty keeping her balance. She could have just been intending to walk down the stairs but one little wave of nausea, one little moment where the world blurred into a drunken mist caused her to stumble forward, that is possible.

There is also plenty of evidence to suggest that Mrs Mills was more than upset about Daniel's departure. They also know that she was angry, she was very drunk, she could have jumped thinking that it would bring Daniel back to her side, just like last time. She could also have jumped, not understanding the danger since she was drunk enough to believe that she could fly.

There is no denying there had been a violent fight either, that always hints of homicide. This wasn't a marriage on the rocks any more, this was a marriage six feet under long before Mrs Mills hit the stairs.

"Who would have something to gain by killing her?" Grimm starts.

"By the sounds of it, everybody."

Grimm sighs. "Okay, let's start with Daniel."

In so many cases, the murderer turned out to be   surprise, surprise – the husband. Usually they look most carefully at the closest person to the victim. The one who gains most in the insurance, the one who gets the house, the kids and the bank account. There is just something about pledging your life to someone, saying "I do" at the altar that just makes you want to kill them. The husband has become the new butler.

"So far only Anne-Marie's mother has thought he is having an affair. I didn't see any evidence of an affair in the house. We need to find his phone," Colvin says. Daniel Mills claimed he didn't know where he left it.

"Yeah, but Anne-Marie was more likely to confide in her mother than with the neighbours." The neighbours they had met so far were definitely not Anne-Marie's friends. Grimm pauses, checking his own phone. "You know what's interesting about Daniel's statement?"

"What?" His lack of emotion? His relief?

"He isn't overplaying the evidence. He isn't trying to convince us that this is a suicide. If he had murdered her, I would expect him to be trying to use the smoke and mirrors more. He isn't even trying to hide that they had been fighting."

"Not that he could." How else could he have got those scratches on his face?

"I would just have expected him to be overplaying how depressed his wife was. Instead, he seems to be still protecting her."

"Hmmm."

"I think Daniel thinks she fell."

"But the same fall happening twice?" Doubt laces Colvin's statement. They both know that drunks and stairs do have problems with each other.

Colvin and Grimm are half-heartedly discussing the possibilities but what they are really doing is watching the neighbourhood from the car windows, waiting to see if any other neighbours appear now the coast is clear. The "Sorry, officer, I didn't hear the doorbell" neighbours. The ones who were purposely avoiding them. The neighbours worth talking to.

"We should have another look at the house, while we are here. Double check for trip hazards and such." Colvin mutters an agreement, still closely watching the Bryskis' house. She thinks she has seen the same curtain twitch with an alarming frequency. "It is possible that Daniel or Peter or even the mother... what is she called again?"

"Sherri Fowler."

"Yeah, Sherri," Grimm says with a slight snort. No wonder her daughter turned out to be an alcoholic. "It's possible that any one of them pushed her."

"Well, duh."

"Not to kill her. Did you see the doctor's notes from Anne-Marie's last hospital visit? She was very close to being sectioned the last time. We know that Anne-Marie had been resistant to treatment and was refusing to get help. Another 'fall'..." Colvin doesn't even have to look at Grimm to know that he is making air quotes. "...and Mrs Mills would have a lot more explaining to do about her drinking. Fool me once, shame on you, fool me twice etc., etc. The nice doctors at the hospital wouldn't be so understanding with a second fall. Clearly she wasn't taking care of herself. It is possible that one of the family members or even all of them orchestrated the fall as an elaborate plot to make her seek help... I am just saying we could be looking at an angel of mercy rather than a cold-blooded kill. That's all."

Colvin doesn't completely disagree. It is a possibility, but she doesn't think they are that smart. Sherri Fowler is in denial about her daughter's drinking problem. Peter Fowler is a possibility. Daniel Mills seemed resigned to his wife's behaviour. He wouldn't be thinking how to help his wife, he would be thinking about how to get rid of his wife, so much easier. Less chance of a relapse.

There is no denying that Anne-Marie Mills was a burden to Daniel Mills. They will look at his and her financial accounts, and whether there will be an insurance payout. But it is already clear that Anne-Marie Mills' drinking habit was an expensive one and would be costing someone dearly. The real question was, who? There is also a possibility that either Anne-Marie or Daniel had been borrowing money off some poor sucker, a friend, neighbour or family member, and that person had come round, already upset because the long-overdue debts hadn't been repaid and the resulting argument took a wrong turn. Or even they were just upset because they could see their hard-earned money being drunk away, with no hope of repayment, just an outstretched wobbly hand and a drunk voice demanding more.

"It could have been either Sherri or Peter Fowler acting alone. They could have seen that Anne-Marie was alone in the house. They might have just seized the opportunity." They could have gone round to comfort Anne-Marie, the comforter saying something stupid like Anne-Marie should leave Daniel or that Anne-Marie should get help. Something that had upset Anne-Marie. From what Colvin and Grimm have heard so far, Anne-Marie was an aggressive drunk most of the time. If the wrong thing was said, or even the right thing with the wrong tone of voice, then Anne-Marie might have reacted violently, another fight ending with Anne-Marie being pushed away. Only this time pushed harder and further.

"Hell." Grimm chuckles to himself. "At this point, we can't even rule out that either Peter or Sherri Fowler were the ones having an affair with Daniel." They both laugh at this but there is a small twinge of truth to it. They don't know enough yet. People sometimes kill for the most stupid of reasons. They discuss the other possible motive, that since Anne-Marie and Daniel both seem to be a burden on the Fowler family, that maybe Peter or Sherri killed Anne-Marie to frame Daniel. Get both of the black sheep out of the family photographs. Peter Fowler especially seemed to be plagued by the couple to breaking point. But he was the only one who had a good alibi, if he really was at work at the time of the death. They needed to make a few phone calls to confirm.

But what would Peter or Sherri really have to gain by killing Anne-Marie? As bad as things were, she was still family. Unlike Daniel! Colvin doubts that Daniel was ever really truly accepted into the Fowler family. Colvin thinks that if either of the Fowlers were going to kill one of the Mills in a premeditated strike, it would be Daniel they killed, not Anne-Marie.

"What would Peter or Sherri Fowler have to gain from killing her?" Colvin asks out loud this time.

Grimm ponders this for a few moments. They really do need to know if there was an insurance policy on Anne-Marie's life, or a will. Or even something stupid like Grandma's treasured brooch going to Anne-Marie instead of Sherri, since Sherri seems the type to hold a grudge. But at the moment, neither officer could see any financial gain for the Fowlers.

However, evidence didn't point to a calculated, cold-blooded kill, but more a heat-of-the-moment kill. The *I didn't mean to but she just came at me* kill. If it was a kill.

"Same with the neighbours, I guess, peace and quiet," he finally says quietly.

Then there are the neighbours. No one so far had been that surprised to see them. It is evident that Anne-Marie Mills was well known within the neighbourhood and they all expected something like this was coming. Some seemed shocked that she was actually dead, not in custody, but no one seemed that upset or sad, just relieved. There was a possibility that it had been someone in the neighbourhood. Colvin suggests, which is why half of them are lying and the other half won't answer the door.

Grimm looks down to his notepad. They have been compiling a list of who lives in which house.

House number one belongs to a Fran De Winters – according to Ludmilla Bryski, she is usually away on business for months at a time, which explains the slightly overgrown garden and extra security on the house.

House number three has no occupant. This house is completely empty and has been for nearly a year now. Maybe now the previous owner will be able to finally sell it.

"We need to find out who actually owns this house and how desperate they are to sell it," Grimm notes.

House number five belongs to Daniel Mills.

House number seven belongs to Ludmilla and Paul Bryski. Whilst it is evident that Ludmilla Bryski was tired of Anne-Marie's temper tantrums, and that living next to the Mills was enough to push even the nicest person to their limits, Ludmilla Bryski had seemed the one most afraid of her neighbour and afraid of confrontation. She preferred to call the police on Anne-Marie rather than deal with her directly. The Bryskis are also very old. At a guess, Grimm would guess late seventies. Whilst they might have the mindset of murder, Grimm doubts that either of them would have the strength to push. Grimm says that if Ludmilla Bryski heard correctly, then this indicates Anne-Marie Mills was still alive when Daniel left the house. But Colvin is quick to point out that Daniel Mills had a few unexplained hours when he was lost. Enough time to leave, come back, kill and leave again unnoticed.

House number nine rented by David Clark, the only one who gained financially from Anne-Marie Mills being alive. He thought he saw two houses with the doors open, but wasn't sure as he was rushing to work at the time. He said he had never met Anne-Marie or Daniel Mills, something that seemed suspicious given Anne-Marie's notoriety. David Clark had also given them the name and contact details of the person he is renting the house from; Colvin thinks this will be another dead end.

House number ten belongs to a Penelope "Lying Penny" Cooper. A little background research showed that "Lying Penny" wasn't completely unknown to the police. There was a complaint on file from her about the house next door, number eight, Don and Gloria Hutchings. According to the complaint, the Hutchings had the audacity to do a little DIY work at 6pm on a Sunday and Ms Cooper had immediately filed a noise complaint. Grimm had Ms Cooper pegged as the local busybody, the nosy parker, there was usually one in every neighbourhood. Interestingly, there were several complaints listed from her, grievances such as littering, other noise complaints, behaviour complaints. But no complaints against Anne-Marie. She was one of the few neighbours who hadn't filed a complaint against Anne-Marie Mills. Grimm looks forward to meeting Ms Cooper, just for the entertainment relief.

House number eight belongs to Don and Gloria Hutchings. They currently know nothing about this household, except that they did their own DIY and didn't answer the door.

House number six – Laura and Derrick Noble and their young daughters, Chante and Lenore. Colvin thinks that there is a possibility that Laura or the unseen Derrick could have done something, people do strange things to protect their kids. Laura did seem slightly nervous to Colvin.

"Who vacuums for four hours?" she asks Grimm.

"When you have two young children interrupting, it's not unusual," Grimm says with a quiet air of personal suffering. Grimm thinks that Laura was another ditzy blonde, another overworked mum.

House number four, Mrs Bryski thought it belonged to "Susie" but knew nothing else. The officers couldn't decide if someone lived in the house now or not. It didn't look abandoned but it wasn't exactly cared for either. They will have to do some research.

House number two, rented by Michael and John Fox. Ludmilla Bryski had told them that this nice couple are currently on holiday to Barcelona and they won't be back for another week. She knew because she is looking after their house plants. They weren't completely off the hook until the airline confirmed they had really left, but they were unlikely.

It is possible that anyone from the neighbourhood entered the Mills' home yesterday, especially as it seemed that Anne-Marie Mills was in the habit of leaving her front door unlocked, sometimes even wide open. Not only could anyone from the neighbourhood have just walked in, pushed Anne-Marie Mills down the stairs and walked out again, but it is also possible that an opportunist burglar was in the area, saw an open door and took the opportunity. They could have become enraged when they found nothing in the house worth stealing. They could have been surprised by Anne-Marie Mills and her violent temper. Both officers know that anyone could have just walked into the Mills' house yesterday afternoon, anyone.

The officers wait a few more moments in the car. It is more overcast today but still warm, a soothing relief from the previous hot, humid days. They can hear a bird tweeting close by, but no other sounds. They have been sat in the car for nearly twenty minutes now and have seen no one, nothing apart from a few curtain twitches. This is a quiet area, Colvin thinks, very little foot traffic coming through, no cars except for those who live here. A noise like Anne-Marie would travel far here, no doubt someone must have heard more than they were willing to talk about.

"Let's go into the house."

They stand outside for a few moments. Grimm notices that

Colvin is inhaling deeply a few times. He understands why when she unlocks the door. The smell that was strong yesterday is even stronger today and they are reluctant to close the front door behind them. They move hastily through the living room into the kitchen, as Colvin wanted to take a second look at the post on the kitchen table. As she remembered, in the pile of bills there is a credit card bill. She reads it more carefully this time, noting that the bill lists over fifteen different transactions, costing between £50 to £200 but the charges are from only two places, the local supermarket and the corner shop.

They tread carefully as they head upstairs, both trying to hold their breath. They carefully run their hands over the first-floor hallway carpet, looking for anything that might have caused Anne-Marie to trip, a piece of loose carpet perhaps. But nothing. They move again into what was Anne-Marie's bedroom. It feels even darker than before. The half-empty tequila bottle still sits in the centre of the room, waiting for its drinker to come back. A child's screech intrudes on the silent room. Grimm, who is standing close to the window, tweaks the blinds to see Laura taking her daughters out. Both children are laughing and squawking loudly as they pass the house. Colvin understands why they drove Anne-Marie mad. This room, with its baby blue walls and elephant curtains was clearly intended for a child, not for Anne-Marie, and every shriek that came from those happy children was just another reminder of something she didn't have.

Grimm pulls out one of the storage boxes under the bed, the plastic tub making a crunching, scratching noise as it glides over the broken glass. On the first look the box contains nothing but spare towels, but underneath the towels, hidden carefully, are two full litre bottles of vodka. Colvin wonders if Anne-Marie had put them there then forgot about them or if Daniel had put them there. It felt like nothing, but also important at the same time. She decides to process them anyway, sliding them carefully into an evidence bag. Grimm raises an eyebrow but doesn't say anything. Nothing is quite right in this case, it is best not to miss anything, no matter how unimportant it may feel. They take the mostly empty tequila bottle this time too, careful not to smear anything. Grimm wonders aloud why the forensics team hadn't taken it. Colvin shrugs, no doubt they had taken quite a few other alcohol bottles as evidence.

They stare for a while at the blood explosion on the hallway carpet.

"By the looks of it, she stood here for a few moments," Colvin says, gesturing to the larger drops and smears in the doorway of the spare room. "Then she moved towards the stairs and stood there before the incident occurred."

"So she could have stood in the doorway, thinking about jumping, and then walked forward, paused and then jumped," Grimm says, thinking back to their earlier conversation.

"Or she could have stood here, talking to someone, and then tried to leave as someone pushed her down the stairs."

"Or she could have had a dizzy spell, leant on the doorway for support, then staggered to the stairs, world spinning as she fell forward." A thoughtful pause and then Grimm continues: "She may have even confused the stairs for the bathroom, judging by how drunk she was."

"They are all possible options, aren't they?"

Grimm nods in agreement.

"Damn it," she mutters.

Grimm again nods in agreement.

They take one last look at the master bedroom, Grimm whistling softly at the devastation. Colvin takes a closer look at the wardrobe, noting that Anne-Marie's clothes aren't in the spare room, they were still in here, a sign perhaps that this altered sleeping arrangement was not thought of as permanent? Or perhaps just another job no one cared enough to do.

Neither Anne-Marie nor Daniel has what Grimm refers to as dating clothes. Nothing special that you would wear to meet a secret lover. Colvin doubts that either of the Mills have bought any new clothes in the last three years. They seemed to be content with the same old, same old. She thinks back to her theory about houses and their occupants, that most houses reflect the personalities of their owner or owners. This house was bland and showed no evidence that either of its occupants ever aspired to anything more. But then it is hard to think of Anne-Marie as a person, as someone who once had dreams or hopes, especially as everything that she had once owned was now in shards.

They had searched everywhere for Daniel Mills' mobile phone but no success. It is only as they are leaving that Grimm spots a small black object, nicely camouflaged in the soil of a half-dead house plant by the front door. It is Daniel's mobile with two missed calls and one voicemail.

CHAPTER TEN

The corner shop is a shop of last resorts. A barely surviving relic, kept alive only by convenience. As they open the door a curious stale odour of dust and old sweets is released. One of the most miserable-looking females that Colvin has ever seen greets them with a nervous but friendly, "Hello." She quickly drops the smile as they come close to the counter, miserably turning to the floor for guidance, once she sees their badges. She knows they are not here to buy any pick and mix.

"I am Officer Grimm, Grimm by name but not by nature," Grimm says with a wink, trying to reassure the slightly shaking mass that she is not in trouble. This is his best joke, it usually gets a couple of nervous laughs but from her, nothing, just the sense that she is about to secrete a tear or five.

She closes her eyes, swallows hard and through gritted teeth, introduces herself as Margie. She flinches as Grimm reaches his hand into his folder, pulling out one of the better photos of Anne-Marie Mills.

"Margie, do you know this lady, Mrs Anne-Marie Mills?" he asks gently. This is a test. They all know she does, that's why they are here. She hesitates, trying to decide whether to tell the truth or lie. It will do the shop no good either way.

"Yes," she eventually squeaks.

"When did you last see Mrs Mills?"

"Yest'day."

"Do you remember what time yesterday?" Grimm couldn't help himself with the automatic correction. This is what having children has done to him. Margie, who looks like she wishes the floor would swallow either her or them, doesn't notice.

It isn't Margie's fault. She and her husband had tried to ban Anne-Marie Mills after several thefts, attempted thefts and verbal abuse, but the ban didn't help. It only made the verbal abuse worse. The un-ban came when Daniel finally visited, paying for the bottles they knew she had stolen, apologising repeatedly and slipped them quite a few extra notes for damages. Daniel had all but begged on his knees for the ban to be lifted, promised that if they noticed her stealing anything else, he would pay for it.

"She is not well," he had said. "We are getting her help. Please don't call the police on her, she is not well," he repeated between apologies. Luckily for him, Margie hates confrontation as much as Daniel does, and her husband is too busy screwing the barber to really care. Truth be told, Anne-Marie Mills is one of her best customers, money-wise. Margie couldn't really afford to ban her again.

"Three o clock." Ah shit, that just made everything a little more complicated, Colvin thinks, if Anne-Marie was still alive at three o clock then that rules out a few theories.

Margie remembers the time well. Anne-Marie had stormed in just as Margie had been about to close for a quick break. The smell of Anne-Marie and her stained pyjamas had made Margie feel sick. At the time she just wanted to get Anne-Marie out of her shop as quickly as possible, she always wants to get Anne-

Marie Mills out of her shop as quickly as possible, before anything gets broken.

"What kind of state was Mrs Mills in?"

Guilt pours into Margie's face, her voice trembles as she speaks. "Very angry," she says meekly.

Grimm stays silent, waiting for her to continue.

"She was very drunk." Margie had taken one look at Anne-Marie's angry eyes and wished she had something to protect herself with. Wished her husband would agree to installing a panic alarm, despite the costs. Margie should have refused to serve her; it was in her legal rights. Should do a lot of things but what was the point? Everyone knows she will always agree to anything Anne-Marie wanted. Margie doesn't know what she will do if she loses her licence for selling alcohol to someone already intoxicated. But if she refused to sell, then who knows what Anne-Marie Mills would do. She never has taken no for an answer. It was easier to give her what she wanted, then she would go away again, at least for a day or two. Anne-Marie Mills had snarled at Margie then pointed at the bottles she wanted, giving Margie a clear view of her wrists. "She had two really large bruises on her wrists." Margie hopes this information will distract the officers from the drunk remark.

Margie had nearly wet herself with fear when Anne-Marie snatched the bottles from her hands. "My husband will pay for these later," she had growled and Margie didn't dare disagree. She knew Daniel Mills would pay and even if he didn't, it was still cheaper to let Anne-Marie take two bottles than argue with her. On one occasion, Anne-Marie had destroyed nearly a hundred pounds worth of merchandise when she had been told no. Margie still shakes at the memory of that horrible day. She is still filled with a sense of dread every time the shop door opens, just in case it is Anne-Marie, or her mother. She opened the shop every morning with a nervous shake and locked it each night with a hurried relief. Countless times she had begged her husband to sell the shop, she begged for an assistant or a security guard and got nothing but empty promises.

"Can you describe these bruises?"

Margie is too scared now to think of the right words, she gestures with her hands, marking a stripe on each wrist.

"What did she buy?"

"Tequila and vodka." Margie won't point out that she hadn't really bought them. Colvin notices that Margie doesn't ask them why they are here; just like everyone they have spoken to, they automatically assume that Anne-Marie Mills has got herself into another mess.

"How frequently does Mrs Mills buy alcohol from you?"

"Erm..." Margie looks to the floor again. "Most days."

Grimm asks Margie a few more questions and receives a few more short responses. He tells Margie that Mrs Mills is dead and Margie starts to cry. Colvin can't quite tell if she is crying out of relief or sadness or both.

They are here because Daniel's discarded phone had a voicemail from *Shop Margie*: "Hi, Mr Mills, this is Margie... Margie from the shop... erm... Mrs Mills came to the shop again today... she has taken two bottles on credit... I am sorry... but she... if you could come down and urm yes. Thankyougoodbye!"

Margie just didn't have the heart or the attitude, even in a voicemail, to say you owe me money, please come and pay. Nor the spine to ever refuse Anne-Marie. Nor the concern to mention the bruises to anyone. What was she supposed to say? Your wife is messed up and scary? Please can you stop her coming in?

Behind Margie, just slightly out of sight but still well positioned, Grimm notices the red flickering light of a CCTV camera.

"Do you have the recording from yesterday?" he asks, motioning up towards it.

"Yes."

The video footage from the shop's CCTV clearly shows Anne-Marie Mills alive and furious at 3pm on Thursday 18 July. She moves quickly but in a slightly wobbly manner towards the camera. Even through the grainy footage, Colvin can see Margie's body straighten in shock and then shake with terror. Colvin watches Anne-Marie snatch the bottles, unknowingly showing the camera her wrist bruises, and then she stumbles slightly as she turns and staggers out of the shop at five minutes past three.

Well this changes most of their theories. Now they believe that Daniel left the house around midday, they know Anne-Marie was heard smashing up the master bedroom room as he was leaving or shortly after. But now they have her visiting the corner shop at 3pm, then presumably going straight back home to drink more before she decided to destroy her own room. If she had destroyed her own room before coming to the corner shop, then Margie would have seen a blood trail on her shop floor and there would also be a slight blood trail in the streets. This is presuming that all the blood splatters in the spare room are Anne-Marie's and presuming that Anne-Marie did smash her own room. Which, judging by the numerous cuts detailed in the autopsy report and the amount of glass lodged in her body, is very likely. One small comfort would be that Anne-Marie was too drunk to feel anything more than a stinging pain.

The officers read through the autopsy notes again, still trying to make sense of it all.

Cause of death: subdural haematoma
Manner of death: undetermined

The autopsy had been frustrating for all those involved. Autopsies are never easy but with this death, there are too many uncertainties. The pathology team are fairly sure she was alive when she fell, but they are unsure of how aware or conscious she was, given the very high levels of alcohol in her blood stream. The toxicologist said that she had around 275mg of alcohol per 100ml, legal drink driving limit being 80mg.

They know the cause of death – a subdural haematoma – they know that a force hit Anne-Marie Mills' head so hard, her brain expanded within her skull. She survived the fall for anything between a few minutes to an hour but it is unlikely that she ever regained consciousness.

Perhaps the cause of death should be alcohol. Even if she had not hit the stairs, she was still on her way to becoming very sick. Another drink or three, and it is possible she would have slipped into a coma anyway, would still be lying on the autopsy table. Cause of death changing to respiratory paralysis. The alcohol contributed in a different way too, her long-term, heavy drinking meant her brain's blood vessels had become frailer, more vulnerable, easier to burst. Without the alcohol abuse, she might have had a slightly better chance of survival.

Some of her injuries are consistent with falling down the stairs, others were not. More bruises had appeared once the lividity settled. Definite handprints appeared across her chest, considerable force had been applied there resulting in a cracked sternum, however, these bruises are consistent with the bruises caused by CPR attempts. Someone had put a lot of effort into trying to restart her heart.

The pathologist had also noted the condition of Mrs Mills' feet, they had spent a long time removing shards of glass and granite out of the dirty skin. The constantly bare-footed Mrs

Mills had picked up so much stray matter and infections without feeling a thing.

The mortuary technicians had checked Anne-Marie Mills one last time before releasing her body. As suspected, more bruises had become visible. Not just the ones across her chest from the attempted CPR, there was more bruising on her shoulders and legs, all worth noting but nothing conclusive. There was nothing that could be clearly identified as a hand or fingerprint. The technicians had photographed the new bruises dutifully, this may be the last time they have access to her body, so everything must be recorded carefully, just in case. They signed the documents to release her body minus a few samples and moved on to the next body.

Daniel thinks that it is finally over. He has spent days in police custody answering the same questions over and over again, until he was on the brink of tearing out his remaining hair, screaming, "What the hell do you want from me?" He didn't know why the officers continued over and over to try and break him. Didn't they know that after so many years of being married to Anne-Marie, he was already a broken man? Finally, they told him he was free to go but he couldn't go home. They were still looking for "evidence" in the house. "What evidence?" he asked worriedly, but received no answer.

When Daniel left the police station, he didn't know where he could go or who he could stay with. Not Peter or Sherri, that was for certain. He knew better than to even ask. His own parents were thankfully long dead, no brothers or sisters, no close family. He just had Anne-Marie: now what he has is not worth thinking about.

Unable to think of anything else, he has spent the last few days in a cheap hotel, alone, not knowing quite what to do. He pretended he was on holiday, getting up late, eating too much for breakfast, then spending his days watching television in his room, always just waiting, waiting for something to happen. What happens now, he asks himself, is she really gone? He shouldn't have left her. He should have left her sooner. What does he do now? What is taking them so long with his house? Why can't he go home? He never wants to go home. He tries not to think about his wife or their last argument but it replays over and over in his mind. He remembers little details that he didn't tell the police officers. He thinks about her just lying there, at the bottom of the stairs, and regrets his last words, the ones that ended in the word "bitch". He wants to say he is sorry.

Finally he has the call saying he can go home. He has been advised, first to use his home insurance to pay for a cleaner, a specialist cleaner! Like he is made of money! The idea is tempting at first, but then he thinks of the increase in premiums, the hassle, the cleaners joyfully describing the state of the house to anyone, neighbours – like he wants to give more fodder to people like Lying Penny. No, he has spent enough time cleaning up after his wife. This time won't be any different... except this is the last time. How bad could it be? He didn't notice much damage before... hopefully she hadn't smeared hand prints into the wall like last time. Those had been an absolute bitch to get off... no, it won't be as bad as last time, he could do this. No point in wasting any more money.

He is given back his house key and his mobile phone. His clothes are still being kept as "evidence". His favourite jeans! He should have protested more but the female officer Colvin had been giving him an *I-will-get-you* look, whilst Grimm continued his good cop routine fooling nobody. He can tell they both think he is guilty, that it's not over. He is not guilty; he really is not. They can stop looking at him like that! Not guilty!

He has to leave the police station quickly before he says

something he will regret. Outside and into a waiting taxi, no Peter to take him home this time. He hasn't spoken to Peter or Sherri yet, doesn't want to either. No doubt they blame him, people like to blame him. He notices the curtains twitching as the taxi pulls in front of his house. He takes a deep breath. They all know, don't they? What have they been told? What are they going to do? Fear grips him tightly, he thinks about turning around, going back to the cheap hotel, just abandoning this life. But the taxi is already leaving. With a weary sigh, he fumbles for his house keys. He might as well see how bad the damage is. He pauses, enjoying the sunshine of another hot sunny day. At least he is not in prison. He would be if Colvin or Sherri got their way. Daniel steadies his hand on the door knob, removing the *Do not cross* police tape guiltily even though they said he could. He is expecting his wife to be on the other side, readying herself to shout, "Surprise!" Anne-Marie always did like to take a joke too far.

He is assaulted instead by an overwhelming stench. What remained of his wife has congealed at the foot of the stairs, soaking into the hallway floor tiles, the stair carpet. He covers his face with a handkerchief. Home sweet home. It's worse than before, a lot worse than he was expecting, but he can still do this. He needs to do this quickly before anyone sees it. Just like before, they can't see this. Sherri can't see this. Daniel knows he is a dead man walking when it comes to Sherri, but if she saw this, he would be a dead man hanging. No, he has to do this, quickly and alone, before they start ringing the doorbell with their "Just checking you are okay." He plods into the kitchen, opens up the windows and the back door. Something smells rotten in here too.

He fills the bucket with lemon-scented bleach mixed with hot water, easing into the old routine. Flicking on the radio for company, talk radio this time, he can't bear the thought of love songs right now, he returns to the hallway, his hands shaking as he pushes the mop down with a splat. He can do this; he is a big boy now.

The water is bloody and useless within seconds, the smell growing stronger. He keeps emptying and refilling the bucket, watching his wife's blood swirl down the drain, feeling nothing except that he is getting nowhere. This is the last time, he reassures himself, but that just makes it worse. The house is too hot and the smell is everywhere. He keeps mopping, sweating, tears running down his face. He fills the bucket, mops more, dumps unrecognisable objects into the bin, refills the bucket and mops again until his back aches.

Trust Anne-Marie to die in such a messy way, a burden even after the end. Trust her to do this to him. No, it wasn't her fault, it was no one's fault, it was his fault, no it was just an accident, a stupid accident, just like before. It takes over an hour before the carpet starts to look better. It still smells, an overpowering fight of blood and lemon, but it looks cleaner. Finally he can relax. He needs to take a carpet shampoo to the spots he can see on the stairs... and the unfortunate large stain on the last bottom step. Wearily, he starts to climb the stairs, ready for a nice hot shower, noting angrily the random holes that have been cut into the carpet.

Oh, holy shit.

Daniel stands for a moment, hopeless surveying the destruction. Oh God, what does he do now? He gazes at the criss-crosses of blood, ruining the hallway carpet, decorating the walls. He looks up in disbelief and catches glimpses of wrecked rooms through open doors.

"Surprise, honey!" He can almost hear her caw. He knew there would be some damage, he had left her screaming and smashing... but this... he has nothing left... why did she do this to him?

The only thing he can do is go and get a large bin bag. There is nothing left worth saving. No wonder the police had been so convinced he was guilty. He feels guilty just looking at the destruction. Why did she do this? He tries to think how he might have reacted coming home to this mess, with Anne-Marie still alive and giggling in her bedroom or waiting in the hallway readying herself for another fight. He would have left or they would have had another screaming match, another fight. Why did she always have to provoke him like this? She was intent on driving him away, screaming into the night, leaving the same way her father had.

Daniel steps into her room. For the first time it hits him, along with the wave of putrid alcohol, that maybe this wasn't another drunk accident. He sees with dismay the big *Fuck you Daniel* written on the wall. This was one big, drunken fuck you. She wrote it loud and proud for everyone to see. She just loved exposing him, knowing how much he hated it. Then she went to the stairs for the big swan dive, so everyone would come and see her work, so everyone would know. Fuck you, Daniel.

What did he do that was so bad that she was driven to this?

Fuck you, Daniel, for not being there when she needed him? For not being able to gather her screaming and biting into his arms and make everything okay? Fuck you, Daniel, for not being able to help her? Fuck you, Daniel, for not forcing her to get help? Daniel is filled with overwhelming despair, what else could he have done? He hears the whispers of accusations pouring out of the walls. Accusations from Anne-Marie, accusations from his own mother. So many drunken whispers, laughs and cries. He hurries out of the room, slamming the door shut behind him. He can't cope with this right now. She just had an accident, he murmurs comfortingly to himself. It was just an accident.

He needs to get the room cleaned before anyone sees.

Needs to get the whole house cleaned before anyone sees. He needs to get that message off before anyone sees. Who cares now? The police have already seen it. He can't hide anything anymore. It really is an ultimate fuck you; he has been named and completely shamed by his wife. What's the point in hiding anything anymore?

He slumps wearily into his – their – his bedroom, finally accepting two things. One, that she is not going to jump out of somewhere and yell surprise. She is really dead. Two, it might not have been an accident. Something crunches under his foot. It is the blasted wedding photograph. He had left it on her bedside table, just as something to fill the space. The frame isn't worth trying to fix, a cheap wedding gift from a cheap, distant relative. Should he keep the photo? They are not even smiling in this photo, there are better ones. He is not even sure why this one made it to a frame, while the rest were banished to the attic storage. Shit, he can't cope with seeing Anne-Marie's face right now, it makes him want to... cry? Even in these pictures, Anne-Marie's eyes hold an accusing glare. The photo is crumpled, he screws it up further. Then he regrets screwing it up, no one is ever going to be able to take a picture of Daniel and Anne-Marie Mills together again.

Bin bags, that's what he needs, an Irish coffee and plenty of bin bags.

It's time to start again.

He drags himself back downstairs, feet slapping uncomfortably against the lemony swamp at the bottom. Through the living room, oh well at least she didn't wreck the TV, as he tries to look on the bright side. Then he remembers that there is no food in the house. Everything in the fridge is out of date and mouldy, the TV really is the only thing he has left.

He is going to have to leave the house at some point. There is no food and there are funeral arrangements to make. But what if he goes out and someone recognises him? What does he say? What have they been saying about him? What does he say if someone asks how she died? He is too drained to cope with any of this.

Two days pass. No one rings the doorbell or calls. No one. He doesn't eat for two days, he just spends his time cleaning, sleeping or waiting. Waiting for something to ring, for someone to care. But mostly just waiting for the post to arrive. There was a small pile waiting when he returned to the house, but it wasn't what he wanted.

A small amount of post arrives each day. Some of it is anniversary cards, addressed to both of them. Congratulating them on reaching five happy years and wishing them a continued happy ever after. He reads each one carefully and unemotionally, looking closely at the handwriting, the names. They are not what he is looking for. He doesn't know what to do with the anniversary cards, including the one he has hidden away upstairs, written to a darling wife. There seems little point in keeping them now. He hates the cards, the images of cutesy newly-weds and teddy bears mock him with their fairy-tale love.

Condolence cards begin arriving, addressed to him alone. He doesn't know what to do with these cards either. Is he meant to display them? It feels wrong to put them up. He wants to bin them but he knows he shouldn't. He thinks about burning them, that feels more appropriate; but then what if the neighbours saw the fire and thought he was burning evidence? What if any of the senders of the cards came round to comfort him and asked if the card had arrived? He is not that great at lying. But he doesn't want the cards, has no need for them, receives no comfort from them; he ends up stuffing them all in a drawer.

The cards are not what he is waiting for. There are the

usual bills, which he dutifully pays, a message from Margie which he doesn't read. Then the usual take-away menus, which he reads through, carefully examining each one for an altered message, a folded note, something hidden for his eyes alone.

He knows now, that the day Anne-Marie died, she went to the corner shop, nothing new or strange about that, but en route to the corner shop is a post box. She could have sent him something. That's what he is hoping for, one last message, something, anything. He has searched the house in vain, whilst piling their broken possessions into bin bags. A note or something, anything, but nothing. Now he waits, he just needs something, one last "I hate you", or "I am sorry", or even, what he really hopes for, is an "I love you". He is desperate for a last goodbye, something that she had written after the *Fuck you Daniel*. Those can't be her last words, not after all this time. There has to be something else.

He waits hopefully, searches fruitlessly, whilst knowing in his heart that Anne-Marie would have been too drunk to think of doing such a thing, that nothing is coming.

There has to be something, his mind insists, it can't end on a fuck you.

It just can't.

CHAPTER ELEVEN

Ludmilla Bryski has decided not to attend Anne-Marie Mills' funeral. Not that she still bears any grudges or ill will towards that poor drunk creature. In fact, now she has had some sleep, Ludmilla can even feel the tiniest bit of remorse at her sudden passing. Remorse and guilt. She still thinks she heard a scream, still hears a scream over and over, but doesn't want to admit it. It wasn't her fault that Anne-Marie died. There was nothing she could have done. She just wanted there to be quiet.

Ludmilla always thought that Anne-Marie would be the death of her, not the other way around. A drunken plague to an early grave. Even now Ludmilla still flinches when she turns on the vacuum cleaner, expecting a hammering on the wall or front door. Now there is no one to accuse her of passive-aggressive vacuuming. Her husband Paul had been no help at the time. "Well you did start at seven in the morning, dear," he had said with an annoyed sigh. What was she supposed to do? She hadn't slept, she couldn't just lie in bed all day like some people.

Paul just couldn't believe the worst of people. Ludmilla caught him yesterday, happily conversing with Lying Penny about what a tragedy it was, for such a sweet young girl to have such a nasty accident. Adding new fodder to Lying Penny's lies. He doesn't listen to anything Ludmilla tells him. He doesn't even understand why he shouldn't talk to Lying Penny.

Ludmilla herself had plotted a far worse retaliation to Anne-Marie than just passive-aggressively vacuuming. In those early morning hours, when she was kept awake by her own anger as well as Anne-Marie's drunken screams, whilst Paul slept peacefully beside her. But the vacuuming was the only thing she was brave enough to do.

Ludmilla had prayed that she would never have to see or hear Daniel Mills again either. But God only laughed and sent him back to his house. She heard him return, slamming the door so loud she feared Anne-Marie was alive again. When her heart stopped thumping with fear, she realised it was Daniel and felt... scared all over again. She doesn't know what happened and doesn't want to know, but she doesn't want to live next door to him anymore. He is not as harmless as she thought he was. Now instead of the constant neighbourhood hum of "How do we solve a problem like Anne-Marie?" They ask instead, "How do we make him leave?" It is too soon to suggest anything, but maybe after the funeral, they can get things moving. Maybe they will have peace in this neighbourhood, one day.

Ludmilla does feel the need to pay some kind of respect to Anne-Marie. Maybe she will light a candle or maybe she will sip a stiff drink in Anne-Marie's "honour". That seems more fitting. A drink would calm her nerves, stop her hands from shaking. From Paul's secret stash, of course.

Daniel has regained his appetite with a vengeance. He has gone from fasting and waiting, to eating everything in sight, unable to sit still. He doesn't know what to do with himself, what to think or how to feel. It started when he watched the first load of bin bags containing the broken remains of his life being crushed in the bin lorry and felt nothing. Not even a sense of relief that it was nearly over. Just empty, just hungry, he told himself. He then scrubbed the fridge clean, showered for the first time in days and finally left the house to go food shopping, stockpiling as much food as he could. He hasn't stopped eating since.

To his immense relief, no one recognised him in the supermarket. No pointing fingers, no whispers, just indifference. Then after the first gorging session, there was more scrubbing to do and then all over again because the stains were reappearing as everything dried. He keeps cleaning the whole house from top to bottom, except for the spare bedroom, which he still can't face. The house still smells odd, a hint of something rotten under the bleach, and feels empty and cold. Everything feels empty including himself, so he keeps eating.

He has carefully examined his face in the mirror every day, convinced that the scratches could still be clearly seen. Even now, on the morning of the funeral, he is frantically examining his face from all angles just to check, hating who he sees in the mirror. Trying not to think of the coming funeral. He still can't think of her as dead, he's still half-waiting for her to come home. *Joke's over now, honey, please come home,* he pleads silently, whilst fumbling with his tie. *No questions asked, just please come home.*

Previously, days or maybe even weeks ago, Peter broke the silence by sending Daniel a text, asking if Sherri could arrange the funeral. They both knew it wasn't really a request. Daniel knew he was being told that Sherri was arranging the funeral and his input was not required. He didn't have the will to argue, Sherri always wanted things to be done in a certain way, her way, she would venomously insist on it. The text had been a relief as well, he had been caught between the decision of burial or cremation. He and Anne-Marie had never even discussed funeral plans, it had felt too early for that kind of talk. He couldn't help but think that if they cremated Anne-Marie, there would be a huge fireball, wrecking the crematorium, as the alcohol in Anne-Marie's veins ignited. A forbidden thought, he couldn't help it but it would have been the way she wanted to go.

Daniel knows that today at the funeral, he needs to cling to this empty feeling, not to allow any emotion to appear on his face. No matter what is said, he can't cry. Sherri will mock him if he cries.

"Man up!" is what his father bellowed at his mother's funeral. "Big boys don't cry," that's what they told him at his father's funeral. He had felt nothing but numb and sick at those funerals too, sitting alone, wishing for everything to be over. It will be over soon, he assures himself. Just don't think about the argument or finding her. Don't think about those accusing eyes, those eyes still open. No, don't think about that. Don't think about how empty the house feels, or how they are all whispering about you. Don't think of anything. Just pull on the funeral suit, finish getting ready and go.

"I can't face the world today," Anne-Marie used to say.

Finally he knows what she meant.

But it's time to go.

It is hot again on this August day, hot and muggy, like a storm might break at any moment. People swelter uncomfortably in their mourning suits. The weather is making Sherri Fowler even more irritable. How dare it be sunny on the day of her daughter's funeral? As if even the sky is glad she is gone. Sherri is displeased because there are not enough people here and those who are, are not acting upset enough. Some even look relieved that Anne-Marie is gone. Sherri has to keep hiding her face in a tissue so they don't see her disapproving glare. She has to keep biting her tongue, her hand itching to slap someone and she badly wants a drink. She has to hold back, can't afford to turn people against her, she needs to gain their sympathy, something which is bloody hard to do when no one cares. Even the newspapers, who printed any old bloody rubbish, ignored her! No one would run a story on her daughter's tragic demise. Even the obituaries clerk was indifferent to her "She was taken far too soon" wail. They just made some indifferent "I am sorry for your loss" twaddle. No one cared that her daughter was murdered.

Sherri hates Daniel Mills. Hated him right from the start. Everything about him just disgusts her. She knows the feeling is mutual and she is aware that Daniel calls her Mrs Foul-er in private. That sort of petty behaviour is just typical of him. At the very beginning, she had tried to be pleasant, after hearing so much from her sickeningly happy daughter squawking about how happy she was, how much she liked him.

Remembering that now makes Sherri sick to the stomach. On that very first meeting, when her daughter had gushingly introduced him and it was going awkwardly fine until Daniel made some comment about her daughter's name: Anne-Marie. A little unusual but very pretty, he had said, causing her daughter to blush like a fool. Sherri had accepted the compliment gracefully and said that it was from an Elvis song. And do you know what the little prick had whined? Oh, I don't like Elvis. What was wrong with him? Who doesn't like Elvis? She had made an excuse about dinner burning and left the room. She wished now she had gone with her first instinct and kicked that stupid twat out of her house.

Later, when her daughter told her about the proposal, she had advised against the marriage. It wasn't just about not liking Elvis, but that had been a good warning sign. She had, right up until the wedding day, urged her daughter to change her mind. There were plenty of other men out there, nicer men. But the more she had urged her daughter, the more Anne-Marie insisted that she loved him. The stubborn fool. Sherri had taken great delight in playing Elvis' greatest hits whenever they came round for dinner, constantly on a loop, not too loud so the little prig couldn't ask her to turn it down or off.

It was a nice ceremony in the end. Daniel and Peter gave nice speeches and Sherri read some miserable poem – but then Sherri had to have the last word. They had all stood for the coffin to be carried out, and the final music played. It was fucking Elvis and *Marie's the Name*. (Sherri had always thought he was singing "Anne-Marie's the name" and no one dared correct her.) Daniel just kept his head bowed and followed the coffin outside, knowing there would be a triumphant gleam in his mother-in-law's teary eyes.

It was not an appropriate song for a cremation.

Peter waits patiently outside, away from the departing crowds, waiting whilst his mother smokes yet another cigarette. He is reluctant to say anything about the ceremony, knowing that whatever he says will be wrong. However, his mother doesn't need prompting.

"I expected better for Anne-Marie," she snaps.

Peter doesn't know if she is referring to the funeral, which she had arranged, or Anne-Marie's life in general. Sherri doesn't elaborate, instead she launches into a full-blown criticism of the funeral flowers, in particular an arrangement that one of Anne-

Marie's neighbours had sent, which "quite frankly, looks like it was taken out of a dustbin".

Peter doesn't really listen. His suit feels prickly in the heat and he didn't sleep well again. It had been too hot and he couldn't stop worrying about what might happen at the funeral. He was determined to keep Sherri and Daniel separate, despite their promises to behave. He just wanted a quiet day for his sister. He is not protecting Daniel, despite what his mother says, he is not.

"It would have been a fine funeral for you," concludes his mother, flinging her cigarette off into a flower bed. "We are done here," she mutters, moving towards the car without even a backwards glance. "Let's get this shitshow over with."

CHAPTER TWELVE

"Guilty," said the doctor.
"Guilty," said the hearse.
"Guilty," said the lady with the black purse.

Fifty-two people attended Anne-Marie's funeral, which meant fifty-one pairs of judging eyes, all accusing Daniel. Twenty criticised Daniel's appearance, noting the fat bulges, straining at his shirt buttons. Four had been holding their breath, waiting for the tell-tale ripping noise as he sat down – any minute now. Two thought he needed a haircut.

Forty have already judged him and found him guilty. They add their own justifications like "He didn't even cry". The jury in the corner agrees, they had expected a crocodile tear or two. "He didn't even look sad." They all agreed. They continue their conversations out of earshot of any members of the Fowler family, discussing what may have killed Anne-Marie and who might have killed her and why. Some were insisting that Daniel would be in prison by now if he was going to be held accountable, others assuring he will be in prison soon.

"Do we know what killed his parents?" Laura Noble asks in one corner, quietly. She is one of twenty-five who are attending only for the gossip. No one knows what or who killed the elder Mr and Mrs Mills. "I know they died when he was quite young," one person ventures, but no one else knows any details. Suddenly it seems important, one sleuth inwardly makes a note to find out. Not directly from Daniel of course, no. In fact, all but five out of the fifty-two are considering cutting all contact with Daniel, cutting him completely out of their lives. Not that they spoke that much to him before.

They all watch Daniel now, out of the corner of their eyes, as he approaches the buffet table, loads up a plate, looks around and hurriedly retreats to an empty table. Some people go up to him with perfunctory, "I am sorry for your loss." Some offer a brave, "Let me know if there is anything I can do." Some people ignore Daniel completely, only offering their condolences to Sherri.

Sherri is being more social, moving around the room, thanking people for coming in an unusually polite way, doing what she can to encourage the gossip. She is trying to get everyone in the room on her side, making sure Daniel has no allies left for the days ahead. She agrees with some people quietly that Daniel shouldn't even be here. Peter had insisted. She is only tolerating his presence because she knows Daniel will soon be in prison, where he belongs. They all murmur agreements. Sherri is also watching all the females in the room carefully, regardless of their age. Watching to see how they interact with Daniel, waiting for someone to linger a comforting hand for too long. She has been waiting for him to move his slut into the house, that poor replacement for her daughter. She seethes, imagining that bitch wearing her daughter's clothes, using her make-up. Why else would Daniel kill her daughter? If not to move in some younger model? The minute Sherri catches one scent of that bitch, she will be moving in for the kill.

Daniel is trying to calculate how long he needs to stay for. Until the end? Or is it acceptable for him to leave earlier? He knows he is not wanted but if he leaves, people will think that it's a sign of guilt, they will all talk about him. They are already talking about him, he can tell by their looks and whispers. When he was at the buffet table, he had heard a familiar voice, not quite out of earshot, say, "Well, I heard..." He had groaned inwardly, realising that Lying Penny was behind him and that she had found a new audience.

He is relieved that no one wanted to hold this part of the funeral at his house. No one has visited since the accident, not even Sherri, something he is slightly shocked about. He has caught some people, namely Laura Noble and Lying Penny, peering through the windows. Laura had given him an embarrassed wave when she realised she had been caught and moved swiftly on. Lying Penny was too short-sighted to realise she had been caught and continued peering for a few more minutes. Daniel is now carefully keeping every blind and curtain closed.

Laura Noble is leaving. Daniel is surprised she had come at all, after the way Anne-Marie had screamed at her children. Probably, like most people here, was just making sure that Anne-Marie was really dead. He watches as Laura quietly offers her condolences to Sherri, no doubt explaining that she needed to collect her daughters from something or other before leaving. Lying Penny hasn't spoken to him, just watched him warily from a corner of the room. Daniel tries to subtly look around the room. Who is left? Who is a friend? Who is looking guilty? Someone in this room is just as guilty as he is, someone here must have been enabling his wife, plying her with more alcohol, it wasn't just him. He sees nothing but accusing eyes.

He is still expecting a fight, despite Peter's assurances. He knows that Sherri is just waiting, that this is just a temporary truce. That look in her eye whenever she sees him promises nothing but revenge. She will get him. It's only a matter of time.

Daniel takes another worried bite of his food, but everything tastes like sawdust. He wants to go home. He can neither leave nor stay. He can only hope, along with the remaining twenty-eight people, that it will be over soon.

Grimm finally caught Lying Penny at home the morning after the funeral. He thought he would try one more time to reach the intriguing lady. She is not what he expected, a peering elderly woman dressed completely in bright, vivid purple. He introduced himself and asked politely if he could ask a few quick questions. As the door closed behind him and he followed her into the musty-smelling house he had no idea what kind of two-hour non-stop diatribe she had been preparing to launch.

He fumed back into the station, intent on taking his anger out on the next hapless person he saw. He cornered an indifferent Colvin at her desk, furiously recounting everything to her, refusing to allow her to escape or provide any input.

"She treats the whole street like it's her own personal soap opera. She has her own trashy story for each person. I caught her lying to me at least four times." Grimm never wants to hear Lying Penny's croaky hideous voice again. "She spent over an hour just talking about the milkman! And whenever I tried to change the subject, she just looked at me and continued on with whatever she was saying." Grimm has heard all about the "idiot family... so stupid" at number six, with three kids, the wife with her second family. "Don't let her looks fool you, dear... And why haven't they arrested that woman at number one? She is a spy, you know, dear, not even on our side."

Grimm growls and Colvin suppresses another giggle. "Just when I thought she was never going to stop, and this is the worst bit," he tells Colvin. "She said, 'It's eleven o clock. I have to go, dear, I play bingo every Thursday afternoon. I don't want to be late.' 'Every Thursday?' I asked. 'Yes, dear,' she said. So I asked: 'Did you play bingo on Thursday 18th July?' And you know what she said?" Grimm angrily pauses, then continues in a croaky, high-pitched voice, "'Yes, dear, I remember that one because I won over £100 that week. I treated the girls to fish and chips. We had the most wonderful afternoon'."

Colvin laughs as Grimm storms off to get a coffee.

He should have, but doesn't mention another incident to Colvin. He should have told her that when he arrived on the street, he was immediately spotted and invited in by Laura Noble calling out, "Can I talk to you for a moment inside, Officer?" Grimm had grinningly obliged. Somehow an "I am scared" led to some verbal comforting and somehow that lead to Laura purring, "Can I count on your personal protection, Officer?" She then surprised Grimm with a strong kiss on his lips. Grimm was caught, he wanted so badly to respond, to see where the kiss would take him. He could taste coffee on Laura's lips, felt her tongue demanding him, all of him.

An unwelcome thought crashed through his desire. "She is married, you idiot." He had wanted to ignore it, wanted to wrap his arms comfortingly around Laura's slender body.

"You are married, you idiot." Another unwelcome thought. Reluctantly he pushed Laura away instead of pulling her close. Tried to ignore the results of that one kiss. For a brief moment Laura looked angry, then she turned away in embarrassment.

"You have nothing to fear, Mrs Noble," he said gallantly, trying to ignore that the kiss happened. He couldn't think of anything else to say and slowly backed out the door. She said nothing, not even a goodbye. He took a few deep breaths out of sight, still smelling a faint trace of her perfume. It was not the first he has been propositioned. Let's face it, he looks damn good in this uniform. But no woman had ever quite had this much of an effect on him... except his wife of course! Did he imagine it or did Lying Penny smirk knowingly as she answered the door? He soon forgets all about it, all he remembers later is Lying Penny. Everything else, the kiss, the smell of her perfume, everything he forgets but Laura remembers.

When he comes back, he notices that Colvin is reviewing the CCTV footage of Anne-Marie Mills at the corner shop again. She is upset but trying not to show it.

"Mrs Fowler called. I told her that the coroner has ruled an open verdict, so unless new evidence is found, there isn't going to be a trial."

"How did she take it?"

"She screamed at me."

Grimm nods, it was the reaction they both were expecting. "Then she told me to get my head out of my arse and find some new evidence." Mrs Fowler had also shrieked: "Does my daughter's murder mean nothing to you either Col-Vine?" Colvin thinks that Sherri purposely mispronounced her name to make her feel small. It had worked.

"She also asked if we had tried dusting for fingerprints."

"Oh no, we forgot about that one," Grimm groans mockingly. Both of them inwardly suspecting that there will be more calls from Sherri Fowler, telling them how to do their jobs. A lot more calls.

They didn't have much evidence to work with. Daniel's

clothes had contained some plant matter, similar to that on King's Park and most other parks. There were no blood drops on his clothes except those close to his neck line, consistent with the face scratches. Samples had been sent to DNA testing. But for Daniel to be guilty, he would have had to have gone back into the house after 3pm, changed his clothes, killed Anne-Marie, then changed back into his first set of clothes, disposed of his other clothes and gone back to King's Park (which was over fifty minutes' walk from the house for the even the fittest of people), all by 4.30pm. Unless he had help or called a taxi, but there was no evidence that he even had a friend willing to do something like that and no evidence that he had called a taxi. Colvin has spoken to all the taxi companies just in case and no one had driven anywhere even close to the two places on that day.

Anne-Marie's stained pyjamas were of no help either, just blood and glass. Samples had been sent away for DNA testing, along with the pieces of flesh found underneath Anne-Marie's fingernails. No prizes for guessing who they will belong to, Colvin thinks, before going back to examining the photographs taken by the forensics team.

Grimm watches her quietly for a few moments before asking, "Do you think we have missed something?"

Colvin shrugs and then nods. Perhaps it was Sherri Fowler's screeched accusation that they were letting a murderer get away or perhaps it is her own gut feeling, but something just didn't feel right.

She is annoyed that they can't even determine the manner of death: if you thought this was a murder case, you found evidence for murder. If you thought this was a suicide case, you found evidence for suicide. If you thought this was an accident, you found evidence for an accident.

"How many cases have you had where 'we had a fight and I

left' turned out to be 'we had a fight, I battered her brains in and left'?" she asks.

Grimm is silent, not wanting to admit that it happened often, along with "she tripped" and "I don't know what happened, I swear". He wearily sits down to review the evidence again with Colvin.

"Well, we will find something or my name is not Nicholas Agamemnon Grimm."

There is a confused pause before Colvin asks. "Agamemnon?"

"I have a very powerful grandmother," Grimm replies with a wise nod.

Daniel's boss called him a few days after the funeral. It was an awkward conversation. Daniel knew already that he wasn't going to be welcomed back. He could hear the relieved intake of breath when he told her that he was quitting. The joy in his boss's voice as she stammered that she would miss him but she understood, that she would write him a good reference. Then she said a quick goodbye, no doubt wanting to end the conversation before he changed his mind.

Daniel is not surprised, he was a good worker, a competent worker, unlike some people. But he knows what they have been saying about him, even before Anne-Marie's first accident. She'd repeatedly embarrassed both him and his work colleagues.

It was his fault too, for trying to include her. He would always take her to the company outings, anything where spouses were invited. She was never purposely left out. She would be excited about going right up until the day, then suddenly she hated every piece of clothing she owned. If they went shopping for a new outfit a few days before, then she would hate that outfit especially. Nothing fitted right. There would be tears and then a shot of something. No matter what he said to reassure her, it wasn't right. She acted as if his company, his workmates and their spouses were a gaggle of harpies, their sharpened claws ready to tear her to shreds.

There were four ways it would go after that, Anne-Marie having a good time was not one of them. On two different occasions she refused to get out the car and he had to drive home, where she would retreat into her room with a bottle. "We realised we left the oven on," or "Her mother is unwell," he would say the next day to the few who had seen them arrive.

Second option, she would stay at his side, drinking, because she was bored. A co-worker would want to discuss something and she would start twitching with boredom. Anne-Marie could never be sober and still at the same time. Her hands would constantly be twitching, waiting for something to happen. If nothing happened and she felt she was being ignored she would take a long gulp of the complimentary wine, then another. Then another glass, more gulps. Until he had to make excuses and usher her away.

"You were ignoring me," she would wail. "I wait all week to see you. You see them every day." It was not his fault that she had no interest in the audit or the inventory. These things were important.

Third option would be that some well-meaning wife, who was usually new to the female group, would take Anne-Marie under her wing, introduce her to others, then someone would start talking about their darling Freddie or Alfie. Someone who didn't know or didn't care that children were a taboo subject. Anne-Marie, having nothing to contribute to the conversation, would start drinking to escape the awkwardness. No matter who took her under their wing, no matter what was said, she was different to them. She didn't have anything in common with anyone. Well, early on, she must have had something in common with him. They wouldn't have got married otherwise.

After a few awkward outings and so many muttered apologies, after Anne-Marie had become loudly abusive on three occasions, the fourth option was the only one left. They stopped talking to her – and him. He couldn't blame them, but that made things so much worse. When they arrived, you could hear the happy chatter reduced to murmurs, smiles became forced. No one could look them in the eye. Anne-Marie had an inbuilt sense for awkwardness, and at any sniff of it she would start drinking at such a pace that Daniel didn't know why she bothered with a glass.

In the very beginning, his colleagues had been nothing but concerned. "Is your wife okay?" was asked around twenty times the following day. "She is fine," Daniel would always insist with an unbelieving smile. "She just had a touch too much to drink, I am sorry for what she said." They would shrug off the apology, citing incidents where they had said something worse. It was always laughed off at first, then it was rarely mentioned, they would just acknowledge his apologies. On later occasions, they would say nothing to him the next day, just avoid glances, whisper when they thought he couldn't hear. Then the complimentary wine was stopped and he became the most unpopular man in the company.

It wasn't his fault that she didn't fit in. She didn't want to fit in, so she drank. He didn't really fit in either. It was a relief to use her as an excuse to leave. They were a perfect partnership really.

Nothing was said. They were all too polite for that but Daniel stopped bringing her, stopped ruining everyone else's day. She noticed, of course. He would tell her that it was because he didn't want to go or that the activity planned wasn't "their kind of thing". Of course, she didn't believe him. It just became fuel for the "you are ashamed of me" arguments. It wasn't his fault that she didn't know how to talk to people. What was he supposed to do? Supply cue cards? Warn everyone ahead of time that they couldn't talk about children, holidays or work? What else could they have talked about?

He knew it was too late to repair the damage at work. If they had got divorced then maybe he would have been accepted again. But for her to die in such a suspicious way – they would be whispering about him for years to come. Even in death, Anne-Marie is still ruining his life. He can do nothing except start again.

Maybe when things quieten down, he will start again.

CHAPTER THIRTEEN

Yes, I killed that bitch.

So what?

She deserved it.

And let's face it, it's not like anyone is going to miss her!

Someone should have done it years ago.

She fucking deserved it. She was blackmailing me! Me! How fucking dare she? Kept increasing her demands with that ridiculous smirk on her face. Did she really think she could get away with blackmailing me for ever? I never should have given in to her in the first place, I should have pushed her years ago, wiped that smirk off her face there and then. I control things, not her!

Well, she is not smiling now, that's for sure.

When you have a problem you should deal with it straightaway, you don't let it fester, you don't let it gain a foothold.

And let's face it, no one really cares that she is gone. I performed a neighbourhood service, a community service, getting rid of her. I should get some kind of reward; they should be thanking me. Even the police know that, which is why they are *only doing a half-hearted investigation, going through the perfunctory motions.*

Everyone thinks Daniel did it anyway, even if the police managed to find a clue, they will blame him not me. They are not going to find anything; they couldn't find their own arses even if they had help.

So long, Anne-Marie, you stupid bitch.

Don't come back.

CHAPTER FOURTEEN

There will be no trial unless new evidence is found. Daniel is relieved of course, the thought of testifying fills him with dread, but he is also disappointed. No trial means he can't silence the whisperers, those who think the worst of him. He can't prove to them that he is not guilty, and he is not guilty! He's not!

He is in limbo now, no idea what to do. He can't go back to work; his resignation has been accepted and there wasn't so much as a Sorry You Are Leaving card. He can't cope with the thought of finding a new job, not until this town has forgotten his name. What else can he do?

He could scrub the hallway again. Despite his repeated efforts, nothing looks clean and a permanent smell remains, intruding like an unwanted guest. He is convinced that he can see his wife's outline from where she lay on the tiles. He needs to get rid of it all. The holey carpet, floor tiles, everything.

But how?

The neighbours already saw too much the day he got rid of that first load of bin bags. He had paused when taking them out and looked up to see almost every curtain on the street fluttering. He suspected this would happen, it is why he left the reeking bags in the hallway until he saw the collection truck approaching, taking them out at last minute so no one could pry inside. If he pulls up the stairway carpet, where would he take it? No doubt it will be stained on both sides, which adds to his problems. Wherever he leaves it, some self-described detective will claim it. He could burn it, along with Anne-Marie's clothes. There is nothing suspicious about that, nothing at all!

He can't afford a new stair carpet right now, not with all Anne-Marie's debts, including her funeral costs. Oh, Sherri had been happy to arrange everything but had left the cost of paying to him. Typical! He can afford it mostly, but he can't stay unemployed for long.

That should be a motivator to start applying for jobs, but it's not. He just can't bring himself to even look, can't bring himself to do a lot of things recently. He thinks about taking a holiday, the one he had longed for so much before, but it doesn't feel like the right thing to do. He doesn't want to leave the house, and he doesn't want to go anywhere alone. He can't stand being alone in the house but hated being alone in the hotel. What can he do? His only hobbies were Anne-Marie and the TV. He doesn't have much else. He tries to tell himself that it won't be so bad to spend a few more days doing a little scrubbing and a lot more TV watching. He needs to give himself time to recover after all he has been through.

So he sits and he eats.

And he eats.

He has always eaten to fill the void inside and food has always been the one thing that he can turn to. It doesn't even matter what he eats, what matters is that he is distracted, preparing the food is a distraction, the endless cramming of food in his mouth is a greasy distraction, the thinking of the next meal is a distraction, then the eating of more food.

Most of the time he doesn't even feel hungry and his clothes don't fit anymore. He plods around the house in unwashed sweat pants. But what does that matter? Does anything even matter? Sometimes he just stares at food, willing himself to be hungry so that he can eat again. Sometimes he thinks of himself as a duck, being force-fed for a fatty liver and he stuffs more food in there.

He now only leaves the house for more supplies. On the first trip, he felt guilty and ashamed by the stares and whispers. He didn't want to be in the outside world, yet he craved social contact. He finally understands his wife, but still doesn't understand everything. Eating, he thinks, helps him to understand. As he burrows through a bag of marshmallows, he becomes convinced that the answer lies somewhere towards the bottom of the bag.

He understands now why Anne-Marie never answered the phone. Before, he was angry when he came home to an answering machine full of messages. Anne-Marie had been at home all day, doing nothing. "Why didn't you answer it?" he would ask. She would stare at the floor and say that she didn't feel like it, that she didn't feel like talking to anyone, not even him.

He used to think that if you were at home all day, talking to nothing animate, then you would jump at the chance to talk on the phone, just to hear a friendly voice. Now he thinks he understands, the phone is just another annoyance, they should have got rid of it years ago. The shrill ring snaps you away from your happy place, with its demand for immediate attention. He doesn't feel like to talking to anyone now except Anne-Marie. Not that people feel like talking to him either, most of the calls he gets are sales calls for things he can't afford.

He stuffs another marshmallow in his mouth. He doesn't even like marshmallows, they are just sugary nothingness, but he had found a packet in the top cupboard. Anne-Marie had liked marshmallows, she had liked to pop as many as possible into her mouth then add a gulp of something spirity, then she would sit, chewing contentedly, like a cow, occasionally giggling to herself. He tried to copy her on occasion, share in her fun, but it only made him choke. Now he keeps eating them, even though they make him feel sick. There is something in the taste; had he once kissed Anne-Marie after one of her marshmallow stuffs? Had he once had this sweet taste on her lips? No, he can only remember tasting the sharp notes of something alcoholic, even in the early days – reminding him of his mother. He wishes now he had kissed his wife more. He tries to stuff that feeling away with another marshmallow, and another, and another, then he takes a swig from the brandy bottle, and another, mixing the bitter with the sweet in his mouth, wanting to remember more and yet wanting the memories to stop.

Peter has had another bad day at work. They all seem to be bad days now, ever since his sister died, as if she had cursed him with her dying breath. She probably did, that would be just like her. He did nothing wrong but he must still be punished. Why? Who knows why? Because Anne-Marie thought that Sherri loved him more? Because he let their father leave? Because he couldn't save her? Because he was glad she was dead? Because he didn't answer his phone earlier? Because he didn't want to take her away from her husband? It wasn't his fault; she wasn't his responsibility. He shouldn't feel so guilty, he did nothing wrong. Why did he end up surrounded by crazy women? Why was everything he said the wrong thing? Why does he feel like he is turning into Daniel?

To make his day even worse, his mother is calling him, again. She calls him now more than Daniel used to. As soon as he gets rid of one annoyance, he gets another.

"Peter?"

"Yes, Ma."

"Daniel could have..." He lets his mother drone on and on, barely listening. God forbid she would at least ask "How are you? How was your day? How was work?" Then he could tell her that his job at the moment is like sitting at a dinner table, when you have had the starters and everything so far was fine, but then suddenly shit is being served, some people leave immediately, some nibble at the shit and then leave and some eat the shit, hoping dessert will be better and if you stay, you have to be positive about eating the shit, so other people will join the table and there will be less shit for you to eat. Not that his mother would understand, she would be the one serving the shit, insisting that he eats up because it is good for him.

"Peter!" His mother's voice is stern, whatever she is going to say next needs his full attention and no doubt it will be difficult to answer.

"Yes, Ma?"

"The day Anne-Marie was taken from us."

"Yes, Ma?"

"You rang me and said Anne-Marie may have taken her own life."

Peter inwardly groans and curses. "Yes, Ma?" He is going to get a *"don't you yes Ma me"* in a minute, if he is not careful.

"Why did you say that?"

"Oh, Ma."

"WHY DID YOU SAY THAT?"

"I am tired, Ma, can't we talk about something else?"

"Oh, you are tired, poor little baby." Her tone turns

mocking. "You just curl up in bed and forget all about your poor murdered sister."

"Ma, I really don't want to talk about this right now."

"Okay."

Peter breathes a slight sigh of relief and then panics; it is not like his mother to give in so quickly.

"Why did you then say she had an accident?"

"Oh, for God's sake!"

"Peter Fowler!"

"Ma, I don't know! I wasn't really thinking!"

"What made you say that? There must have been something that made you say that. What is being kept from me, Peter? I know there is something you are not telling me." His mother starts to cry.

Peter can't tell if she is crying to make him feel guilty or genuinely crying. He wishes his mother wouldn't manipulate him like this. He wishes it didn't still work on him. A voice inside him starts to resonate: well, her daughter did die and she deserves an explanation.

"I said suicide because Anne-Marie had been sad for a while," he began, not knowing how else to phrase it.

"Well, married to Daniel, who wouldn't be?" Sherri immediately snaps.

Peter knows that no matter what he says now, his mother will still insist that it is Daniel's fault and Daniel's fault alone. Peter isn't entirely sure that is true.

"What has brought this on, Ma?" Peter asks gently, trying to change tactics.

"Those useless police officers. They said that they are not going to charge Daniel..." Sherri practically spits his name. "... with murder. Can you believe it? They need more evidence! How much evidence do you fucking need? You know what I think, Peter?"

Peter tries to murmur a response, but knows it's a trap no matter what he says.

"I think someone is not telling me something. Something is being kept from me." Her tone is dangerous now.

"Ma."

"What happened to Anne-Marie in January?"

"Nothing, she fell down the stairs, it was a stupid accident, that's all."

"You sound just like your father, Peter."

Sherri means that he sounds like a spineless coward, a good-for-nothing bastard. Peter has had enough now and seeing no better option, he slams the phone down. One single mindless motion that he knows his mother will punish him for over and over again. She always knows when she has hit a nerve. She doesn't let go, especially when she knows something is wrong and he is not telling her something. But if he tells her Anne-Marie had been drinking heavily, then she will start with the why wasn't I told sooner? She will insist Anne-Marie's drinking wasn't that bad, that Daniel was lying. Peter will be punished if he tells her what really happened and he will be punished if he doesn't. Peter closes his eyes; this shit is beyond overwhelming now.

It has been two weeks since the funeral. Laura Noble rings the doorbell, eager for something to gossip about and to get a plan moving. Her cheer fades into shock as a bloated Daniel opens the door.

"Maybe it's time to move on," she blurts out, not thinking about what she is saying. She is about to apologise and in the same breath suggest gym membership. Daniel doesn't give her the chance; he takes one look at her and slams the door shut.

He should feel guilty, he is not normally this rude, but he is tired, so tired. He lurches back into the kitchen, his feet loudly slapping against the dirty floor.

Later, "Maybe it is time to move on" echoes in his mind.

"Maybe it is time to move on." The thought interrupts his evening feast, making him childishly add another plop of butter to his already saturated meal.

"Maybe it is time to move on" echoes more annoyingly than any TV advert as he pours his fourth beer.

You should move on; it's so fucking easy to do. You should stop destroying your life. Because it is just that fucking simple, just move on, jeez. Why didn't I think of that? Sure, I will just click my fingers and all the hurt will just magically disappear, everything will be rainbows and sunshine again. All new and improved.

He finishes his fifth beer as the air around him grows hotter and stuffier. The smell from the stairs is growing so strong, he can't bear sitting in the room any longer. Daniel treads carefully up the stairs, the wet carpet squelching underfoot. He grips a bottle of brandy in one hand and recalls the bittersweet memories in his head. The heat has been unbearable ever since the funeral. There is the constant threat of a storm in the air. It's so muggy he can barely breathe and all the while there is a smell emanating from all parts of his house. He needs to get out. But how? He takes a long drink of the brandy before stripping down to his underpants and climbing into bed, without brushing his teeth – well, it's not like he will be kissing anyone tonight.

It's too hot to sleep. He takes another long gulp of the brandy, trying to wash away the accusations and the feelings of guilt that have followed him upstairs. His eyelids grow heavy and he finally closes his eyes...

Daniel wakes up at 4am. The air feels colder, and heavy taps of rain hit his window. Daniel thinks that it's Anne-Marie tapping and bolts upright. But it's just the rain, he sleepily assures himself. He is still alone, alone in the bed he used to share with his wife. All that remains of her now is a wrecked room and a lingering odour. Even in here, he thinks he can still smell it, pressing down on him, suffocating him. A gush of wind howls outside, sending shivers down his spine as lightning flashes, briefly lighting up his bare room.

Neither awake nor asleep, he imagines his room as a court, and the thunder striking as a judge hammers the court to order.

"Guilty!" roars the rain and the jury. "Guilty! Guilty! Guilty."

"I am not guilty," Daniel shrieks. Did he really say that aloud?

"You wanted her to die," the voices accuse. "You hoped she would die. You gave her the alcohol knowing it was killing her. You wanted her gone but you were too cowardly to kill her any other way. So you helped her drink herself to death."

"You killed her and you need to be punished."

He wasn't guilty, the police even said so.

"Guilty, even the police thought so."

He often wished she was dead. He couldn't help it; he didn't really mean it. He just wanted something to change.

He bought her alcohol, but even if he didn't, she would make his life a living hell and do unspeakable things to his toothbrush. He didn't buy her that much, not as much as she had been drinking, and it still worries him where else she might have been getting it. What she might have done to get it. He had looked around at the funeral, trying to find her collaborator, her enabler, her lover? But everywhere he looked, the accusing stares were aimed at him alone. She had stolen alcohol, but she was a terrible thief and she was always caught. He always paid quietly for those bottles, but there were other unaccounted for bottles, so someone else was helping her, someone was as guilty as him. It wasn't just his fault.

There isn't going to be an official trial but he has already been judged and found guilty! Sentenced to a lifetime of loneliness and greasy food.

Daniel lies under the sheets, longing for warmth. He closes his eyes but can't go back to sleep. He is too tired to be awake, doesn't ever want to be awake again. Rain continues to thud against his window. He feels cold and very much alone. His head is pounding from the brandy and his heart is pounding from the fear.

Rain, he had fallen in love with her in the rain. One time they were coming home from the pub, laughing drunkenly together as it started to rain. Instead of running for cover, Anne-Marie just took off her shoes and started to dance, dragging Daniel to dance with her. Anne-Marie had taught him how to laugh – and then she wiped the smile off his face just as quickly.

He thinks of the bottle still by his side. Would that not bring warmth and much needed sleep? Is that not how this all started? She started drinking because she couldn't sleep? Maybe he should follow her example. They could become a modern Romeo and Juliet. Though unlike Juliet, Anne-Marie was not faking. Daniel remembers her pleading open eyes. The blood. The sickening stillness and the longed-for silence. I never should have left her. But I couldn't take any more. No one was willing to help. They are all so quick to judge but no one came when he called, when he was broken and begging for help like the weak little man he was. Still shouldn't have left her.

I didn't kill her. It wasn't me. I didn't do anything. His words sound empty even to himself. He is not sure he believes himself. Should he just confess? Anything just to make them stop. He wants everything to stop, for the accusations to go away. He pulls the spare pillow over his head, trying to block out the rain and his thoughts. Make it all go away.

He shouldn't have left her.

He tosses to one side, and a painful twinge starts in his neck. The rain seems louder on this side, so he switches again. Now his leg is too bent, twinging with protesting pains. He shuffles around again. He needs to relax, shut down his thoughts. Maybe think of that stunner from the afternoon's movie. The one with the perky breasts and long dark hair. She was very nice… no, it's no use. It's deader than dead. Cold and unresponsive, just like she was. Oh God. Didn't want to think about that. He removes his hand, feeling ashamed and dirty and tries to turn over again. He becomes more aware of his ever-expanding belly, crushing against his lungs, and turns again.

It's 4-fucking-30 am. Why can't he sleep? As a final bolt of lightning lights up the room, Daniel half-expects to see the broken Anne-Marie in the corner. That would be just like her, tormenting him even now, beyond the grave. He watches for a few more minutes, waiting for another strike, but the storm is moving on. Everything is moving on except him. He is stuck here and he doesn't know what to do.

It's nearly 5am now and he is still restless. Hell, it's not like he has to go to work tomorrow. He needs to stop thinking and go to sleep. He thinks of the bottle again, that would help. No, he doesn't want to end up like her. Can't end up like her. But then what's the point of going on without her? The bed she hadn't slept in for nearly a year feels empty. He wants her back so badly but then did he ever really have her? Angry tears splash down his face. He gives in and takes a gulp of brandy. As the warmth spreads down his body, he thinks he can feel Anne-Marie lying next to him and closes his eyes once again.

Daniel wakes up alone, with an ache in his neck. He expected to see someone next to him, had dreamt she was there.

He feels like shit. He doesn't want to get out of bed. Best just to lie here for a while. There is nothing he needs to do today anyway. It's either lying here or lying in front of the TV.

"Maybe you should move on."

Maybe they should shut up.

It takes two days for Peter to work up the nerve to call his mother and apologise. He doesn't want to admit he was enjoying the silent treatment. Sherri spends the next ten minutes telling him it's her fault for not raising him better, for not finding a better replacement father figure, for raising him to be a coward. Peter just murmurs agreements whilst sipping on a cold bottle of beer.

"I want to know everything, Peter," his mother finally demands. "I want to know what happened in January. Why YOU said it was an accident. Why YOU said it was a suicide. I want to know how YOU found her. EVERYTHING."

"Ma, can't you just move on? Let the police deal with this?"

"They are as useless as you are. I can't move on, Peter."

"Ma."

"It's a crock of shit when they say that time heals all wounds. Peter, let me tell you, the wounds may scab over but they are still infected."

Silence. Peter takes another sip of beer, wishing he had something stronger to drink. He can't argue with that. His mother isn't going to let this go.

"I can't let that shit get away with murder, Peter. You have to help me." Sherri thinks of her daughter, crying for her mother at the bottom of the stairs, scared and hurt. Sherri couldn't help her then. The only thing she can do is make sure that her daughter's murderer doesn't get away with it. She doesn't understand why her son is being so difficult.

"I am waiting, Peter."

Hesitatingly, but knowing he has no other choice, Peter tells his mother a condensed, well-rehearsed version of the events. She listens, interrupts occasionally, like when Peter tells her that Daniel said he left Anne-Marie alive and trashing his room.

"Did you see the room?"

Peter admits that he didn't.

"How do you know he wasn't just making it up?"

Sherri then wanted to know everything he told the police. He tells her mostly everything, except that he purposely ignored the phone call on his lunch break, knowing what her reaction would be. Sherri is still in denial about Anne-Marie's drinking, still insisting that her daughter was not an alcoholic, that she just liked a drink every now again; married to Daniel, who could blame her? Blah blah. Sherri reuses her old excuses, her old denials and stories that she used to use for her own drinking.

When he finishes telling her everything, Sherri is quiet. Peter holds his breath, waiting anxiously for a reaction. His mother's voice is quieter and firmer than he expected when finally she says, "I need you to go back to that house, Peter, look for more evidence. We need to find more evidence."

More days go by. Daniel has eaten so many fish and chip dinners, he can feel grease oozing out his pores. He gets out of breath just moving around the house and has lost sight of his toes. But still he eats. None of his trousers fit and on the rare occasions when he leaves the house, complete strangers shout insults at him. But still he eats. His face has more pimples than the average adolescent and his hair is pure grease but still he eats on, and on, and on. It's the only thing he can think to do, keep eating until it goes away. He doesn't even know what "it" is but just wants it to go away.

He goes out again for yet another fish and chip dinner, to the shop with the woman who used to greet him with a smile and a "How are you, sweetheart?" Now she scowls at him, sullenly serving him as quickly as possible. The only time he sees a smile these days is on television. He considers driving out of town, just to eat at a place where people don't know him, but then he might have to explain why he left town, even for one night. They are watching him, he knows that, every move he makes, he can feel their eyes watching, tongues mocking and whispering.

Daniel staggers out of his car, clutching the tepid fish and chips to his chest. He can smell the unmistakable scent of eggs, even over the vinegary scent of the chips. His front door has been completely splattered. He shrugs. What does it matter? It was probably Sherri getting some kind of petty revenge. He won't give anyone the satisfaction of reacting. Plus, he thinks cheerfully, it will give him something to do after he has eaten, in that long boring period before he is due to eat again.

Maybe he should sell the house. That would make the stain and the smell someone else's problem. He has never liked the house anyway. They had bought it because they couldn't find anywhere else. It seemed a good compromise at the time. They were just so eager to get the baby's room ready. His little girl's room. Now the house is just another monument to bad memories. Perhaps it is time to move on. He doesn't want to grow old in this house with nothing but the lingering smell of spirits.

Selling would mean getting rid of every last trace of Anne-Marie. It would mean going through what was left of her stuff. Then there would be estate agents, quotes, the hassle of finding a new place, then the viewings, the nosey onlookers, everyone asking questions. Daniel doesn't have the energy for any more questions. But he doesn't want to die in this house either.

He fills a bucket up with warm soapy water and scrubs hard at the eggs plastered to his front door. Maybe it is too soon to sell, people will start making presumptions. But then did they really expect him to stay in the house where his wife died? Who would want to buy a house that someone has died in? There is nothing quite like a death in a house to lower the property value. Also, he would have to repaint all the walls. At least the fresh paint smell will distract potential buyers from the lingering scent of stale blood. If it didn't then he would have some explaining to do. Was it really worth all that effort? He could just sell the house *as is*. But that would mean a loss on potential profits, and he needs all the money he can get right now. Most wives got into trouble for running up large bills shopping for clothes or jewellery, but not his wife, oh no, she spent everything they had, and money that they didn't have, on alcohol. At least the other wives had pretty things to show for it. She had nothing but cirrhosis. He is partly to blame for the large bills and the constant buying of food isn't helping either. He needs to get back to work or sell the house or his car. He has to do something soon, no one will employ a bankrupt accountant. He finishes scrubbing the front door with a relish, it looks cleaner now than it has in years. Invigorated, he decides to get some fresh water and scrub the hallway walls again.

Maybe he should start with baby steps. Maybe it is time to finally evict Anne-Marie out of his house and mind. Finally go into her bedroom and scrub away the last traces, and then maybe she will stop haunting him. Not today though, he doesn't think he can do it today. Tomorrow, first thing tomorrow. He keeps scrubbing at the hallway for a while, the walls are looking better, he thinks the smell is starting to go away. It is time to move on. He is going to order a pizza to celebrate.

Daniel opens the door to the pizza guy and sees Ludmilla Bryski and Laura Noble gawking from across the road. The look of anxious worry on their faces suggests they were just gossiping about him and are anxiously praying he hadn't overheard.

Daniel grunts his thanks to the indifferent delivery guy and closes the door again on the outside world. Fuckers have egged his front door, AGAIN. He is so fucking tired of this neighbourhood. He tries to think who would be doing it. Was it still Sherri? It wasn't the sort of thing Lying Penny would do but maybe Gloria... or Laura, maybe even Ludmilla, though she wasn't the type to waste food. No, his neighbours wouldn't do that, they weren't the type. Sherri was that sort of person; it must be her.

There is no point calling the police about the egging. Daniel knows what the police think of him, they didn't like him. They would probably try to frame him for the egging, say it was attention seeking. Why is everyone so determined to push him to his fucking limits? Anne-Marie always took so much joy in pushing him – push, push, poke, push, until he snapped. She took such great delight in making him snap. Sherri did too. They all just wanted to break him, humiliate him. Ever since he was young, he has been the world's punching bag. He just wants to punch them back, keep on punching until he is revenged for every insult, every humiliation, everything.

He needs power, biceps. He needs to lose this soft victim look, he needs to work out until he becomes something more dangerous, something even the old wives wouldn't dare gossip about, something that finally makes people respect him, fear him.

They already fear him.

The blood stain on the stairs screams out to the neighbourhood that he is a slaughterer, a murderer, a slayer, and they all hear. They all believed Anne-Marie's lies before and now instead of a beating heart, she has placed a megaphone beneath the floorboards. It is so fucking typical of Anne-Marie, always lying to get other people's sympathies. There is no way of shutting her up now either. It isn't fair, where were his condolences? His supporters? His comforters? Why did they always believe her?

Daniel feels so angry, he stuffs another pizza slice into his mouth, imagining it will give him superhuman strength, the power to crush everything so the others can feel his pain. He would take particular pleasure in crushing Sherri's stupid house whilst she sobs outside, regretting all her vicious lies. Hell, he would make sure he crushed it whilst she was still in the house.

Oh God, this isn't him.

Look at what they have made him into. An animal! A monster! He never used to think like this. He needs to get out of this house; if he doesn't get out soon, who knows what they will make him do. He is not a monster. He is not. He is not guilty!

Daniel stuffs more pizza into his mouth, hating every cheese-filled bite. This was supposed to be his celebration pizza and they wrecked it. It was wrecked anyway, by this stupid house and his stupid wife. After years of living with Anne-Marie the now-empty house feels too cold, too dark, too quiet. He is not used to being this alone. He needs to hear reassuring bangs, he needs his broken bird creeping around in the shadows, stealing food from the cupboard when she thought he wasn't looking. He can't believe it, he finally got what he wanted, peace and quiet... but now it's too quiet.

And everyone hates you, a thought whispers.

And everyone hates me, he agrees.

He picks up another slice, he is already feeling very full, uncomfortably full but he still shoves it down. Chewing quickly, trying to block out his thoughts, readying his hand to reach for another slice. He can hear the kitchen clock ticking; how fast can he eat this slice? How fast can he eat the next slice? He needs to feel more than full so he doesn't feel... anything else.

This is how it's going to be for the rest of your life, he thinks sadly. I have to get out of here before it is too late.

It is too late, another voice insists. It's much too late. He has become the neighbourhood bogeyman. His monster reputation will follow him wherever he goes.

He swallows, forcing the food down. He feels sick. This can't go on. How often did he say that when Anne-Marie was still alive? This really can't go on. He can't go on like this.

"He put ice on the stairs!" Sherri's voice shrieks down the phone.

It is nearly midnight, and Peter had just closed his eyes when the phone rang.

"What?" he finally manages.

"Daniel put ice on the stairs."

"What?" Peter can feel the return of a throbbing headache.

"Daniel put ice on your stairs?"

"No, you moron, he put ice on the stairs, that's how he killed her. He put ice all down the hallway, making it slippery. We need to get a copy of the autopsy report. They would have noticed if Anne-Marie's feet were wet." Under her breath, she says, "Unlike those idiotic police."

"Ma."

"This is why the police couldn't find anything, the evidence melted."

"Ma."

"Don't you Ma me, we need to find a way to prove this."

"I don't think Daniel..." He can feel her displeasure already hissing down the phone, an unforgiving silence as his tired mind struggles to think of something to reason with. His mother doesn't want to be reasoned with; she wants him to agree with her. "Ma, it's late." What other excuses can he use? He is too tired to think of why she is wrong. Daniel wasn't a criminal mastermind? The police would have noticed puddles of water? Then a sudden thought springs to mind. "How would she slip on ice on a carpeted floor?"

His mother is silent. She had forgotten that little detail.

"Maybe you need a break, Ma."

"Maybe I need my daughter's killer brought to justice."

Peter is too tired to cope with this. "What do you want me to do, Ma?"

"I want you to go to the house," Sherri says with exasperation.

Peter is equally exasperated, this is the fourth in a series of calls, all demanding the same thing. The first call she blabbered on about hiring a private detective, since her son was too cowardly to go into the house himself. Then the next day she was talking about getting in touch with a clairvoyant, to try and find the truth, as she is sure her useless son still isn't telling her everything. Even though they were a waste of money at least they would try to help her. Next call she was talking about some nice people on the internet, who agreed with her that Anne-Marie had been murdered. Could Peter get them a copy of the autopsy report? Could he talk to them directly? No, she didn't know who they were exactly but at least they were helpful.

"Ma, can we talk about this tomorrow? I will call you after work."

"Oh sure, because work is more important. I can't believe–"

"Goodnight, Ma," Peter quickly interrupts, and he hears a howl of rage as he hangs up the phone. Maybe he should go to Daniel's house, if he finds evidence that Daniel killed his sister, then maybe he can blackmail Daniel into killing his mother too.

CHAPTER FIFTEEN

"I do not feel safe living here anymore!" Laura Noble wails to an indifferent audience.

There are the usual mutters of agreement but nothing more. She wails the same thing at every meeting and it is getting old, especially since they have been meeting for over a year now.

The meetings began as a way to vent their frustrations over Anne-Marie Mills, then they started discussing ways of getting rid of her, legally and then illegally. Now the topic has changed from Anne-Marie to Daniel Mills. Daniel, the one they used to see as a bumbling, quiet man, who had their full sympathies, they know now he is a cold-blooded killer, a psychopath, a potential pervert. The real danger to the neighbourhood. Someone smart enough to fool the police. Someone with no morals or common decency. They fear him now more they ever feared Anne-Marie. At least she was predictable. Who knows what Daniel will do next? They have been watching him closely, waiting for the mistress to move in or new things that suggested a lavish insurance pay out – but nothing. He didn't kill Anne-Marie for love of another or for money. He could have just left her, committed her for being dangerous, done something kinder than pushing her down the stairs. Whilst no one amongst them could honestly say that they wished she was still alive, the general agreement was that killing her was a step too far.

"I went to his house," Laura continues, to gasps of astonishment and admiration for her bravery, "and he slammed the door in my face!" Laura conveniently doesn't mention that a small token bunch of flowers was delivered to her house this morning, along with an apology for being so rude.

"Well, I heard..." Usually when Lying Penny starts talking, people in this neighbourhood stop listening but not this time. "I heard him going out at 11 o'clock last night. I think he was going to meet a lady." Penny waggles her eyebrows suggestively.

"Don and I are talking about putting the house up for sale," Gloria says. They are not just talking about it, the *For Sale* sign is going up next week. She doesn't mention that Lying Penny is also part of the reason that they are going to move. That lying bitch nearly ruined her marriage. This starts off another angry discussion, as Michael and John also want to move and number three has been up for sale for over a year now, so won't it look odd if three houses on the same street are all up for sale at the same time? Won't it lower the value of the houses? Can't they wait? Soon there will be no one left in this neighbourhood.

"I am not leaving," Ludmilla says firmly, as the argument starts to turn nasty. "I like my house."

"Well, what else can we do?"

Daniel's post-breakfast snooze is interrupted by the doorbell ringing. At first he doesn't want to answer it, he is not expecting any visitors and he hasn't ordered anything. The doorbell rings again and he groans as he pushes himself to his feet. It is probably the police. They have come to harass him or something similar.

It is with some surprise that he sees Laura Noble and Ludmilla Bryski on his very clean doorstep. Ludmilla is even holding a chocolate cake in her hands.

"Hi, Daniel, we thought we would come and see how you are," Laura says, with forced cheerfulness. Daniel is hesitant, why are they really here? He knows he is supposed to invite them in, but should he? Will they notice the stain? The smell? But then if he does invite them in, perhaps the chocolate cake will be for him. He hasn't had a home-made chocolate cake in years and it does smell irresistible.

"Would you like to come in?" he finds himself saying. A look of fear crosses Ludmilla's face, but Laura is eager.

"Yes, please."

He ushers them quickly past the stairs, into the dirty lounge, suddenly feeling ashamed. No doubt they are noticing the strong scent of the take-away pizza, the empty beer bottles. Well, what did they expect? He is single again. They sit on the sofa gingerly, Ludmilla holding out the cake for him to take.

"Oh, is this for me?" he says eagerly.

Ludmilla nods.

"Shall we have a slice? Would you like a drink to go with it?" He is only offering to share because he suspects that the cake has been tainted with something nasty, bleach perhaps, a belief that is reinforced by the look on Lady Bitchski's face. But to his surprise, Ludmilla nods and says she would like a cup of tea to go with her cake and so would Laura.

He bounds into the kitchen, rushing to put the kettle on, hoping they can't hear him frantically washing three cups and plates. He hopes the milk hasn't gone off.

Neither Laura nor Ludmilla move from the sofa but both have turned their heads, so they can see the stairs. There is nothing worth noting there now, except a few small holes in the carpet. Daniel blunders back and forth, handing a cup of tea and a slice of cake to each lady, wishing he had replaced the ugly side table after Anne-Marie broke it, wishing they had more chairs.

They never really had visitors, except for Peter and Sherri. He awkwardly brings a chair in from the kitchen and sits clumsily holding his own tea and cake. There are a few awkward sips of tea and bites of cake. Then the inevitable praising of Ludmilla's home-baking skills. She doesn't mention this is the first time she has baked in a long time, just hasn't felt like it, for some strange reason. She accepts the praises with a modest comment and the charade continues. Daniel wishes he had showered this morning and put some clean clothes on, if only he had known they were coming! They are being polite about it but he knows what they are thinking.

"So, how are you?" Laura asks brightly, dropping her voice into what she thinks are caring tones.

Daniel stammers. It has been so long since he interacted on a social scale with other humans that he has forgotten quite what to say.

"It has been difficult, I imagine," Laura continues in her special tones.

Daniel nods.

"You are very brave coming back to the house, I wouldn't want to stay in a house where Derrick... I mean all those reminders!"

Daniel stares intently down at his cup of tea.

"How are your daughters?" He changes the conversation.

"Oh, they are fine, as noisy as ever, ha ha. I will have to go soon to pick them up from a party."

"And Paul?"

"He is fine," Ludmilla says quietly. Paul is bumbling along

quite happily, oblivious to everything. He had been annoying her lately, more than usual, tearing the house out, rooting around everywhere, leaving everything out of place. He was looking for some kind of present, he wouldn't say what it was or who it was for, so naturally she refused to help.

Daniel starts to feel sorry for all the times he called her Lady Bitchski over the years... and for Anne-Marie's... well for Anne-Marie's behaviour in general. He thinks back to the last argument he had with Ludmilla, both of them tired and at their breaking point. Nasty things had been said by both of them. But still, she is here now, she brought cake, there might be hopes of a reconciliation.

More silence.

"Well, we best be heading off now." Laura stands. "I need to pick the girls up before lunchtime!" It's not even eleven o clock yet, her cake is half-eaten, tea not even slightly cold. Ludmilla also quickly stands, saying nothing but not wanting to be left behind.

Daniel feels a pang of desperation, he doesn't want them to leave, doesn't want to be left on his own again but can't think of anything to say that will make them stay. He grudgingly rises from his seat. He wants to clutch their hands, plead with them, make them understand that he is not guilty.

"If there is anything you need or anything we can do to help, then you know where we are... oh! And I just wanted to let you know that one of my friends is an estate agent, if you were thinking about moving on then let me know, he will be able to get you a good deal!" Subtlety, thy name is Laura.

Colvin has gone through every witness report, every interview recording and transcript, all the CCTV footage they can find and the bloodstain pattern analysis, everything that was recorded about the sudden demise of Anne-Marie Mills. It is one of the most puzzling cases she has come across so far. Senior officers have advised her to let it go, that it was either a nasty accident or a suicide. They didn't think it was murder. "If you didn't know there had been a fight," they had said, "what would you think had happened? You would think suicide or accident, what other evidence is there for murder? None. Let it go."

Colvin will let it go, after they receive the DNA results, the last thing they are waiting for. After that there are no more leads to look into. Nothing that will stand up in court either. If Daniel did it, he didn't do it for the money, Anne-Marie's life was not insured. Daniel's life was a policy all set up to take care of his wife in case of an accident. No inheritance either, Anne-Marie had nothing hidden away, except maybe a bottle of vodka; Daniel gained nothing financially by her death.

If Daniel did do it, someone must have helped him. Colvin has gone through both Daniel Mills' home phone records and his mobile. It is a pitiful record, the only numbers belonging to Sherri Fowler, Peter Fowler, Daniel's work place and some take-away places. Unless Daniel was working closely with a pizza deliverer, then this was unlikely.

There is still a small possibility that Anne-Marie had surprised or even tried to attack an opportunist burglar, also the possibility someone in the neighbourhood had entered the house with the intention of getting rid of the street's problem for ever. There had been too many smudges for the forensic team to lift any clear fingerprints or footprints from the hallway and it was evident that no one in the area liked Anne-Marie Mills, that she was more than just a problem. There had been too many guilty looks of relief when they were informed of Anne-Marie's passing. But then Colvin thinks of the people they interviewed: an elderly frail couple, a chaotic family and an eccentric old lady. None of these were really people who would win a fight against someone like Anne-Marie, as drunk as she was. Most of her other neighbours were at work, their alibis confirmed, the only person who didn't have an alibi apart from Daniel Mills was Sherri Fowler.

"Sam?" Grimm interrupts her thoughts.

"Yeah?"

"We have to go."

She grabs her camera and notepad.

"Female found dead in a flower bed," Grimm tells her as they walk out of the door. "Throat slit, she has a number..."

And that's the last Colvin thinks about Anne-Marie Mills, for a little while.

"Murderer!" The word pierces through him. "Murderer! Murderer! Murderer! Murderer!" The unrecognisable voice chants.

"I am not a murderer!" he protests weakly.

"Murderer! Murderer! Murderer! Murderer! Murderer! Murderer! Murderer! Murderer! Murderer! Murderer!" That horrible word over and over again until Daniel slams down the phone. He feels shaky and sick, and a panicky feeling spreads through his body. He already felt guilty for eating the rest of Ludmilla's chocolate cake in one sitting. He couldn't help it he had sat down with a fork, intending to only have a little bit more, trying to figure out why they had bothered to come round in the first place, then before he knew it, the plate was empty. He should clean up in case they came back. They will come back; Ludmilla Bryski will want her plate back.

His fingers rub over a noticeable chip on the faded plate. No, they won't be coming back, they probably just wanted to see where Anne-Marie died. Something to gossip about. He is everyone's favourite topic after all.

The phone rings again. Daniel picks it up without thinking. "Hello?"

"How does it feel to have murdered your wife?" a voice hisses.

Daniel slams the phone down and marches back into the kitchen.

He doesn't know what to do. Should he call the police? It seems such a trivial matter and he doesn't want the callers to know they are getting to him. If he stops reacting, they will go away. His eyes fall on a stray bag of doughnuts and automatically his hand reaches out. Sugar will help him think, despite the fact his head is already pounding from the chocolate cake overload. He needs something to help him think about what his next move will be.

You need to stop eating, he tells himself, in the exact same tone he used to tell his wife that she needed to stop drinking. As an incentive he tries to picture what would happen if he does keep eating. The protective blubber would continue to swell, shielding him and steering him towards death. No one would know if anything happened to him, he is alone. He could have an accident and only the local pizza place would notice he was gone. They would be the only ones to miss him. And because life is a bitch sometimes, he would probably end up dying at the foot of the stairs, right in the arms of Anne-Marie. Everyone whispering that it was karma or guilt. At least he wouldn't have to deal with the aftermath this time, the funeral fees and so on, that would be someone else's problem. If there was a funeral, Sherri would have him thrown to the dogs if she could.

Daniel is feeling like a man who has eaten a whole bag of doughnuts can feel, which is not that great. He thinks about cleaning again, about showering, about washing his clothes, but it's another hot day and he is tired and feels sick, very sick. He sits in front of the television for a quick rest and later wakes to darkness, the only light coming from the television. There is an annoying repetitive sound, not coming from the television, and he blinks and looks around in confusion before finally realising that it is the phone. He jumps to his feet, no one ever calls him this late at night, it must be an emergency.

"Hello?"

"Murderer! Murderer! Murderer! Murderer! Murderer! Murderer! Murderer! Murderer! Murderer! Murderer!"

"Fuck off!" he shouts and slams the phone down. The shaky feeling comes screaming back and his neck is burning from an afternoon sleeping on the sofa, plus his head hurts. He thinks about calling someone, asking if he can stay with them just for one night, just so he can have some peace, away from the phone, away from her. But who can he call? He has no one left. He shivers, alone in the dark. Daniel doesn't like the dark. It's not that he is afraid, well maybe he is a little afraid. But the dark brings loneliness and Anne-Marie's ghost; at night she is back in the spare room, trapped, hammering noiselessly at the door to be let out. Every time he dares to look at the stairs, he expects to see her standing there, staring. If he goes to sleep, she wakes him up, calling for him or singing or whispering, "Danny, I need a plaster."

Not that a plaster would have fixed that huge bleeding hole in her forehead. "Danny, I need a plaster."

What was his line again? Something uncaring like, "Go back to sleep." Something like that. He can smell her perfume of alcohol and blood. It has become a reassuring smell now, she won't leave him.

"Danny, I need a plaster."

Alone in the living room, he can hear her singing – Elvis again. A broken-hearted voice promising that he was the only thing on her mind. He takes a deep breath and charges up the stairs as fast as he can manage, feeling her behind him, giving chase. He goes straight into his bedroom, slamming the door behind him. Loud enough to startle the Bryskis. He throws himself onto the bed with a loud thud and dives underneath the sheets. Not that he can sleep now. He lies panting, heart racing, on his bed, frantically looking around the room. It's not fair, why won't people leave him alone? Why must he be harassed, hunted and haunted? His wife had been a ghost before she died, a ghastly figure wailing in the night and bumping into walls. She was barely here before, now she should be gone. It isn't fair. He spent so much time waiting to be rid of her and just when he was starting to think that it was all over, she comes back to haunt him.

He can hear the phone ringing again, then it stops, then it starts again. Someone must want him for real this time, there must be some kind of emergency, He staggers down the stairs and rushes to the phone, his heart pounding.

"Hello?"

"Murderer! Murderer! Murderer! Murderer! Murderer!"

Day breaks and there have been no more phone calls. It doesn't really matter to Daniel, because after the last call at 4am, he didn't go back to sleep. He spent an hour inwardly raging against whoever is calling him, thinking about what he would like to do to them. The sun begins to rise, the light banishing Anne-Marie back into the spare room. He glumly thinks of the day ahead. It's going to be another hot day; he needs to go out before it gets too hot. He needs to shower before he goes out, if he is going to shower then he needs to clean the bathroom, if… it just hasn't seemed worth it lately. But he is running short of everything. He needs to go out today. It will do him good to get away from the house and the ridiculous notion that Anne-Marie is still here.

Today is going to be a better day, he promises himself, heaving himself up off the bed and finally into the shower. He piles some malodorous washing into the machine and leaves the house. He is tired but cheerful, despite the egg stains on his front door, despite Gloria Hutchings obviously hiding as she sees him, clutching something in her hand. He is not going to let anyone bother him today. It doesn't matter that even the sheer effort of walking up and down the aisles at the supermarket is exhausting him, it doesn't matter that he has filled his trolley with some essentials, but mostly with things that are bad for you. He has got some sleeping aids (a bottle of brandy and a bottle of whiskey) and he is happily steering his trolley towards the check-out, looking at the shelves rather than where he is going, when BANG, he collides with another trolley. He starts to apologise as he looks into the unsmiling face of Sherri Fowler. Oh shit!

"Murderer!" she snarls.

She expected him to ignore her, keep walking, pretending he didn't hear anything, his usual cowardly manner, and an obvious sign of his guilt.

But Daniel's temper flares. "What did you say?"

An even more obvious sign of his guilt.

Sherri is not even in the least bit intimidated. "I said you are a MURDERER!" she yells loudly enough for people in the next aisle to hear.

A few heads turn and some other people suddenly become very intent on studying the shelves in front of them.

"I did nothing to her," Daniel retorts pathetically. Then he thinks of the prank calls, his repeatedly egged front door, and now he is certain of who has been harassing him. The question is, how did she know to find him here? Is she stalking him now? What else is she planning?

"This has got to stop, Sherri, I didn't do a fucking thing to your daughter."

"You killed her!"

"It was an accident!" He is going to regret saying that. "It wasn't my fault."

The onlookers are whispering now, and Daniel suspects a manager has been called. "Walk away," a voice inside him reasons. "Walk away now! You are not going to win in a fight against Sherri."

He rages against the voice. Whatever happened to Anne-Marie wasn't just his fault, wasn't his fault at all. Sherri was partly to blame; she was in denial about Anne-Marie's drinking. Daniel used to believe that Anne-Marie only married him to get away from Sherri. Sherri and her "nothing is ever good enough" criticisms, Sherri and her temper. Sherri and her "you are just like your father" manipulations. Daniel inwardly fumes, trying to hold himself back. This is not the place, he keeps repeating to himself. But still, one more retort, one more. Something to feed the crowd.

"If you loved her so much, why did you break her arm?"

Sherri's eyes shoot open, and she manages a weak, "That was an accident." Direct hit! Sherri is so upset that the unmentionable incident has been mentioned, she can barely even speak. She can sense the crowd is shifting in allegiance. All accusing eyes on her now, especially when Daniel says, "What kind of accident does an eight-year-old have that ends up with a broken arm?" The look in her eyes warns him against asking further questions. He is not that stupid.

Sherri feels anger shake through her veins, her hands clench and beg to tear Daniel limb from limb. She clenches her jaw and pictures sinking her teeth deep into his flesh and then she will shred, shred and shred until nothing but an unrecognisable pile of flesh remains. She clenches unrecognisable muscles, trying to hold herself back. Wait, just wait, she promises herself. You will get your chance, when no one else is around. No witnesses. Her hands begin to throb, little red crescents forming in her clenching hands, as her fingernails dig into her flesh instead of his. She has never felt like this before, so tense, so angry... so strong. Just slip up once, fat boy, just once. One excuse, that's all she needs, one excuse and no witnesses. Her eight-year-old daughter breaking her arm had been an accident, an accident Daniel shouldn't even know about. He had no right to bring that up. No fucking right. How dare he!

Daniel struts off quickly before she manages to speak again, paying for his shopping and leaving, before someone official asks him to leave.

A fresh coat of egg has been added to his door whilst he was out. Daniel carries the shopping bags, taking extra care not to touch the slime. He knows who is doing this now and he is going to catch her and report her to the police. Problem solved; he might even get a restraining order against her! Ha! That will teach her. He suspects she will retaliate soon after what happened in the supermarket. He will have to set up some kind of surveillance, he almost hopes that she will do something more substantial, something that will force the police to act against her. He can't believe he stood up to her! Finally! He should have said more! Dragged all of her skeletons out of the closet! All those drunken "secrets" Anne-Marie slurred at him over the years are becoming useful.

He stays exuberant as he cooks brunch, he is going to feast on some nice fresh food for once, things are finally sunny-side up! His hand automatically reaches out and grabs two plates.

Then he stops, his happiness crashing down around him.

He realises he has cooked two brunches without even

thinking about it. He has flipped the eggs the way she liked them. This time he won't be eating, wondering if she is going to come downstairs or what state or mood she will be in, because she is not coming down. The plates crash out of his shaking hands, and the brunch, his special brunch, begins to burn as tears cascade down his face.

Daniel is just finishing shovelling the burnt remains into the bin as the phone rings, hesitantly he answers it.

"Hello?"

"Murderer! Murderer! Murderer! Murderer! Murderer!"

He slams the receiver down, but that doesn't feel enough. He picks up the entire phone and hurtles it into the wall as hard as he can, with a loud, satisfying smash, frightening the life out of Ludmilla Bryski. Then he paces up and down the corridor, trying to calm himself down before grabbing his mobile and dialling a different number.

"Hello?"

"You tell your mother to leave me the fuck alone!" This comes out more slurred than he likes to admit, anger seizing his tongue.

"What? Daniel is that you?"

"You tell your mother to leave me alone," Daniel repeats more firmly. "I don't know why you are all so adamant that I killed her. I didn't! Leave me alone!"

Peter is silent. Daniel deflates, he is tired, sad, angry and he is yelling at the wrong person. The Fowlers no doubt will be laughing at him later, all he is accomplishing with this phone call is confirmation that they are getting to him.

"I am sorry, Peter."

"It's okay."

"I keep getting phone calls from people saying I am a murderer. I know it's Sherri's doing. Just ask her to stop, okay?"

"Okay." Peter is too stunned by Daniel's outburst to really say anything. Even on the really bad Anne-Marie days, he has never heard his brother-in-law so angry.

"She keeps egging my front door, too," Daniel adds, feeling childish. There is a brief silence where neither of them know what to say.

Daniel abruptly says goodbye and hangs up.

Peter doesn't know what is going on, all he heard was a pig squealing things that didn't make sense. He knows better than to ask his mother not to do something, Daniel should know that too by now.

Daniel examines the broken house phone. Nothing left to do except throw it in the bin. Use it to force down the burnt brunch and empty crisp packets. He should probably empty the bin but that means going outside, and going outside means having to smell the intoxicating aroma of raw eggs, of having to acknowledge the slime and the hatred. One good day, that's all he needs, one good day, where nothing goes wrong, no one bothers him. He should feel more remorse over denting the wall, but then it wasn't like the walls upstairs are in pristine condition. What did it matter? He isn't going to get a good day. He wasn't going to be left alone. The look in Sherri's eyes promised that there will be more to come.

He can't just leave the door, it will rot in the heat, the smell of rotting eggs is already starting to penetrate the house. He has had enough of bad smells. He will just clean the door again; it is easier than anything else. Just like it was easier to just clean the house, instead of arguing with Anne-Marie. Just like it was easier to stay with her rather than leave her. Just like it was easier to hand over his money to the school bullies, instead of getting his nose punched. He can either mope, remembering every time he was someone's punching bag, the victim, or he could just empty the bin and clean the door, force the lid shut on his memories.

A few monotonous hours of scrubbing and then eating and more eating later and Daniel is sitting alone in the living room. Nothing unusual about that but for once the television is not on. The room is in complete darkness. The window is open but only slightly. It is 3am and he is waiting, has been for hours now. Hiding out of sight, slowly sipping a cold beer. Straining his ears, desperate to hear a sign, listening for the tell-tale thump and crack of an egg hitting his door. This must stop. He keeps repeating to himself, in a desperate attempt to keep his tiredness at bay, this must stop. He doesn't know what he will do to make her stop, he has never been any good at standing up to schoolyard bullies. But each sip of beer is giving him new-found strength and courage. He should go to bed, he knows that, but he has a chance to end this. She must know he is awake, despite his best efforts, a witch like her would sense it. She is just waiting for him to go to bed and then she will strike. He won't give in.

He keeps turning to stare at the hallway, Sherri isn't the only thing he is waiting for. The stains seem more visible in the darkness, even though he has gone over and over them again with the cleaner. It is comforting in a strange way, right now, like his wife is finally standing with him, supporting him. Perhaps that chill is her hand resting on his shoulder, her other hand trying to steal his beer.

It is 4am and Daniel thinks he is losing his mind along with everything else.

The irony is not lost on Daniel, he knows he is turning into his wife, finally after all these years he understands how she felt.

He doesn't want to end up like her but this eating, drinking, sleeping or not sleeping cycle is so hard to break. He thinks of all those times when he looked at her, wishing she would snap out of it, stop being so bloody mopey, make an effort for once. Now he knows it's not that easy. Every day he wakes up telling himself today will be different, today he is going to change things, today is going to be a better day and each evening he goes to bed a broken man.

"I am just a little depressed right now, my wife died after all," he says to himself.

Man up. You are a fucking pansy, a disgrace to your gender. Snap out of it, you fucking pussy. A voice similar to Sherri's answers from inside him.

You are always depressed. You have been depressed for fucking months now. A voice similar to Peter's answers with a sneer.

"I am doing the best I can," Daniel whines.

But you don't do anything, you do nothing to help yourself. You just eat and eat and eat. You are making yourself this depressed and what do you do to compensate? You ignore everyone, you shout at people, pick fights in supermarkets. How is that HELPING?

"FUCK OFF." Daniel is constantly saying that to no one now. Fuck off. He sometimes wakes up in the middle of the night, from dreams, screaming for the vultures to fuck off, then he sits in the dark, shocked at himself, worrying if Ludmilla heard him. Spending his nights waiting for a knock on the door, waiting for the singing to start, waiting for the "Danny, I need you".

He is drinking in the morning now, just like she did. If he is not careful, he is going to end up just like her. Daniel feels a small pang of jealousy. If he suffered a similar incident to Anne-Marie, he wouldn't have anyone like Sherri demanding justice.

He wouldn't be missed. No one would even care to find out what happened. He would just be dead and gone, forgotten before morning. The police would take one look at the credit card bills, those mounting bills and think they know why he jumped. Oh God, he should have insured that fucking bitch years ago. Her death payout would have got him out of this financial sinkhole. He is going have to sell the house anyway before the bank seizes it. He will have to start again, start again with nothing but a wish that he had never got married in the first place. He should have just killed that stupid bitch years ago and been done with it. Daniel finishes his beer and decides finally to go to bed. If they want to egg his door, then they can just egg away, he doesn't care.

CHAPTER SIXTEEN

"I saw him in the supermarket." No pleasantries, she just ploughs straight in.

Peter knows better than to make a joke and say, "Who is this?" Peter can also guess who she is talking about, he knows better than to play dumb. His mother will only talk about one thing now.

"What happened?" he groans.

"He practically admitted to murdering Anne-Marie! Said that he didn't murder her, it was an accident! He practically admitted it, Peter! But that shit of a store manager wouldn't tell me if they got it on their cameras."

"Uh huh."

"And he threatened me."

"And what did you say to him?"

"You are just like your father!" Sherri spits.

What? Reasonable? Peter wants to reply but knows it's not worth it. Sherri is becoming more and more irritated with her least favourite child. He doesn't react how she wants him to react, he doesn't even seem interested. He won't do what she wants him to do either. She has been reading as many true crime books as she can get her hands on. She has become convinced that something incriminating is still hidden in the house, but will her ungrateful son go and look? No. She wanted Peter to go and endlessly question Daniel, over and over until he snapped, whilst recording everything that was said, but no, he won't do that either. It's not like Sherri can do it, she hates the bastard.

"He is threatening me now, Peter."

"What did you do to him?"

"Nothing."

Her snarls are met with disbelieving silence, and finally Peter says, "I will talk to him."

"Sure you will! I am sure you two pansies will sit down and have a nice little tea party."

"Ma."

"Why do you keep defending him, Peter?"

He tries to change the subject. "Did you give Daniel's phone number to your friends on the internet?"

"No." Sherri hadn't thought to do that. It wasn't a bad idea though. Her friends have been very helpful so far, not like her son. "You didn't answer my question, why are you defending him? Are you two...?" Sherri is too revolted by the thought to finish the question.

"I am not defending him! I am trying to move on!"

"Does your sister's death mean nothing to you?"

"Why are you here?" Sherri snarls at Peter. She has waited weeks for her son to visit now and when she doesn't want to see him, he bloody well turns up.

He holds out his phone, like a small child proudly revealing a handmade creation. Peter shows his mother a text message, silently praying that it will be enough to placate Mount Sherri.

She snatches the phone, lips moving as she reads a text message from Daniel.

Hey, sorry again about yesterday. I am going to put the house up for sale. Please ask your mother if she wants any of Anne-Marie's things, thanks, Daniel.

"I thought I would volunteer to help him clear out Anne-Marie's things," Peter says quickly.

"And bring everything to me?"

Peter nods.

Sherri could almost hug her son in her excitement. He hasn't redeemed himself quite yet but if he brings back something incriminating then all is forgiven.

Hi, Daniel, yes Sherri would like all of Anne-Marie's things. Peter

Grimm and Colvin had been ordered to give a talk at one of the local schools on knife crime. Colvin presumes that they are meant to be against it. She is happy to let Grimm do the talking on this one, since he is under the belief that children like him. As Grimm begins lecturing on knife crime and how really uncool it is to carry a knife, Colvin gazes around, looking up at the three hundred or so bored young faces, some of whom she recognises. She notices at least seven children and one teacher sneakily chewing gum. One girl is nonchalantly checking her phone, ignoring a nearby teacher's warnings, but there is something else.

Something is not right.

Colvin takes a few slow steps into the audience, ignoring the whispers of the more boisterous pupils and teachers. She stands in front of one boy, a tough-looking boy who looks like he has more spots than sense. She meets his challenging gaze for a few moments.

"Hand it over," she commands, holding out her hand, not to him of course but to the weedy-looking boy behind him. The boy looks around astonished and seeing no other option, drops a small knife quickly onto her palm. The other children chant their disapproval or support in an "Ooh Caleb" chorus.

After the uproar had died down, after the boy had been marched out of the room for more than a stern talking to, Grimm has to finish his speech as calmly as possible, ignoring the excited whispers. Those kids will be talking about Colvin for weeks to come. Caleb Bullrush will never forget her.

"How did you know?" Grimm asks later.

Colvin just smiles, mutters something and changes the subject as soon as possible. Why that one boy out of all those assembled today? She can't quite say why, there had just been something about him. She noticed something odd and acted on it. She is just quietly grateful that her hunch paid off.

She goes to bed that night, still wondering, still running over the assembly in her mind. Maybe if she could understand what it was, maybe she could use that superpower to catch the new bad guy.

At 3am her eyes snap open with a sudden clarity, a single thought comes to her mind.

Sleeves.

Sleeves?

Sleeves, something to do with sleeves.

She had noticed the boy, Caleb constantly touching that pocket, assuring himself that nothing was visible, unconsciously signalling the very thing he wanted to hide. Someone else had done that too, someone more confident than Caleb. She had missed it at the time, they didn't do it constantly but they had still checked a few times. Colvin rubs her eyes, trying to think. Did it matter? Her mind starts dredging up her last few cases: the rape victim; the unfortunate Mrs Mills; the stabbing victim;

that flower bed victim, the one that they are trying not to think about; the hit-and-run; and that's only the recent cases. She tries to remember each suspect, each interview, but her mind is refusing to co-operate, only hints that she has missed something. She can't quieten her mind long enough to go back to sleep. Colvin yawns and grabs her phone, sets herself a reminder – sleeves – a notification that will mean little at 7am. Then she lies back on the pillow, trying to sleep. It has been a hot summer, no one has been wearing sleeves unless they really had to.

Margie, she thinks. Margie the corner shop assistant in the Mrs Mills case, she had been wearing sleeves, constantly fiddling with them nervously and the boy today had the same nervous expression as she did. That must be it. She has watched that video too many times. Yes, it just must have been Margie, she thinks. She wants to go back to sleep but now the thinking won't stop.

That woman, the woman they still can't find a name for, the one found dead in a flower bed, her death remarkably similar to another poor woman's death, the one found three weeks before. It wasn't one of Colvin's cases, she doesn't know too much about it yet but the rumours are hinting that both deaths are incredibly similar to a whole spree of deaths that happened two years ago. A spree that slashed a gaping hole into the heart of the city, one people have only pretended to recover from.

No one is using the word serial killer yet, in fact they are using every word they can except serial killer, even amongst themselves, making sure that no details are being published. No one knows just how similar this new serial killer is to the old one, no one trusted anyone, after what happened last time. Colvin transferred to this city eighteen months ago, but even she knows about the scars the last serial killer left. She knows the legend of the woman she replaced and knows she is wearing outsized shoes.

She is trying to get her mind focused, concentrate on outsmarting this new bastard but she can't stop thinking about Anne-Marie Mills, can't let go of the case that everyone else thinks is solved. She can't stop thinking about the sleeves, the giveaway twitches, the feeling that they had missed something big. She knows they missed something, just like she knew that boy had something he shouldn't have. The only thing she can do to get rid of the feeling is to act on it, talk to the source, talk to Margie.

It's not Margie, her feelings insist, but she can't think who else it might be. That's why, the following morning, bleary-eyed Colvin walks slowly up and down the cul-de-sac where Anne-Marie had lived, terrorised and died. She is trying to deduce who might be home and what questions she could ask, a stall before she goes to see Margie.

She stops in front of each house, trying to recall its occupant, what information they gave, what they wore the day they interviewed them. She hears a door creak open behind her, she spins around to see a middle-aged woman wearing a distinctive bright red and purple patchwork top, coming out of number eight.

"Excuse me, are you Gloria Hutchinson?" Gloria looks up in surprise, her eyes widening at the sight of Colvin or perhaps at the sight of the police car behind Colvin. The look of sheer alarm on Gloria's face is worth the risk of guessing, since Colvin has now caught her off guard by guessing her name. This woman is hiding something, she just knows it.

Gloria stammers a "Yes" then regains control of herself. She laughs the moment away with a nervous high-pitched laugh.

When Colvin asks if she can talk about Anne-Marie Mills, Gloria lets out an over-exaggerated sigh of relief.

"Oh thank goodness, you had me worried that something else bad had happened," Gloria tries to gaily trill. "I am sorry,

Officer, but I am on my way to a really important meeting. I really must go."

She darts off before Colvin can stop her, trotting nervously down the street and quickly out of sight.

Colvin finishes her patrol of the neighbourhood, lingering at Lying Penny's door, still regretting that she hasn't met this particular occupant yet – the only person who has ever made Grimm lose his temper. She debates ringing the doorbell but can't think of a decent reason why she should.

"Beware of giving fodder to fools." Her grandmother's advice echoes in her mind. She slowly walks away, peering occasionally to look for giveaway curtain twitches.

Someone is watching her, she knows that, but can't figure out who. Lying Penny? Ludmilla Bryski? Or even Daniel Mills? She tries vainly to catch them but fails. Maybe she is just tired, she is overthinking this, exaggerating a small event to give meaning to something that had little meaning. What happened to Anne-Marie was a senseless accident, she tells herself echoing her commander's words, she needs to stop making it into something else and get back to the bigger picture. But she can't, she is drawn back to this case over and over, to the point that Colvin is starting to drive herself crazy. Sighing heavily, Colvin decides to revisit Margie's shop; might as well, she still has an hour before she is due to meet Grimm and it is the reason she came here today after all.

Moments after she enters the shop, after Margie nervously greets her, Colvin just happens to look up automatically, checking out the security mirror, just in time to see a familiar patchwork top hastily leaving the premises.

"What did she just buy?" Colvin asks abruptly.

Margie knows better than to pretend she doesn't know who Colvin is talking about. "Just... just... just some milk and eggs." Margie doesn't want any trouble.

CHAPTER SEVENTEEN

Daniel had expected Sherri to say she wanted everything that belonged to her precious Anne-Marie, Sherri didn't like to miss out. She is welcome to everything Anne-Marie owned, although she is going to be disappointed.

Still, Daniel is in a jolly mood, no one has egged his door since last night, the phone calls have stopped, standing up to Sherri was worth it. He should have done it years ago, should have done a lot of things years ago. He has even come round to the idea of moving house, there is nothing left for him here. They hadn't intended to live in this house for long. The plan had been to have the baby and then move to somewhere bigger, comfier, once Anne-Marie was working again. It had never really felt like home. He will be glad to leave, he lies to himself. This is no more a home than his parents' house was and look at how little he misses that place.

A strong scent of decay fills the air in Anne-Marie's bedroom, mixing with the smell of stale alcohol – the smell of a dead lover's embrace. He crunches his way to the window, twirling the blinds to finally let some light in, but not enough so the neighbourhood can see in. Forcing the window open for the first time in over a year, it helps a little, but not a lot.

He decides to start by collecting the broken glass. He should get a broom, start by sweeping up the big shards and then see what the vacuum cleaner will pick up. He turns, expecting to see his wife in the doorway, demanding to know why he was in her room, screaming at him to get out.

She isn't there but the *Fuck you Daniel* blazes from the wall.

His wife's final words to him. Words more heart-breaking than anything else she had ever done. He can get another pen and cover it over, or even some paint, but he will still know it's there. It will always be there. He thinks about going back to the sofa, but if he does that, then he will never get out of here. He has to get out of here. He has to get Anne-Marie out of here too.

He fills the bucket with the usual lemony water, he is really starting to hate the smell of lemons. Soon, he promises himself, he will never have to smell lemons again. He collects a mop, broom, dustpan and a bottle of beer for courage.

He sweeps carefully, not wanting to add any fresh blood to the dried blood spots. He fills two double-bagged bin bags with broken glass and two more carrier bags with empty but intact bottles. He cautiously carries these outside along with the broken bedside table, straight into the boot of his car. Then he has a second bottle of beer, since the first went down so well. He sweeps again, half filling a third bag, then he vacuums, but even after all of that, he can still see tiny diamonds of glass, embedded in the wooden floor, mocking him. He knows he will have to sweep again. Tomorrow, there is no rush. Baby steps, he reminds himself.

He is going to do two more things in this room, then he is finished for the day. He starts with the bed; it still looks and smells like Anne-Marie has just left it. Hesitantly, he picks up the pungent duvet, the pillows and the mattress and drags them downstairs. He strips the duvet and pillows of their polka dot covers, putting the covers into the washing machine and then, panting heavily, he wrestles the single mattress, stained duvet and pillows into the now full car.

Nearly there he tells himself, heading back upstairs. Last job is to carefully mop the floor, scrubbing hard at the dried spots and smears. So it can dry overnight, and he can start again tomorrow. He thinks of all the times he has had to do this, but this time is the last time. His anger has gone now, he doesn't feel sad either. He just wants this to be over. He is going to leave here he tells himself, although he hasn't figured out where he is going or what he is going to do but it is a start. He is not going to end up like Anne-Marie.

He takes the carload to the tip, windows down the whole way, carefully watching in his wing mirror for any followers. He unloads as quickly as he can.

"Goodbye, Anne-Marie!" he says quietly as he throws away the spoiled mattress. "I love you." A choked whisper as he tosses the bin bags, the final goodbye.

He arrives back home with a Chinese take-away, settling comfortably in front of the television with another bottle of beer. Already the house feels lighter, less haunted. He is doing the right thing, he assures himself with a gulp of his drink.

The next morning, he wakes up with a sore head and sore muscles. He overexerted himself yesterday but it was worth it. He needs to keep going. He hangs the wet polka dot covers outside. It has been a long time since he has been out to the garden, sometimes he forgets he has one. He needs to mow the grass, before that he needs to pick up all the stray bottles and cans Anne-Marie had flung outside. So many times he caught her outside at two or three in the morning, sitting on the long grass, staring up at the stars... or at the houses that overlooked them. He never intruded, never asked her why she was out there. She was being quiet, that was the main thing, except when she flung a bottle into the neighbours' gardens, cackling as she did so. When Daniel had begged her to stop, she denied it was her. No wonder the neighbours hated her so much. He should apologise to Ludmilla Bryski before he goes. He leaves the covers flapping in the autumn wind as he retreats back into his house.

He goes back into the spare bedroom. Now the mattress is gone, he can see clearly what was under the bed. A plastic tub, containing towels, clearly rifled. He shakes each towel out carefully, before placing into the bin bag, still hoping for a note, a last goodbye. Nothing. A half-full bottle of vodka lies discarded, out of reach. Most likely she dropped it, it rolled under the bed and she forgot about it or accused him of stealing it. He sniffs it gingerly and then takes a sip, it is definitely vodka. Waste not, want not, he thinks, taking a gulp to help his muscle ache.

He looks at the half-torn curtains. He should have taken these to the tip yesterday too. He remembers the day he put these up, a proud expectant father. It didn't matter if the baby was going to be a boy or a girl, Anne-Marie had decided she liked the curtains so these were the curtains that were going up. Another gulp of vodka. He carefully takes them down, examines them, folds them carefully, hugging them close to his heart and then drops them into the awaiting bin bag. Anne-Marie said she thought it was a girl. She had wanted to call it Lisa Marie. Daniel had happily agreed, not realising the Elvis connection until Sherri had gleefully pointed it out. Another long gulp of vodka. He was going to nickname his daughter LizzieBee. Another long gulp to drown the sobs threatening to emerge. He finishes off the vodka, adding that to the bin bag, and then surveys his handiwork. There is nothing left in this room except some dusty blinds, a bed frame and a *Fuck you*

Daniel screaming from the wall. He will get some paint soon, he assures himself. One job at a time one room emptied, two more to go.

"Their" bedroom next, no longer will he wake up with an instant reminder. Everything must go. He starts with their wardrobe, folding her clothes into a bag, ready to give to Sherri. It is a miserable collection of stained outfits. Sherri will no doubt blame him. He crouches down to lift her two pairs of shoes out of the bottom of the wardrobe. They are strangely heavy. A small bottle of something lodged in each one, four little bottles all hidden in plain sight. He places the bottles tenderly on his bedside table, where their wedding picture used to be. Oh, what the hell, he thinks and opens one. Tequila on top of vodka? Why not. He might as well get rid of some of his clothes too, the ones that no longer fit. He is going to take some more stuff to the tip anyway. The alcohol has left him feeling warm and reckless, ready to start cleaning out the last place, the attic. Whatever doesn't go to Sherri he will take to the tip, he promises as he pulls down the attic stairs and unsteadily climbs up.

Before the drinking really took off, Anne-Marie had gone through several manic shopping phases, buying workout gear, jewellery-making equipment and cookery books, so many impulse buys that weeks later, she couldn't stand the sight of, couldn't return either. They had all been shoved up here, out of sight. He carefully examines each piece, still checking for hidden notes before dumping each item into a bin bag. No doubt Sherri will look through all this junk whilst angrily exclaiming, "What is this shit?" It is her problem now. She won't be able to return it to him because he will be gone, gone, gone!

A wrapped Christmas present from years ago lies on the floor. *To Sherri, with love from Anne-Marie and Daniel.* Anne-Marie and Sherri had had a massive row that year, and it had easily been the best Christmas ever. Just him and Anne-Marie, blissfully drinking in front of the television, eating crap.

To make it even better, Anne-Marie and Sherri didn't speak to each other for nearly three months, not until Anne-Marie announced she was pregnant. A vodka-induced thought stirs at the back of his mind, the forbidden thought resurfacing, that he tries to ignore. Now that thought won't go away. Daniel goes over the evidence again in his mind. Anne-Marie never bought maternity clothes, never bought anything for the baby except the elephant curtains. But they bought the house because of the baby. He had stopped threatening to leave because of the baby, his little LizzieBee. They had never even attempted to try again. He hadn't wanted to try again until Anne-Marie was better. Anne-Marie had found his weight gain too repulsive to want to try again.

But he had collected her from the hospital that day, she had sobbed when she told him the baby was gone. She had gone to therapy sessions alone. She could cry on demand, he reminds himself, and he fell for it every time. His mind starts listing the other evidence: she hated her job, maybe she had been fired and used the baby lie to leave. Maybe she had used the baby lie to reconcile with her mother. To keep him on a chain. But then she had been so sad afterwards. They never talked about the baby that might have been, but he caught her longingly looking at other children. He always wanted a family, she knew that. She wouldn't lie to him like that. Just like she wouldn't lie about stealing her brother's wallet or about the haircut. His head hurts, he is drunk, he shouldn't think such things. It wasn't true. LizzieBee had existed, she wouldn't lie about something as important as that. She wouldn't!

He puts everything into boxes and carries them down, panting drunkenly as he ferries the meagre collection consisting of three bags of clothes, four boxes of random impulse buys and a box of alcohol. That's all that is left to remind the world of Anne-Marie Mills. He struggles down with the last two boxes, one containing their wedding album and stray photos, the other a box of paperwork. He is muttering over and over to himself, trying to reassure himself that it doesn't matter now, it is over now. He can finally leave this house, the baby, Anne-Marie behind. He closes the empty attic door behind him.

How little they both have. He thinks of what remains now in the house, his own things would probably amount to another bag, maybe two, plus the TV, that's all he has left now. That and some worn out kitchenware and furniture. Maybe he should just bag it up now and end it all. Take the stuff to charity and himself to the cemetery. He can't see a reason not to.

He moves all the bags containing Anne-Marie's stuff into the hallway. The rubbish bags go straight into his car, he thinks about driving to the rubbish dump now, get it over with, he is not that drunk... he is that drunk, he can't give the police an excuse, he never wants to go back to the police station again. He locks the front door and sits in the living room with the boxes of paperwork and the pictures. He opens another bottle and begins to flick through their wedding album, wanting to remind himself of happier times. Had he been happy at their wedding? It had been a small, rushed affair. They had nearly cancelled. He had been drunk that day, so had she. He stops in disbelief, and slowly flicks over a page and then another. Someone had already gone through this album, with a marker pen, scribbling out the faces, defacing every page. Another *Fuck you Daniel*, courtesy of Anne-Marie. Daniel gives a howl of pure rage, his hands trembling.

She got what she deserved. He wants to scream that now but chokes it back, she got what she fucking deserved! He takes a long drink. He has spent every day since the day she died looking for a sign that she loved him, something to show that it had been an accident not a suicide, that she didn't mean to leave him. And what did he find? Nothing but *Fuck you Daniel* everywhere. Well, fuck you right back, Anne-Marie. Hell, she probably jumped out of malice, knowing what pain she would cause him, her ultimate fuck you.

Drunkenly he stumbles outside into the garden, ignoring the forgotten polka dot covers still waiting for him. He dumps the wrecked album on top of the rusty BBQ, pours on a little alcohol and then throws a match. Burn, baby, burn. He giggles, throwing on the rest of the photos, the paperwork, watching their past melt away into chunks of burning love.

CHAPTER EIGHTEEN

The smash screams through the night, shattering Ludmilla Bryski's sweet dream. It's that awful woman again, she thinks, her heart thumping waiting for another sound, for another long night of screaming, smashing and swearing to begin. But she hears only the sound of Paul's snores, he is oblivious as usual.

What has that woman done now? Should she call the police? Why won't that awful woman go away? It is only after a few minutes of careful listening that Ludmilla remembers the awful woman did go away, permanently. Something else made that noise. Someone else maybe. Probably the same person who made the awful woman go away, the same person she heard shouting weird accusations to an empty house. Ludmilla tries to hide under the blankets. She is more scared of Daniel Mills now than she ever was of Anne-Marie. Ludmilla remembers with a shudder, tears trembling down her cheeks, how he opened the door with a crocodile smile. He had been waiting for them; long before they even decided to visit, he had been waiting with anticipation. They had gone there to try and subtly talk to him about moving, but she had been useless, scared from the moment he had smiled at them. She had wanted to flee before they had even sat down. She forced herself to stay, only because she couldn't leave Laura alone with a murderer. They never should have agreed to go in the first place. It was a stupid idea. Their other stupid plans aren't working either and she doesn't know what else to do. They need to do something else, something more.

Daniel had been burning something earlier. Ludmilla had smelt the smoke and gone to check, worrying that the garden was on fire. She had seen Daniel huddled over the flames, heard him drunkenly singing something about Anne-Marie being the name of the latest flame. She had hid quickly, not wanting Daniel to know she had seen him. He must have been burning something incriminating and if he knew she had seen him, then she would be next. She wasn't safe whilst Daniel Mills still lived next door. How many nights had she stayed awake, forced awake, wishing Anne-Marie would go away, praying, begging for something to take her away, to make her be quiet and now she is starting all over again with Daniel. She can't go through all this again, she can't. Daniel has to go; they have to get him to go or she doesn't know what she will do.

CHAPTER NINETEEN

They had almost missed the skin. The three little chunks of flesh under Anne-Marie Mills' fingernails. They had expected it to belong to Daniel Mills but sent it for testing anyway. Just in case something went to trial. Just in case they needed something to mark the difference between falling and being pushed. The DNA testing gathered from the two dead women at the flower bed scenes had taken priority over Mrs Mills. Taken over the minds of most of the police force too, including Grimm and Colvin.

Even now, Colvin is only skim-reading the results, expecting it to say male, matching to etcetera. She is anxious to get back to that other case and this report means she can finally let this stupid case go. She reads and rereads it and rereads it again. Surely there has been a mistake? A contamination perhaps?

"What's wrong?" Grimm asks from behind his own stack of paperwork.

"Do you remember the Anne-Marie Mills case?"

"Yeah?" Who could forget? That mess? That mother? Those neighbours!

"Do you remember the three pieces of skin we found under Anne-Marie's nails?"

"Yeah."

"One of the pieces of skin belongs to Daniel. The other two pieces belong to an unknown female, no match to Anne-Marie." Colvin remembers with a sinking feeling Sherri Fowler's affair accusations. Her insistence that her daughter had been murdered, combined with her own feelings that they were missing something big. She had ignored Sherri's repeated demands that they find the guilty woman, dismissing it as quickly as she dismissed Sherri from the investigation. Colvin doesn't want to have to admit to Sherri that she may have been right.

They watch the corner shop surveillance for the eleventh time, thinking perhaps Anne-Marie Mills had scratched Margie, the corner shop assistant, but no, Margie always carefully kept her distance from Anne-Marie. A lesson well learnt from a previous encounter. They keep watching, going past the moment, making sure that Margie doesn't close the shop for a convenient break. Nothing. It is time to do another round of interviewing, this time with swabs. Colvin wants to start with Gloria Hutchinson.

CHAPTER TWENTY

"It's not my fault... Anne-Marie..." Daniel whines, oblivious to Peter moving behind him, a rope held tight in his hands. Peter enjoys the sheer satisfaction of pulling the rope tight around his flabby neck, cutting off his air supply mid-whine.

"This is for my sister," he whispers whilst Daniel is still conscious enough to hear, listening to Daniel's final gasps for air, with a quiet satisfaction. Then he suspends Daniel's body from... from... this is where the fantasy breaks down, what could he suspend Daniel from? There are no rafters, no ceiling beams. How would he even lift Daniel's weight? Where would he even get a rope from? Inconveniently, Daniel did not keep pieces of rope in the house for hanging purposes and it would look suspicious if he went out to buy one now. What if they found a piece of his skin in the rope? His DNA in something. What if the rope broke under Daniel's weight and Daniel survived? No, hanging is out, it's not as easy as it looks.

What other options were there? He could get Daniel drunk to the point of passing out, then carefully slice his wrists, but what if the pain woke Daniel up? What if he screamed for help?

Anne-Marie has made Peter well aware that blood gets everywhere, so it was too big a risk, he can't risk having a drop of Daniel's blood on his clothes. Also, how long does it take for someone to bleed to death? He didn't have time to wait around to make sure the job was done. No, whatever he did, it needed to be fast. It would have been nice to see Daniel suffer slowly for what he did. To let him know who had killed him and why. He could even get some things off his chest and Daniel would be forced to finally listen to him. Peter could finally tell him just how boring both he and Anne-Marie were, always whining. "Oh he doesn't love me!" "She doesn't love me!" "Why don't they love me anymore?" Always demanding attention but neither of them attempting to reconcile or even talk to each other, or even listen to Peter's advice! Just the same old whining loop playing endlessly.

"Neither of you are perfect," he wanted to yell. "Either live with it or leave. I don't care. Just stop whining at me!" He had to listen to all their shit over and over, and did they ever listen to him? Or even care about him? Did they ever ask, 'How are you? How's your work going?' No, it was just me, me, me; whine, whine, whine.

Peter mused over feeding Daniel sleeping pills, diluted in whiskey, but where would he get the pills? Wouldn't Daniel taste them in the drink? What if he vomited? What if the police found his fingerprints on the bottle? He never realised before how hard it is to kill someone.

Did he really want to kill Daniel? It was fun to fantasise about it but deep down, Peter knows he has no real interest in killing Daniel. Too much effort required and Daniel wasn't worth it. Daniel wasn't worth spending his life in prison for, if things went wrong. He is not going to murder someone just to make his mother happy, not even Daniel deserved that.

Daniel wasn't completely to blame for his sister's miserable life and death, he was just the easiest person to blame. It wasn't like he was having the time of his life without Anne-Marie either. It would be a mercy to put Daniel down, and Daniel didn't deserve mercy. Besides, it is only a matter of time before Daniel ate himself to death. Just like it was only a matter of time before his sister drank herself to death. Good things come to those who wait.

Peter rubs his face tiredly; here he is, caught up in his mother's drama and goading again. Every time he swore he wouldn't let himself be drawn in and every time she got him baying for blood. Damn his mother. Peter knows she is only using Anne-Marie's death as an excuse to get angry and bully new people, her two favourite activities. Look what she was goading him into doing now – going to the house, taking all of Anne-Marie's stuff. She was always doing things like this to his father, using threats and fake pregnancies. Every time he threatened to leave, she would use anything she could to force him to stay. Which is why their father left late one night, whilst everyone was asleep and was never heard from again. He was the smart one. Peter is trying to do the same now, he is trying to move on with his own life. He has been applying for new jobs in different cities, even one in a different country, just to get away from it all. He wants to move on, but his mother is so insistent. He needs something to shut her up, something to untangle him from her claws long enough to escape.

Why hadn't he told her the truth about January? Told her the truth about what happened when Peter had visited Anne-Marie alone in the hospital. He had asked her what happened, only out of obligation though, and not expecting an honest answer. She only protested that she had had an accident.

"You were drunk again, weren't you?"

She wouldn't look him in the eye.

"I am worried about you. You are really going to hurt yourself soon."

Anne-Marie had only laughed a self-depreciating laugh and said, "Daniel would never be that lucky."

"What happened?" he asked again.

"I was just enjoying a little drink and I noticed the bottle was empty. The next thing I know is that I needed a plaster." She had looked him straight in the eye then, with a mysterious smile, she then said: "I should tell Mum that Daniel pushed me." Peter never stops wondering what other lies Anne-Marie told Sherri... or told him or told about him.

His mother wanted so badly to believe it was murder, not an accident. She wouldn't listen to anything that suggested otherwise. She wouldn't listen when he told her that all this drink was killing Anne-Marie, insisting loudly that she didn't have a problem, ignoring all warnings that she should stop supplying Anne-Marie with more alcohol. Sherri would never admit that she was to blame for anything. Sherri would never acknowledge that sometimes Anne-Marie did some really stupid things, that the fall in January was just a stupid accident, that Anne-Marie's death was just another stupid accident. The big accident, the one they all knew was coming.

Peter knows that Anne-Marie's death was an accident, that she had fallen in a drunken stupor, that no one was to blame. He had suspected at first that she had jumped, not to kill herself but to hurt herself. She had done similar things when they were children. Stunts to attract attention, stunts to make people forget how naughty she could be. Sherri had taught her that and Sherri had fallen for it every time. It had gone wrong this time, that's all, she had made a stupid mistake, no one could blame for her. They all did stupid things sometimes. Especially his family.

Just get Anne-Marie's things he tells himself, take them

straight to Sherri. Don't get caught up in this anymore. Let his mother find all the "evidence" she likes.

He pulls into the cul-de-sac, remembering with a shiver what he was met with the last time he came to this house, on that hot July day. This is the last time you will have to come here, he promises himself. He pauses to admire the damage done to Daniel's car. Daniel will be fuming. Peter wonders idly if his mother or one of her friends are to blame. Don't get caught in the cross-fire, he urges himself, let the police handle this, that's what he will tell Daniel if he starts whining.

Dried egg stains cover Daniel's front door. He knocks gingerly, trying to avoid the splatters. He feels sorry for Daniel, although not quite sorry enough to help him. To his surprise, Daniel doesn't answer the door. Another feeling disturbingly close to worry, sparks inside of him. He tries the door handle and to his astonishment it's unlocked.

He swings open the door, half-expecting to see Daniel in front of him, waiting just like Anne-Marie. No one, just some bags waiting by the front door. Anne-Marie's possessions presumably. An open invitation to get her stuff and get out perhaps. Peter peers inside a bag to confirm that they are indeed Anne-Marie's belongings and then slowly carries the bags out to his car, still waiting for Daniel to appear but the house remains silent.

He tries to convince himself that everything is okay, that Daniel wasn't as stupid as Anne-Marie, that he was probably just eating or something.

But still.

Resignedly, he locks his car and waits outside for a few moments for any tell-tale signs of life. He stares at Daniel's broken windscreen, the indentations, that word written in lipstick on his bonnet, written in a shade similar to his mother's. What if Daniel had already seen this? What if he had already gone charging over to confront Sherri? No, he would have heard the sirens.

Peter treads slowly back into the house, still expecting to see Daniel, still even half-expecting to see Anne-Marie. It smells like she is here, that whiff of spilt vodka and frustrated tears.

He checks the living room, nothing but a few empties. Upstairs, nothing, Anne-Marie's old room strangely empty, the cleanest he has ever seen it, Daniel's room mostly empty, the bed not looking like it has been made in weeks. Peter checks back downstairs again, his phone in his hand ready to call the police. He doesn't like this one bit.

The back door is open and a faint smell of smoke wafts through the gap. With trepidation, Peter steps outside.

For many nights when Anne-Marie was still alive, Peter stayed awake at night, trying to figure out a contingency plan for the day when Anne-Marie finally pushed Daniel too far. What he will do, what he will say, where he will send his sister? Peter, in all of his planning, never thought that his sister would manage to accomplish this from beyond the grave.

But then Anne-Marie had always been a special kind of person.

Peter takes in the burnt remains of the defaced wedding album, fluttering from their funeral pyre. His sister had cried genuine tears when she told him what she had done, begged him for any photos he had so she could fix it. She was supposed to replace the album before Daniel found out, not that Daniel would have been fooled by a new album with slightly different pictures, but it may have helped with her apology.

And here is Daniel, lying passed out on the grass, looking like he has been there all night. He looks like he is barely breathing and for a brief moment Peter considers just leaving him out here to his fate. How happy that would make his mother. No one has to know he came out into the garden: "The house was empty, Officer, I swear."

Something would go wrong, it always does. He can't let someone die just to make his mother happy. It's just not right. Finally he calls the ambulance. Then he decides he might as well call the police too.

CHAPTER TWENTY-ONE

"I do not feel safe living here anymore!"

They paid her little attention; she said this every time they met. Laura Noble likes to pretend she is practising for a play. You've got to stress the right word, sound out the right syllable, got to get that mummy tone just right, ready for when she starts hysterically talking about worries for her daughters' safety and their fear of the neighbourhood bogeyman. Got to get the small roles, the little lies right, ready for when she is leading with the big lies.

She started rubbing at her eyes, feigning distress. Not that they really noticed, they were too busy arguing. Ludmilla Bryski, bless that old bat, was refusing to leave because she likes her house. Probably can't face packing away all those precious crappy knick-knacks.

Laura chimed in with "I like my house too. I think he should leave, not us." She scanned the room, hoping her face portrayed how much she loved her house and neighbourhood, except for that small problem known as Daniel Mills.

They all echoed their agreements, Daniel should be the one who left, they need to make him leave. Nothing too nasty, they are decent people after all. They will start with gentle cajoling, dropping a few gentle hints. Laura volunteered for this, any chance to practice using her special voice and pleading eyes.

Gloria Hutchings volunteered to use a few more irritating tactics, starting with egging Daniel's front door. Not quite what she originally wanted to do; Gloria had wanted to do something more extreme. Laura was quick to counsel against it, for now. That they should give him a chance to leave of his own free will before they went too extreme. He might leave quickly, she reasons with them, not believing her own words. She knows their hints and little irritations won't be enough to convince Daniel to leave, but she wants to be the one remembered for saying "That's enough!" To be seen as the meek one, the nice one, too scared to go along with their plans. They all had their suspicions about each other even before Anne-Marie's death, she doesn't want to encourage the suspicions about herself.

Derrick is just as easy to manipulate. He likes to think he is the one who came up with the idea of prank calling Daniel. Derrick wasn't at the neighbourhood defence meeting and had laughed along with Laura at their weak and pathetic plans. "What do you expect from a bunch of old ladies?" he had thundered, not knowing that it was Laura who kept those plans at the weak and pathetic stage. She had responded by kissing him and then soothed him by reading him stories from the newspaper. She was halfway through a story about an accused murderer, forced out of his home by harassment.

"It says here they had been subjected to a series of threatening phone calls, property damage... what's wrong, Derrick?" She didn't really need to ask; she could see the lightbulbs going on in his head. Of course, he had just had a great idea! Well, Laura didn't marry him for his brains.

They discussed the practicalities of his plan in great detail. Laura on Derrick's instructions brought a cheap pay-as-you-go

SIM during her out-of-town shop, paying cash, of course. Now they had a mobile number that couldn't be traced to them, now the fun could begin.

Old Lady Bitchski insisted on coming with her to Daniel's house, to Laura's annoyance. "I won't let you go alone, not after how rude he was to you last time," she had quivered. The old bat even brought cake with her. Well, that was one way of getting rid of Daniel Mills – poisoned cake.

At first Laura didn't think the fat fuck was going to answer the door, then he looked like he wasn't going to invite them in. She braced herself for another door slamming in her face. He looked even worse than he had before, smelt worse too.

"Hi, Daniel, we thought we would come and see how you are." Her voice sounded fake, even to her, she needed to practise more. He stood there, staring, then his eyes fixated on the chocolate cake and finally he invited them in.

His house looked a lot cleaner than the last time Laura had seen it, though the scent of stale beer and pizza was overpowering. Laura was grateful for it, as it blocked out some of the stench from Daniel. He ushered them quickly past the stairs and into the living room. Laura and Ludmilla gingerly sat on the faded, still-warm sofa, Ludmilla holding out the cake to Daniel. The poor old bat looked like she was going to piss her skirts out of fear. Laura chuckled to herself. The twit probably wasn't used to dirt, squalor or giving suspected murderers cake.

Daniel had seized the cake a little too eagerly and bounded off to make tea. Laura peered around the room the best she could but didn't dare get up off the sofa. She longed to have a peep upstairs but knew Ludmilla would object if she left to have a snoop. They both ended up staring at the stairs. It is amazing how everyone just knows that's where Anne-Marie died, despite the tight-lipped police officers. Laura imagined she could still see the stains and puzzled over why small chunks of the carpet were missing. She wanted to ask Daniel for any updates but the look on his face warned against it. He handed them both a cup of tea and a small piece of cake before bringing in an extra chair from the kitchen. Laura noticed then, with a slight smile, that he had cut himself the biggest slice of cake. He took a large bite and then another, praising Ludmilla's baking skills with his mouth still full, oblivious to the fact that Ludmilla was shaking. Laura wished again that Ludmilla had not agreed to come, the stupid old bat made this harder than it needed to be. She squeezed Ludmilla's hand, as she joined in with the praise, hoping to relax her.

"So how are you?" Laura asked brightly, trying to ease away the awkwardness.

Daniel bumbled on and neither of them wanted to mention the previous door slamming incident

"You are very brave coming back to the house." Laura noticed the look on Daniel's face as she said this, she had touched a nerve.

He stared down at his tea, then tried to change the subject by asking how her daughters were.

Well this was a waste of time, not what she hoped for at all. Laura stood up then, ready to leave, but unable to resist firing one last shot. "One of my friends is an estate agent, if you were thinking about moving on." A look of eagerness had passed Daniel's face then it was replaced by something darker. They quickly saw themselves out.

"He is tempted already, I can tell," Laura recounted later to Derrick. They still proceeded with their plan, after all the effort they had put in to it, they couldn't resist. First they recorded various people saying "Murderer" from the television and then played the recording on a loop to Daniel over the phone, taking care to call only using their special SIM card. They could tell by the tremors in his voice that they had got to him. For Derrick, it was damning evidence of Daniel's guilt. Then to their disappointment, Daniel's number became permanently engaged. He must have taken his phone off the hook. They considered that to be a success.

Daniel stopped answering his door at that point too, so she couldn't drop any more subtle hints. Laura and Derrick discussed the possibility of threatening letters. They were both addicted to the mild thrill of doing something wrong – Laura more than Derrick. They have to do more, they decided, he is at breaking point. They wanted to egg his door too, why should Gloria Hutchings have all the fun? And she looked like she was having a lot of fun. They kept waiting for the right moment, but the kids were always around, always watching, listening. Kids have a nasty habit of repeating things at the wrong moment, in front of the wrong people, especially hers. Laura and Derrick were about to move on to a new idea, when Laura just happened to catch Daniel outside his house, tossing bin bags into his car. He had smiled when he saw her, asked her if she wouldn't mind contacting her estate agent friend, if the offer was still open.

"I have decided that I should be moving on." He tried to smile. Laura hoped he wasn't fishing for a plea for him to stay.

"Of course, I will go get his details now," she said, trying not to let her disappointment show. She hadn't expected him to break so quickly, she was having so much fun tormenting him. He said nothing but a thank you when she brought over the business card. He looked tired and defeated, she noticed with glee. He said nothing in answer to her "Are you all right?" just retreated back into his house, pretending he didn't hear.

Derrick was overjoyed when she told him their plan had worked and he wanted to celebrate. They sent their daughters to Grandma's house that night, then later when Derrick passed out from too much celebrating, she crept out of the house, wanting more. She always wanted more, that's how all of this started.

It was a warm night and she could smell smoke in the air. She noticed several half-opened windows in the neighbourhood. She would have to be quick, she warned herself, quick and quiet. She wanted one more thrill, something to ensure that Daniel didn't change his mind. She didn't have anything against Daniel, she just enjoyed tormenting him. She has always enjoyed tormenting people; it is why she worked in management.

She started by writing *Murderer* across the bonnet of Daniel's car, using a nice blood-red lipstick, not a shade she would normally wear, of course. It didn't feel as thrilling as she had hoped, it would just wash off, no big deal. She paused and took a long stare up and down the quiet street again. Do something bigger, her mind urged. She spied one of Ludmilla's prized gnomes, only recently moved back into her front garden. She grabbed one, took steady, careful aim and threw the gnome as hard she could, aiming towards the windscreen. She immediately started running. She heard the sound of glass smashing as she ran, direct hit! She could admire the damage later, but right now she needed to get out of sight. She ran down one street and then another, stood gasping for breath in an alleyway, her body tingling with pleasure. She waited for a few minutes before calmly turning around and sauntering back home. The neighbourhood slept on, oblivious. Finally she made it back to her own home. She checked on Derrick, he was still dead to the world, he would never know she had left, would never know a lot of things really. He would never know that she had gone into the Mills' house on the 18th of July.

This all started because Anne-Marie didn't know when to keep her mouth shut.

The stupid bitch.

She had heard them arguing, of course. She had watched Daniel Mills leave the house, laughed hard on seeing the scratches on his face. She watched Daniel scurry out of sight, completely unaware that he was being watched. She could hear the sounds of screaming and smashing coming from inside their house, as Anne-Marie worked through her anger issues. Laura wandered around her own house then, putting a few toys away, enjoying the rare peace. No daughters whining or bugging her every five seconds. She was about to settle down and do some work when she saw Anne-Marie out alone in the streets, out again in her dirty pyjamas, a bottle of something in each hand and she was staring at Laura's house with pure hatred, before turning and disappearing back into her own hovel. Laura sighed; she had hoped that Anne-Marie had forgotten about this week's payment. She would have to go round; she couldn't risk Anne-Marie making a scene.

She heard more smashing and screaming again, the sounds of a radio being turned up. Laura waited, watching keenly, waiting for Daniel to come back. Finally the sobs died down, and she made herself a cup of tea and waited a little while longer, just in case, before finally walking across the road, a vodka bottle in hand.

She entered the Mills' house with trepidation, pushing open the unlocked door with the bottle. At the time she just didn't want to touch the door, now she is pleased that she didn't. It seems so silly now, if Anne-Marie had locked her door for once, then she would still be alive. Stupid bitch deserved it really.

The house was quiet, except for the faint sound of a radio coming from next door and a faint slurred sobbing from upstairs. Laura took to the stairs, determined to get this over with, as a voice cried out, "Danny?"

There were some shuffling sounds then Anne-Marie Mills appeared in the doorway of one of the rooms, clutching the wall for support, as Laura reached the top step. Laura stopped in shock, staring in horror at the dripping cuts on Anne-Marie's arms, hands and bloody feet.

"What happened?" she asked. She wasn't that concerned, it's not like she was friends with the extortionist.

"Nonnne of your bussssiness, bitch," came the slurred reply.

Shit, she was really drunk this time. She probably won't even remember Laura bringing over the bottle. Best to leave as quickly as possible. Just get out of here. "I brought your bottle... I am just going to leave it here." She was just keeping her side of the deal, a litre of spirits every week. It's not her fault that Anne-Marie was stupid drunk this time, wasn't her fault that Anne-Marie refused to take the bottle.

"I donnn't wannnt it."

"I shall just leave it here, in case you want it later," Laura had said in the same tone that she used when Lenore was being difficult.

"I wannnnt Dannnnnnny."

"I am sure he will be back soon."

"Heeess nnoott comminnng bacck!" Anne-Marie had wailed so loud, Ludmilla next door must have heard despite what she says.

"Okay, I shall just leave this here," Laura had said brightly, just wanting to get out of there. Laura had stood aside slightly to set the bottle down away from the stairs, then suddenly Anne-Marie was there beside her, blocking her way.

"Iff myyy marrrriagge is ovvveer, sooo isss yooours," Anne-Marie had dared say!

Laura was filled with disgust that this woman, this woman who stank of vomit, piss and alcohol, that this woman would dare threaten her marriage, AGAIN! Laura took a step forward, hands raised, still holding the bottle of vodka, ready to slap some sense into the stupid bitch. She felt Anne-Marie's nails dig into her arm and Laura had pushed back, using the bottle with all her strength. Then Anne-Marie was gone.

Without even a scream, she was lying at the bottom of the stairs, a dazed expression in her eyes. Laura had walked back downstairs slowly, still holding the wretched bottle. Ready to do something else, she wasn't sure what, but something. Perhaps she would have hit Anne-Marie again with the bottle. Perhaps she would have poured it over Anne-Marie and then lit a match. Fury had made her capable of doing almost anything. But by the time Laura reached the bottom step, Anne-Marie's eyes were closed and blood was seeping out of her forehead. Laura decided that even if Anne-Marie did get up again, she wouldn't remember what happened and that it was best to leave now, before anyone came to investigate the noise. Still clutching the bottle of vodka, she made it back to her own house and took a long gulp from it, to steady her nerves. Her heart raced, body trembled with fear and excitement, but ding dong! The bitch was gone!

She had watched excitedly as Daniel arrived back. She watched with joy as the ambulance took Anne-Marie away, body covered, signifying that the bitch was truly dead.

Then as the euphoria faded, the doubts stabbed in. What if someone saw her? What if the police found evidence she had been in the house? What would she say?

She found a small spot of blood on her shoe and immediately soaked both of her shoes in bleach, then carefully binned them before Derrick could see. She had washed and checked her clothes carefully before slipping them into a donation bag.

Then she practised her lies. Rehearsing over and over, practising with different unknowing people. Trying desperately to prepare for every question, every scenario. Rehearsing lies, saying that she went round to comfort Anne-Marie, should the police discover that she went into the house. Lies about what Anne-Marie did when she was being comforted. Lies about why Laura was wearing long-sleeved tops in July, lies about how those scratches got on her arm. But only if they asked. Never volunteer a lie, only use it if confronted, people are always suspicious of an unprovoked explanation.

This is what Laura would have told the police truthfully. If it had come to it. If they weren't fooled by her bullshit. She would tell them that she was giving Anne-Marie a bottle of spirits a week, something they had agreed on to make Anne-Marie leave her daughters alone. She heard Anne-Marie and Daniel having an argument and went round to comfort her, taking the bribery bottle with her. Anne-Marie was an aggressive drunk (everyone would back her on this bit) and had become hysterical, lunging for Laura in a fit of anger. She had missed and fallen downstairs instead. Laura had ran out the house at that point, convinced that Anne-Marie was following her, not realising how badly Anne-Marie was hurt. She honestly didn't realise that Anne-Marie would never get up again, otherwise she would have called an ambulance. She was just so scared and she didn't know what to do. As a mother, she couldn't bear the thought of losing her children. She is sorry about all those lies.

When the police arrived to interview her, she felt ready. It had been easier than she expected, she had slipped away quickly to find an outfit that hid the scratches on her arm. Her daughters had helped so much there; she took Lenore to Chante's room, knowing they would start fighting within minutes, a welcome distraction for once. She still can't believe that the police actually believed her first lie, that she didn't hear anything because she was vacuuming. The stupid fools.

She even had a story ready in case Derrick asked about the scratches, but he didn't even notice; he rarely takes an interest in her now, which is why she was having an affair in the first place. That's why Anne-Marie had been blackmailing her. She had caught Laura passionately kissing her lover and demanded a bottle of alcohol, a full litre of the good stuff not some cheap crap, in return for keeping quiet. Laura had paid, not wanting Derrick to know, she couldn't risk him even starting to question the paternity of her daughters. Then she asked for another bottle then another, then it became a bottle a week to keep quiet.

Laura tried to feel remorse for what she did. She had killed someone after all but then really, wasn't she just performing a kindness? The bitch was past help, she was a nuisance to everyone. Laura didn't deserve to go to prison for killing her, no, she deserved a medal, she had practically performed a community service. She had made the neighbourhood safe and quiet again.

The bitch deserved it really.

Now the charade is nearly over, but she can't relax. Her lover has dared send her a message. One that reads *I don't think we should see each other anymore.* She is enraged, he can't leave her! They are not done until she says they are done. She has asked to see him one last time and he has agreed, not knowing he is about to be hit by the full wrath of Laura Noble. She has so many things he doesn't want his wife to see. She will make him regret even thinking about dumping her, then regret daring to send that message. She has to admit, it is absolutely delicious to have so much power over someone.

She needs to get rid of Derrick. He had been fun but now he is holding her back. Maybe another push will do it, another tragic accident. She starts practising her lies again, practising what she will say to her lover, to the police, to Derrick. It is with happiness she steps outside her house, noticing the police car parked in front of Daniel's house, a small crowd of her neighbours gathered outside. She puts on her best friendly smile and goes over to investigate as any good neighbour would do.

She can see Lying Penny talking animatedly to the sour-faced Colvin. To Laura's horror, Lying Penny points a finger in Laura's direction. "I saw her leaving the house this morning. I knew she was up to no good," she yells excitedly. Laura fights down the urge to smash her face in with another one of Ludmilla's prized gnomes. She tries to facially indicate how crazy Lying Penny is but Colvin is looking at her in a way that she doesn't like. "I saw her smashing the car!"

"Shut your lying face," Laura finally manages to snarl. She hasn't practised for this. Lying Penny has caught her completely off guard. She starts to back away, noticing the shocked expressions on Gloria Hutchings' and Ludmilla Bryski's faces. They all heard. They all believed that stupid cow! She feels a hand on her shoulder, warning her not to go any further.

"I think you better come with us, Mrs Noble," Grimm says quietly, trying to steer her towards the waiting police car. She shoves against him hard, catching him off guard. These fucking fools. She raises a foot, firmly intending to smash down onto Grimm's cursing face. She is going to get Lying Penny for this. Make it so she can never open her lying face again. Her foot is just reaching Grimm's nose as she is yanked backwards by Colvin. She tries to push against her, tries to hit but feels the click of a handcuff against her wrist.

"Laura Noble, you are under arrest." Whatever Colvin tries to say after this is lost beneath the sound of Laura's angry screams. Something about attempted assault. She still has one hand free and she intends to use it. Colvin has to very quickly recall everything she has ever learned about restraining a violent offender, whilst Grimm curses and slowly manages to stagger upright. Together they drag Laura kicking and screaming to the car. As the car door slams shut behind her, as she hears the request for assistance echo over the radio, Laura finally realises where she is and that it is going to be very hard to talk her way out of this one.

How much do they know? What do they know? What else did that lying bitch say? If Laura is going down, she is taking all of them with her. Does Gloria think that she won't talk about their neighbourhood plots and what she has been doing? Does Grimm not recall that kiss? No, she plots, as the car starts up, she has dirt on them all and she will use it.

They have nothing to link her to Anne-Marie's death, she reassures herself, they can't blame her for that. They have nothing, no idea whatsoever. No evidence, no clue, not so much as a skin flake.

CHAPTER TWENTY-TWO

"Ah, Daniel!" Paul Bryski's voice bellows out, just as Daniel is putting the last suitcase into the taxi. Daniel cringes, he had hoped to get in and out without seeing any of his neighbours. He knows that Laura Noble has been arrested, is still finding it hard to believe that they have found evidence linking her to his wife's death. He can't even start to comprehend what it meant or even why.

"I have something for you." Daniel doesn't want it; he doesn't know what it is but he doesn't want it. He wants to get in the taxi and leave but Paul is already reaching him, a package clearly visible in his hands.

"It's from your wife," he says with a chuckle. "I forgot I had this until Luddy reminded me. Annie had asked me to hide it." He thrusts it into Daniel's hands.

"She was a nice gal, your Annie. Bit wild but her heart was in the right place." He chuckles again. "Luddy won't admit it but she was similar at that age." He says this in what he thinks is a conspiratorial whisper but is actually a loud bellow.

"Well, aren't you going to open it?" he asks impatiently, peering at the shocked Daniel through thick glasses. Daniel swallows hard, the present feels heavy in his hands. He doesn't think he can take any more fuck you messages from Anne-Marie, but Paul is watching him expectantly and he feels forced to oblige.

He runs his fingers across the gold paper and decides just to get this over with. He pulls back the paper to find a large, hard-backed white book. Daniel shudders as he notes the elegant gold writing across the front of the book. *Our Lovely Wedding*. It is a very fancy wedding album, almost too fancy, Paul must have picked it out. Warily, Daniel flicks through the pages, expecting the worse, but sees only pristine, untainted photos. He had forgotten how beautiful Anne-Marie had looked that day. How happy they both were. How hideous Sherri's outfit had been.

"She said she did something stupid to the first one and asked if I could hide this... I don't know until when. I didn't see her again after that and, well, then, |God rest her soul." Paul is unaware that Daniel is barely listening.

Daniel smiles for the first time in months, flicking through the pages again and again. Paul says something else before shuffling off but Daniel doesn't notice. It's only when the taxi driver beeps his horn that he is brought back to reality. He slowly climbs into the back seat and is driven away from his old house for the last time. He doesn't look at the house, or the street, his tear-filled eyes are staring at the inscription at the front of the album.

I am sor– had been written by a wobbly hand, then crossed out, followed by a second illegible scribble, but the words *I love you* are unmistakable, signed by *A* squiggle *M* squiggle finished with large *X X X*.

THE END

ALSO BY CM THOMPSON

What Lies In the Dark

A NOTE FROM THE PUBLISHER

Thank you for reading this book. If you enjoyed it please do consider leaving a review on Amazon to help others find it too.

We hate typos. All of our books have been rigorously edited and proofread, but sometimes mistakes do slip through. If you have spotted a typo, please do let us know and we can get it amended within hours.

info@bloodhoundbooks.com